Déjà Vu

FELICIA JEDLICKA

For those who feel like they have more than one person living inside of their head. And for those who actually do.

More titles by FELICIA JEDLICKA

DESTINY REJECTED

SISTER WITCHES

THE NEBRASKA APOCALYPSE NOVELS
Corn Cows and the Apocalypse
Cow Tipping after the Apocalypse
Corn Husking After the Apocalypse

THE WARDEN SERIES
Successors
Rivals
Lovers and Liars
Bad Blood
Tenants and Tyrants
The Ring Bearer
Gods and Monsters
Beasts and Burdens
Magic and Mayhem

Déjà Vu

1

I was in yet another motel room. The 1970s wood paneling and orange floral curtains told me that it was a cheap one. The noxious smell of menthol cigarettes was still in my hair and I could taste an ashtray skid mark on the back of my tongue. I seriously needed to buy myself a nicotine patch.

Thankfully, I was alone, but that didn't mean I came here alone.

I half crawled, half fell out of the bed. My head throbbed like my brain was trying to break open my skull to escape. I couldn't blame it. I wouldn't want to hang around with someone that starved me of oxygen either.

Unfortunately, it was taking out its frustrations on the wrong person. This bender wasn't my idea. I couldn't even remember the fun of being carelessly drunk. All I got out of it was the hangover.

I managed to make it to the bathroom in a bipedal fashion, albeit not in a straight line. I flipped on the light just inside the door along with the fan. I was a little happy to see the vomit around the toilet. At least I didn't have to remember that. Knowing I didn't have to clean it up made me feel a little better about the motel room, but I made a mental note to leave a decent tip for the maid staff.

I peered at my reflection in the mirror through hooded eyes. My long brown hair was snarled into a frizz. My heavy mascara and eyeliner had reached the raccoon stage. I looked like shit. I felt like shit and smelled like shit, so I supposed that should follow. I needed and wanted a shower, so I stripped naked. Every body part short of my pinky fingers protested against my movement.

I slipped into the shower and let the water hit my face to finish waking me up. Once I had returned to the land of the living, I started to scrub off my body with the diligence of someone unsure with whom they might have spent the night. I hissed in pain as my washcloth hit a sore spot on my lower back. I reached around and touched the sensitive area. The tender puckered skin instantly alarmed me.

I threw open the shower curtain and twisted to see the reflection of my back in the mirror. The swollen red tissue encompassing the black design was typical of a new tattoo. The detailed feminine curves of the ink and its position designated it a tramp stamp.

"You fucking bitch!" I wasn't usually so sharp-tongued, but Deja brought out my inner sailor.

I stomped out of the bathroom wet, naked, and unconcerned about either. I searched the bedside tables, ransacked the dresser drawers, and stripped the sheets off the bed in search of my update.

She always left me a note. It was usually illegible, riddled with profanity, and hardly informative, but it was a mutual respect we offered each other. One of very few things we agreed on.

It wasn't there. That wasn't good. That meant she was mad. I couldn't begin to think what I could have done to warrant that. Me being mad at her was pretty standard, but vice versa meant trouble.

The door to the hotel room clicked open and I whipped around to see a man entering with a grocery sack in hand and a duffel bag slung over his shoulder. He tugged his key card out of the door and stepped inside. After a moment's pause to unload his baggage, he noticed me standing in the center of the room. Frozen in place, he gaped at me with wide eyes.

I remembered much too late that I was naked. Social etiquette demanded that I squeal and grab the comforter at my feet to conceal my nudity. However, I had been in so many of these awkward morning-after situations that my heart just wasn't in it anymore.

"Stay there," I instructed him as I walked back to the bathroom and slammed the door shut. I finished drying off and attempted to brush my teeth with a hand towel. I really needed to start carrying an overnight bag.

There was a slight tap on the door. I chose to ignore it. He could wait or he could leave. I looked down at my smoke-scented clothes strewn on the bathroom floor. There was nothing worse than dirty socks and day-old panties. Eck!

"I bought you some new clothes." The stranger's voice filtered through the door.

I bypassed the obvious strand of *what-why* questions and opened the door. My towel was now tightly affixed, but he had graciously turned his head to salvage what was left of my propriety. He blindly handed me the paper sack. I took it and closed the door again.

At the top of the bag—God bless him!—was toothpaste and a toothbrush. I was thrilled at the prospect of scrubbing the tar off my taste buds. At this point in my life, freshly brushed teeth was ranking higher than sex, coffee, and chocolate. Well, maybe not chocolate.

"Oh thank you, thank you, *thank you*!" My gratitude was intended for a less earthly being, but the man outside didn't quite catch on to that.

"You're welcome," he murmured outside the door and I didn't dispel his misunderstanding.

I pulled a pack of fresh white cotton underwear from the bag, surprisingly the right size and not covered in lace. I ripped it open and slipped one on.

Deeper down I found fresh socks, a gray t-shirt, and a blue cardigan not unlike one I already had in my closet at home. Lastly there was a pair of fashionable relaxed fit jeans. I checked the tag and scoffed. This guy must have had a good time last night if he was buying me $180 jeans.

Glad I showered.

I slipped on the denim and not only did it fit, but it looked better than the jeans I had arrived in. I tucked the t-shirt in so the waistband didn't rub against my fresh ink.

Despite my dislike for tattoos, it wasn't my first one. It was, however, the biggest I had ever discovered. I was running out of money for laser removal. Not that I could technically afford it the first three times.

I left the bathroom in search of my tennis shoes and found them stuffed under the bed. I yanked them free and sat on the mattress to slip them on.

My *guest* was relaxing in a chair by the window, watching me. He was attractive, which was no shock. Deja always managed to get men that I wouldn't have the guts to talk to, let alone aspire to sleep with.

He wore a pair of gray canvas pants with a black T-shirt. The silver chain around his neck was a little too long for men's jewelry, in my opinion. His hair was a mop of thick muddy-brown curls and silver highlights that he didn't look old enough to have.

He was fit. Maybe a little tired in the face, but romantics would call him seasoned.

He didn't look like Deja's usual pea-brained hipster type. His little round glasses made him look bookish and she didn't like smart men. She preferred her men just a little on the stupid side. I could only assume it was because *she* wasn't very smart.

"Look..." I offered my hand to ask for a name. He didn't get it at first.

"Cantry. Layne Cantry," he stuttered, shifting in his chair before checking his watch. Was I boring him? *Well, I'll get to the point.*

"Thank you for the clothes. I can't begin to explain the many reasons I have for not hanging around, but rest assured it's not you. It's not technically me either, but for the sake of argument let's just say it is. Before I go though, I do have one question. Did we use protection last night?"

"What?"

"I'm sorry. I don't remember. I just need to know if I should take any precautions." He stared vacantly at me. "Plan B?   Penicillin? Tetanus shot?" My attempt at humor baffled him even more. Maybe he *was* Deja's type. "Crap man, did you use a condom!"

His eyes widened and narrowed back into exhaustion. "We didn't sleep together."

"We didn't?" I glanced around the room for evidence to the contrary, because it just didn't seem to fit any pattern of Deja's not to sleep with the hot man she just met.

"Of course not. I know better than to get involved with Siamese minds."

2

"What did you say?" I asked, holding back my anger until I had more information.

Siamese minds was an old term for my kind. These days they usually called us a split soul or twin souls, depending on if you view yourselves as one or individuals. Deja and I definitely viewed ourselves as separate minds. Souls? Well, that wasn't our department.

Twin souls were rare, and even rarer was admitting that you were one to people you just met. It's way too easy to take advantage of someone when you know they'll pretend to know who you are just to save face.

"Did D tell you about us? That girl is dumber than the gum she chews. Look, I don't know why she told you anything. That is a very private issue and not meant for strangers."

"I'm not a stranger to her."

"I don't need the sordid details, but one night of binge-drinking with Deja does not a friend make. Trust me, I've had to deal with the fallout of ex-lovers time and time again. Let me give you some advice: She's not monogamous and no matter what she says she doesn't actually *like* men."

"I didn't drink with her last night. I stopped her binge before it got out of hand."

"Out of hand? I've got a fucking tramp stamp on my back!"

Layne tried to cover his smile but it was obvious that this had been a point of levity in the night. "She insisted on that. I couldn't have stopped her short of knocking her out, and she advised me that it would be unwise to try."

"It *would* be unwise," I agreed with a bit more zeal than I intended.

"Why is that? She didn't elaborate."

"Like *I* would." I glared at him, not-so-subtly reinforcing my desire to keep *my* life private. "Could you have at least stopped her before the hangover from hell set in?"

"I'm sorry. I tried to get her to take something but... she was very angry with you."

"Angry? I'm the one who should be angry."

"She disagrees."

"Then she should have written me a note. She knows this whole thing doesn't work without communication."

"She did write you a note. I have it."

I stared blankly at him. Appalled and livid, my mouth gaped before I could formulate my argument. "How dare you take that? That is our personal communication! It's like listening in on a phone conversation."

"I didn't read it."

"Thank God for small favors."

"I wrote it."

"What?" I stared at him, contemplating the

cultivation of a violent streak just for the occasion.

"The first part is her, but after she spent an entire page calling you a fucking bitch, I thought I would help the process by taking dictation. Trust me, if I hadn't, there would have been a novella of cusswords and nonsensical sentences."

"Yeah, well, that's how she communicates. I've never known any different. What gives you the right to interfere?"

"Because I'm the one she came to for help."

"Help?" My voice pitched with concern, though it may have been selfishly motivated. "Not gambling debt again. Whatever money you loaned her, I assure you I have no way of paying you back, and despite what she may have told you, neither does she."

He smiled to himself. "She told me you fret over little things."

"Little things? *I'm* the one who wakes up in the hospital when the loan sharks come to collect. And don't talk to me like you know her better than me. I've known her my whole life."

"Yes, but you've never met her. You've only ever spoken to her on paper. And I think we both know she's not very literate."

"You've known her one night and suddenly you're an expert."

He shook his head and checked his watch again. Was I keeping him from something?

"I didn't meet her last night. Technically, I met her last week, but I've been watching the both of you for a few weeks now," he said casually, as if it wasn't the creepiest thing a stranger could ever say to you.

I was at the door in record time. There was no further explanation needed. This guy was a stalker and I wanted nothing more to do with him. If I could have left Deja behind too, I would have—and a thousand times before that.

I could hear him shuffle behind me, but thankfully I was quick when I needed to be. There were too many shady experiences in my past not to be. I jumped the stair rail early to get some more distance between us. I spotted my car and took a bee-line to it.

It was typically unlocked, since Deja had no comprehension of what personal property meant. I found my purse stuffed under the front seat, as it often was. I pulled the keys out and started the car just as Layne came down the final leg of the stairs. In a moment of pubescent irritation, I flipped him off and tore out of the parking lot like a teenager with a brand new license.

3

I picked up speed on the highway while I was still outside of city jurisdiction and the penalties for speeding weren't as high. It took less than a mile to realize I had no idea where the hell I was. These were not my stomping grounds. Judging by the arid, rocky terrain, it wasn't even my state.

The sign I passed on the highway informed me that I was only 93 miles from Las Vegas. I cussed and wrenched my steering wheel as if it was were Deja's neck. It wasn't unusual for me to wake up in a town several hours away from Boulder, but to be two states away? Whatever had happened in the last couple of days must have been big, but without a note there was no way to know what it was.

I couldn't believe Deja had involved someone in our lives. She was always resistant to get close to anyone. I never even tried to make friends, and forget about dating. Even if I could find a guy willing to tolerate my whackadoo-brain roommate, there wasn't a chance in hell that Deja was going to be monogamous, and most guys weren't up for sharing. As it was, *I* wasn't even that fond of it.

Deja might have known that this sicko Layne was stalking us, but she wouldn't have told me about it. It was somewhat endearing because she didn't want me to worry, but it was also condescending as hell. She wasn't the only one who could take care of herself. If anything, *I* took care of *her.*

Deja meant well, for the most part, but she regarded me as a burden. Don't get me wrong, I felt the same way about her, but I had always thought of Deja as a child, whereas she thought of me as a pet.

I dug through my purse to find my cell. I untangled the earpiece from a knitted scarf I kept around to cover Deja's hickeys, and fastened the device to my ear. "Call work," I said, and the device pinged in acknowledgment.

I couldn't remember what day it was, but I assumed that I had missed work. It wasn't a big shock to find out that I had been fired.

I took my manager's abuse with concealed shame. It was a shit job, but it had paid the bills. When things settled down again, I was still going to have to beg for it back because it was the only work I could get with my *condition.* AKA: pain-in-the-ass alter ego.

I called home and found one message on the voicemail. It was from me to Deja. It was a backup message reminding her of the work schedule because she usually threw away my notes right after reading them—if she even read them.

So much for that.

I was almost out of power. My little energy hog Front Runner took a good two weeks to run out of juice, but with Deja's travels I scarcely had an eighth of a tank. I saw a Plug 'n' Pump and pulled in.

The old gas station had been retrofitted for battery

charging, but they didn't take government power vouchers. Technically it was illegal not to, but since they still pumped gas, the government considered them grandfathered in under the old system, which meant I was going to be racking up another eighty bucks of credit card debt.

Yippee.

I swiped the card and walked around while the car charged. Fifteen minutes would be all it would take to charge, but it was still too long. I was anxious to get the hell out of there. I was already going the wrong direction, but I wasn't sure how persistent Layne the stalker was going to be.

I kicked a rock over the dusty soil, because that's what you do when you're waiting. I noted how nice my jeans were again. Even on sale they had to be over a hundred dollars. Why would he spend so much on me? And if he knew that I wasn't Deja, why did he even come back? He could have waited two days for her to reemerge.

There were too many questions to answer and as curious as I was, I wanted no part of them. My next note to Deja was going to be a whopper. *Stop drinking, stop smoking, stop getting tattoos, and for the love of chocolate, buy a vibrator and stop bringing weird men into our lives.*

The light turned green over my car and I nearly sprinted to it. I unplugged and got in ready to hit the open road. As I backed out of my spot, three cop cars pulled into the station. I stopped to see where they were going to park, but they flipped on their lights and

blocked me in.
Son of a…

4

I sat in a police station on the outskirts of Vegas wondering what fresh hell my shadow had gotten me into. I'd been stalked, fired, arrested, and if I wasn't mistaken, I was having a nicotine fit.

I looked around the police station, in awe of the technology. Hundreds of flat-screens lined the walls with operators monitoring stations of twenty or more at a time. The traffic station, like most these days, was almost entirely automated. They sent out emails to speeders and light runners informing them of their fines even before they finished committing the illegal act. Public properties were monitored for violence as well as vandalism. One call from the operator and the police would arrive before the crime was even done.

The private property stations were in fogged glass cubicles—a paid service that business owners couldn't afford to be without. There was even a division for private homes, but the cost was too high for most people. Depending on the city, it was better not to have anyone monitoring your home, lest corrupt cops use the video footage as their own personal home shopping network.

"Elise Welch," a sullen uniformed cop called from one of the entrances to the waiting area.

"Yes, sir." I jumped up, prepared to be compliant

and generous with my puffery.

I followed him through the soundless monitoring stations. Then we passed by a long line of desks piled high with paperwork and manned by very bitter government employees. When we finally reached the interrogation room I was feeling a little worried about my prospects of sucking up to anyone in this precinct.

"In here," the man mumbled and opened the door to a terrifyingly simple room: metal table, metal chairs, big-ass mirror. I had done a lot of prostrating in rooms just like this.

"Can you tell me why I'm here?" I asked before going through the door.

"In here," he barked gruffly and pointed inside like I might not have heard him the first time.

I stepped inside and the door slammed behind me. Nothing was ever friendly in these places, but this was beyond answering for public intoxication charges. I was either in a great deal of trouble, or this was a horrible mistake. I was willing to put money down that it wasn't the latter.

After a few agonizing minutes, the door opened and Layne Cantry walked in holding a file. The door slammed just as he smacked his file down on the table. He barely looked at me before sitting down in the chair across from me. I immediately noticed the new addition to his wardrobe: a black leather shoulder holster with matching gun.

For a moment, I just stared at him with a thousand questions demanding to be first in line. Instead I held my tongue. If I needed to get a lawyer, it was probably best I shut up early. This man already knew too much about me.

"Not going to ask me anything?" He leaned back coolly in his rock-hard chair, making it seem more like a comfy plush recliner. "That's new. Deja said you were a nervous talker."

I bit my cheek hard. I didn't like Deja talking to this guy about our situation, but I loathed that she had told him about me. It was just wrong. Everything about this was wrong. Call it self-preservation, call it anti-social, but whatever it was, it meant that Deja and I were our own business. Not his.

"You don't like me talking about her, do you?" He eyed me quizzically. "She said you had a maternal streak. Actually she said you had a maternal stick stuck up your ass."

I shot up out of my chair—to do what? I had no idea, because he shot up right after me. My chair clattered to the floor, upsetting the momentary standoff. I shrugged off the excess anger and walked away from the table to breathe. There wasn't any *fresh* air for about two hundred and fifty miles, but I looked out the dirty glass brick window anyway and pretended I wasn't there.

Layne came around the table and set my chair back on four legs. "She told me you would have trouble sharing her with someone else."

I shook my head. Deja had her name in every bathroom stall in Boulder. I had no trouble *sharing* her.

"She didn't want us to meet, but this wasn't going to work with an on/off schedule. She was really messed up last night." I glanced back at him, hearing a twinge of concern in his voice. He was leaning against the table watching me. "I want you to know I've been doing my best to keep her on track. Last night was beyond me, though."

"Why is she so mad?"

"She found out about your research," he said after a beat.

I turned around, slack-jawed. I must have lost some color in my face, because I was instantly dizzy. "Shit," I hissed. "Oh shista-lavista." I cradled my head in my hands for a moment, trying to catalog exactly what she had seen, and what she had gleaned from it.

Out of desperation to qualify my actions to a woman I could never speak to, I turned to the only common link in our life. I wasn't on board with Layne's presence in our lives, but if he was going to be hanging around, he might as well relay my urgent supplication.

"When you see her…" I pressed my hands on his arms and he noted the contact but didn't interrupt me. "Tell her the research is old—*so* old. I'm not pursuing that path any longer. It was a dead end. Well, it wasn't a dead end in that it had no answers, but dead as in I don't want to kill her just to unburden myself." I squeezed his arms a little tighter to make sure he relayed my compunction properly. "I wouldn't do that. Never. *Ever!* You have to make her believe that." I was panicking and it wasn't pretty. He cupped my elbows and ushered me back to my chair. I sat down, but before I let go I squeezed his biceps hard. "Promise me."

"I will make sure she understands." When I didn't

release him, he added, "You have my word." I exhaled deeply and retracted my claws. He returned to his seat. "Maternal is definitely accurate," he mumbled as he sat back down.

"Look." I leaned over the table clasping my hands as if in prayer. "I don't know what she did, but you obviously know that *I'm* not responsible for it. Maybe you can manipulate your police work and call this a case of mistaken identity. I'm sure with as much video surveillance as goes on around here it's easy to mistake one drunken reprobate for another. Let's face it, I can't afford the fine, you'll have to imprison me, and I'm already on public assistance, so why burden the government with yet another lowly prisoner to feed?"

"There she is." He smiled. "Elise… or do you prefer 'Miss Welch'?"

"Um… Elise."

"Elise, you aren't under arrest. I'm not even a cop."

"You're not?" I asked, genuinely surprised. He acted like a cop, mannerisms and everything.

"I used to be a cop. When surveillance systems took over, I lost interest. I'm a private investigator now, but I keep in contact with my former colleagues. They did me the favor of bringing you in, since you left without saying goodbye."

Enlightenment dawned on my hungover brain. "That's why you've been watching us. You're investigating us."

"Not exactly." His eyes shifted downward. He wasn't comfortable with what he was about to say. "I've been protecting you." I narrowed my eyes, wary of his admission. It seemed genuine, but I couldn't help but wonder why he was taking it upon himself to guard us free of charge. "Your name has come up in some communications. Communications that, shall we say, aren't on the books."

I nodded. Crime bosses and mastermind thieves were on the rise since the sudden downfall of petty misdemeanors. There was big business in being smart enough to outsmart technology. The police had to go to great lengths to keep them under control. Illegal wiretapping was common and despite being illegal, everyone knew about it and didn't care. We were all officially desensitized to our lack of privacy.

"I was in the middle of another investigation that sent me your way. I've been trying to figure out why your name was mentioned. It didn't take long to figure out that you were a Siamese mind. Deja was onto me from the beginning. At first I thought she was just… Whatever. She finally confronted me and asked me for help."

"Why?"

"Because someone's trying to kill her."

5

"Kill?" I was out of my chair again. There was no hope of not panicking now. "Why didn't she tell me this?"

Layne stood up with me and blocked my pacing path. "She didn't want to freak you out. She didn't think you would do so well with the truth."

"Ha!" was all I offered since I clearly *wasn't* doing well with it.

"Deja wanted to get this figured out before we had to involve you, but the attempts on your lives have been getting closer together."

"Attempts! What the French! There has been more than one?"

"Four, to be exact."

I wasn't one to swoon, but the thought of handing off the reins to Deja and never waking back up again was alarming to me. I was hyperventilating at the prospect of being murdered and not even knowing why. Layne offered a hand to steady me, but I didn't take it. Regrettably, I should have, since my knees locked and I just fell forward for no apparent reason.

Layne caught me as best he could while still

keeping a margin of professional distance. He put me back in my chair and kneeled before me. He looked concerned, but only in that do-I-need-to-call-a-paramedic way. He took my pulse and advised me to slow my breathing, which was easier said than done.

"I'm sorry," I said when I was a little more myself again. "I guess she was right about not telling me. I hate it when she's right."

"She wasn't right," he mumbled, checking my pulse again. He left his hand on my wrist after. It was a small touch, but as with any touch from an attractive stranger it felt like something important was happening. "She said you would be cowering in a corner crying after I told you."

I looked to the corner of the room before answering. "It does look rather appealing over there." He chuckled at that and I smiled. I enjoyed making people laugh. It wasn't something I got to do often since I didn't want to make friends, but it was nice to know I still had a knack for it.

"There you go, Elise, a sense of humor is good in situations like this. Keep the heart strong with laughter and you'll always have enough strength for hope."

"That's poetic, did you just make that up?"

"No, actually… Never mind." He stood up and returned to his seat. "Listen, this situation you and Deja are in, it's getting worse. I've been trying to figure out why you are on a hit list, but so far I haven't dug much up on you two."

"There isn't much," I said resolutely. "Is that how you found my research?"

"Deja found that when we were searching the apartment. We were looking for some accidentally muled drugs, but she found that instead."

"So last night she has a rebellious binge to hurt me," I said, attempting to recount the last 48 hours. "You tried to keep her out of trouble, but neglected to keep her from tattooing me." He smirked at the mention of the tattoo, but I refused to ask why. "That still doesn't answer the question of why the hell we are in Nevada."

"Three of those attempts on your lives have been in the last 48 hours, so you, me and Deja are on the lam." His brow rose in emphasis.

That corner was looking better and better by the minute.

6

I stared at the hybridized gas-guzzling sports car before me. Layne opened the door to the low-riding vehicle. I couldn't help but wonder if this was all just a really good trap. Maybe Layne was the one trying to kill us and I was about to get into his blue sports car, never to be seen again.

At first it sounded preposterous, but then a question popped into my mind. What if Deja told me in her note that this guy was trouble and that's why he took it? There was no mysterious crime boss gunning for me. It was just this guy kidnapping a drunken girl after she got a tattoo.

Galvanized by logical paranoia, I bolted again. It was another beautiful escape. I dodged the traffic behind Layne's car just right, so he couldn't have followed if he tried. "Elise!" I heard him holler behind me. He didn't sound mad, just frustrated and I almost turned around to look at him, but resisted the curiosity that begged to see his expression.

I jogged in and out of blocks until I was lost enough to feel safe. I stopped at some point and leaned against a white stucco wall. It was then that I realized my theory was all wrong and I was being stupid.

It was all in the jeans. Kidnappers don't buy

expensive jeans.

The truth was I had no idea what was going on for sure until I read Deja's note. Without it, I was lost. Without it, I was alone. As messed up as it was, my stupid other half was the only family I had.

I crouched down, piled my purse in my lap to protect it and cried into my hands just like Deja said I would. I hated it when she was right.

I heard the rumble of a car pull up on the road next to me, but I didn't look up. I already knew it was him. Come to collect the pathetic hysterical—

"Get up, bitch!"

What?

I looked up between the two set of legs that had towering torsos above them, and saw the shiny silver sports car. Wrong car.

Craptastic!

I stood up eye to eye with the two Hispanic men before me. I was taller than both of them, but that made little difference. Even if they weren't stronger than me, the guns tucked under their arms were definitely faster.

"You got a lot of nerve coming back to this town." *Back?* "We told you last summer not to come back. This town is hard-wired, sweetie. We knew the minute your face hit town." These weren't murderers, these were loan sharks. When did Deja have time to go to Vegas? Suddenly my difficulty holding a job was starting to make sense.

"I'm sorry, I got arrested. It won't happen again. I was just trying to get a bus out of here."

"You know that's not how it works. You've got to

pay the toll. So what will the payment be? Cash, credit..." He winked at me. "...or check?" He cracked his knuckles, while his friend cracked his neck.

"Cash!" Layne approached down the sidewalk, pulling out his wallet. "What's the going rate for misdemeanors?"

"A grand." The speaking man turned his attention to Layne.

Layne chuckled as he positioned himself between me and the two thugs. "A grand? She's only been in town an hour. That's bullshit."

"Bullshit is this skank touching Mr. Devitti's son."

"Oh," Layne drawled. "This is a toll for that incident with Artie. In that case, you boys can have this." Layne handed them a one-dollar bill. "If Mr. Devitti has any problems with that, you tell him that Layne Cantry gave him that dollar on her behalf. If he doesn't remember me, tell him I'm the owner of the bullet still lodged in his leg."

The men looked flustered by this new information.

"Mr. Devitti and I have an understanding. A peace treaty, if you will. Tell him that his son is a handsy asshole when he's drunk, and he got what he deserved. I will consider today's matter closed, but if he has any questions, I can visit with him anytime."

The men exchanged looks, but decided that even a grand wasn't worth getting shot over, which was strange, since they had two guns to Layne's one. Apparently, Layne Cantry had more of a reputation in this town than Deja.

7

I was glad to be getting out of Vegas. Even if Layne seemed to have the locals under control, it was still a crazy town to get stuck in.

I looked over at Layne. He hadn't chastised me for bolting again. He seemed to understand, or at least he just didn't want to waste his time with a lecture. He was driving fast and determined, like he had an agenda and needed to get on with it. I remembered that he had been checking his watch that morning.

"What?" He glanced over at me when he noticed me watching him.

"That was pretty bad-ass what you did back there."

"No, it wasn't." He smiled. "Devitti's wife put that bullet in his leg, but his lackeys don't know that or he would lose face. It was a risk, but there was no way I was going to pay those idiots a grand."

"Won't that make enemies with Devitti?"

"Nah, those two won't even mention that they saw me. They'll gossip about me with the other lackeys until the story changes into Blaine Suntry the seven-foot giant with testicles as big as grapefruits and fists the size of hams." I laughed. He was funny, too. "They'll have to make their surrender seem more reasonable."

"Grapefruit testicles, huh?" I smiled.

"Well, I admit oranges to grapefruits is a pretty big leap, but…" He chuckled, unable to finish. I laughed again. It was nice to laugh, but something occurred to me.

"Wait a minute… How did you know Deja assaulted Devitti's son? And don't tell me it was a lucky guess."

"It could have been, given my knowledge of his son and Deja's personality, but no, she mentioned it in passing when I suggested we hide out in Vegas."

"Oh." I felt a pang of jealousy as I remembered that I was the odd man out in this little adventure.

"Look, Elise, I know today has gone from bad to worse for you, but I'd really like you to trust me. I can't protect you if you don't trust me. I also can't protect you if you keep running away from me." He said it apologetically, like he was sorry that I had to stay with him. It made me feel guilty. I hadn't intended to make him feel rejected. I hadn't actually taken his feelings into consideration at all.

"I know," I said, shifting uncomfortably in the bucket seat. I felt like I could stop the car if I just pushed on the floorboard hard enough. "I just wish I could hear it from Deja."

"I have the note in my duffel bag. You can read it at the next stop."

"You know what it says?"

"I wrote most of it, so yes." He glanced over at me. "That bothers you, doesn't it?"

"No," I lied.

"I know I've invaded your privacy on a

monumental level, but being as this was supposed to be the note that introduces me, I really needed it to be… coherent. I'll avoid doing it in the future, unless it's a life or death emergency, if that makes you feel any better."

"Sure," I said, still not wanting to admit to how much it bothered me to have him in between us. I barely knew this man, yet he knew private details about my other self that I didn't even know. He wasn't so much invading my privacy as dwarfing my relationship with Deja, such as it was.

We stopped at a diner to eat a late lunch. Layne brought in his duffel bag that he had come into the hotel with that morning. He flopped down in the booth across from me and handed me the letter. I grabbed it like gold and pressed it to my chest.

I chuckled at myself. "Wow, talk about pacification," I said and he smiled before looking down at his menu. "It's just…" I paused, not sure how much of myself I wanted to offer this man. "It's all we have, you know?"

"I know," he said, and I suppose he did. Not many people knew about twin souls. It was a relief to be able to speak freely around him, not questioning what I should say or how I should act. "She gets pretty territorial about your letters too."

"Really?" I asked, somewhat touched.

"She pretends not to care, and she rants about your lectures, but I think she likes having someone to boss her around. Even if it is just so she can disobey."

"Speaking of disobeying." I reached across the table and touched his hand. It was mostly to express my fervor on the topic, but I also liked to test my boundaries. He glanced at the touch, but didn't move away. "Can you please get her to stop smoking? My lungs hurt." I put my hand back to my chest to emphasize my point. "They literally hurt if I breathe too deep." I took in a demonstrated breath and it made me cough. I took a drink of my water to calm the burn.

"I'll see what I can do, but I might have pressed my luck by talking her out of tattooing 'Fuck Me Hard' on your ass."

I sucked in water with my shocked gasp and spat it all back out again. Layne was doing his best to control his laughter while I tried to breathe, cough, and ask a question at the same time. "What?" was all I could choke out.

A waitress came rushing over to offer me the Heimlich maneuver, and when I declined she patted me on the back and left us extra napkins to clean up.

"She did not seriously request that?" I asked when my voice returned.

"She more than requested it. If you look at that tat close enough, the bottom portion looks a lot like an arrow." My eyes widened in shock. I clenched my teeth with forever-unsatisfied rage and smacked the letter onto the table. "She said…" He looked around and leaned in to whisper so he didn't appall those eating with the godawful language that regularly left Deja's mouth. "She said if you were going to— I'm sorry, I shouldn't tell you this." He chuckled.

I rolled my eyes because I could tell he really wanted to tell me. "Just tell me. It can't be any more embarrassing than what she's already done with this body."

"She said if you were going to have a stick up your ass, you might as well get off on it." Layne looked down at the table, amused, but when he saw the fake smile I was offering him, he looked sheepish. "Elise, I'm sorry, I shouldn't have said that." He sighed. "It's just, she's so…"

I narrowed my eyes at seeing the admiration in his eyes for her. It shouldn't have bothered me. I should have been pleased, but it made me feel like a third wheel on a dinner date that I couldn't get out of. *Ever.*

"Fun?" I offered, and he lost all humor in his face.

"No, outrageous. The things that come out of her mouth are like verbal Ripley's Believe It or Not." He reached over and touched my hand like I had his moments earlier. "I just wanted you to know that despite the result of last night's excursion, I *was* defending your ass." He held back his smile until I smiled at his joke. He squeezed my hand reassuringly and gave it a slight caress that made me take stock in the moment. Unfortunately, the arrival of our food split our hands like nervous teenagers.

9

Dear Elise, YOU ARE A....

I skipped a page ahead to where the writing switched to Layne's.

*I found your research you ****

I noted the footnote at the bottom of the letter indicating that all asterisks were to represent threads of unnecessary, unconscionable profanity. Well, at least Layne kept the spirit of the letter if not the tone.

*I found your research you ***. I can't believe you could consider sectioning us. You're a *** for even considering that. That is selfish, even for you. You should know I would never hurt you that way.*

*Layne here wants me to discuss him. He's a selfish bastard too. You two will get along great. You should *** him. Have babies and shit. It'll be great.*

Here's the thing, someone is trying to kill us and we don't know why. Layne's going to help us. He's saved me once already, and you too, you just didn't know it. I don't know a lot about him, but he's a good guy and you should trust him.

I'm not going to apologize for the tattoo. I know it probably hurts like hell, but you hurt me first. Just do what Layne tells you and don't freak out. I'll figure this out... somehow.

It was short, sweet and to the point, just like Deja—

minus the sweet. It would have been better to hear the details about their introduction, but that was probably irrelevant.

I tucked the letter into my back pocket as Layne came out of the diner from paying. "Well, was it enlightening?" he asked, knowing full well that it wasn't.

"A little terse, but colorful as usual."

"Yeah, I think I should have left the profanity in, just to give you something more to read."

"That would have been nice. She didn't say much about you."

He shrugged. "I told her to, but she said I could tell you, and I didn't want to put words in her mouth." He opened the car door for me and I climbed in. The sun was starting to go down and I wanted to ask where we were going, but I also didn't want to badger Layne with questions.

The ride was quiet for a few miles and I didn't mind since I still had a headache. Finally he broke the silence. "Aren't you going to ask where we're going?"

"I'm unemployed and supposedly being targeted for murder. I'm kind of carte blanche right now, so I'll defer to you."

"Supposedly?"

"It will be supposedly until it's not." I paused. "Okay, where are we going?"

He smiled. "I'm heading to Arizona."

"Are they really going to follow us? I mean, it's one thing to have a hit out on someone, but tracking them across the country seems to drain the resources a bit."

"These people are very determined," he said with threat in his voice.

"Why can't you just put me in a safe house under armed guard?"

"If saving your life was the only goal—and if I could find enough trustworthy men—I would. But I'm not interested in the men pulling the triggers. I want the men that hired them."

"Do you have any idea who those men are?"

"Pick your favorite mob boss. It could be any one of them."

I squinched my face up trying to consider that idea. I was well aware that there were three infamously rich and dangerous men surreptitiously running the country through underworld connections. However, to me they were like characters out of a bad bedtime story. Layne saying that the triad was targeting me was like saying Santa Clause, the Easter Bunny, and Jack Frost were coming to get me. Or I suppose in this case Krampus, Freddy Krueger, and the Boogieman.

"Why would they want to kill me? I couldn't be more than a fleck of dust on their radar."

"I'm not certain. That's what has me so intrigued, and why I began investigating you two. I suspect that it has to do with another investigation I am working on, but until I can prove it, the suspicion is useless. I'm hoping to figure more out from you, which in turn will help me put my investigation to rest and put some very bad men in prison. Yet another reason I can't put you in police custody. If we do come across any of these guys, I'm sure I'll be able to get information from them as well."

"So you're protecting me because I might be able to help your case. However, if I can't, you'll just let me be killed so you can interrogate my killers?" I glared at him.

"What? No! That's not what I meant. You're over simplifying it." He glanced at me. He was annoyed, but clearly it was partly true. I was only alive right now because I might hold the key to breaking his case.

10

Layne checked us into the motel and all hopes of a clean room left my mind when I smelled it. The residual smell of smoke, incense, and rotten food made my stomach lurch. Layne stepped past me while I lingered in the doorway to acclimate my nasal passages. He was either oblivious to the smell, or just didn't want to dwell on it. He kicked off his shoes and dumped his duffel bag and keys on the dresser beside the television.

"Just one room?" I asked, looking over the single queen bed and no couch.

"We're on the lam, not vacationing. Besides, my budget doesn't account for duplicate charges." I nodded, still hanging out by the door. The air wasn't any fresher in Arizona, but it was fresher than this room. "Don't worry. I can call up a cot or something. They'll charge an extra $20 for it…" He trailed off as he yawned.

I shut the door and stepped inside. I placed my purse next to his bag and stared at the sparse surroundings. It was almost identical to the motel room I had woken up in that morning. Instead of the 70s motif, though, they were rocking the 80s pretty hard. The pastel paradise was accented by brass lamps topped with oversized ivory shades. Even the Santa Fe-style comforter on the bed was marred with pinks and purples instead of the traditional oranges and reds. I was in décor hell.

I meandered over to the bathroom to finish my evaluation. It was probably technically clean, but the peeling linoleum, warped counter top, and cracked plastic shower liner were so deeply stained, even a hard scrubbing wouldn't have helped it look sanitary to me. I reluctantly decided against a shower. I wasn't exactly dirty and there was no point in exposing more of my body to the room.

"You're just going to have to relax, Elise," Layne said, moving to the bed to call the front desk. "The coming days are going to be boring. Hiding out is a lot like waiting in a doctor's office. If you don't prepare yourself to be bored for a while, you're just going to get antsy and pissed off."

Layne spoke with the front desk while I scanned the channels for something reasonable to watch. I was not surprised to find that of the eight channels they had, two were scrambled porn.

"Bad news, no cot," Layne said dropping the phone less-than-gingerly on the base.

"Worse news, the porn channels are scrambled and the remaining channels deserve to be scrambled."

He smiled at my joke. "Which reminds me." He pulled the top comforter off the bed and threw it in the corner of the room. "Rule number one in cheap hotels: don't touch the top blanket."

"What's rule number two?"

"Don't let the bed bugs bite." He winked and I

couldn't help but give him a coy grin. "Seriously though, is this going to be really uncomfortable for you?" He nodded to the bed. "I could potentially sleep in the bathtub, but I'm not touching that floor."

"What do you and Deja do?"

He hissed through his teeth before answering. "We were sleeping together." The phrasing threw me off and for a second I couldn't quite remember what we were discussing. "I mean sleeping in the same bed." I nodded, trying to hide my relief. "She's not easily offended by strange men in her bed though."

He meant it as a joke, but it was true. Deja was the free spirit. Somehow that tended to imply *slut*, but in truth she didn't do it that often. Just more often than me, which was never—lately anyway. "I'm sure it's big enough," I conceded, not wanting to sound like a prude.

I crawled onto the bed to give it a try. Layne leaned back on his side and offered me a forced smile. "How's that?"

"It's fine. So, speaking of Deja and you, what exactly *is* your relationship? I know you said you didn't sleep with her last night, but is that circumstantial or are you two seriously just business?"

"Nothing is just business with Deja, but we aren't lovers and I don't intend to be."

"Oh."

"Why do you ask?"

"You said this morning that you don't get involved with Siamese minds. Is that a lesson learned through knowledge or experience?"

"Ah, knowledge, I guess. It's got nothing to do with

me. It's the twin mentality. No matter how you look at it, I'd be getting between you two."

"It's not like that. I know most twin minds are like two halves to a whole. Not with us. She hates me, and I resent her. We just live our separate-but-same lives, and pretend the other isn't there."

"How can you say that when a note from her clearly means so much to you?"

"I live a half-life, Layne. That note is important because I might have missed something. She's the yin, I'm the yang, but without the dots, we're just two people hanging out back to back, but never seeing each other."

He looked at me piteously and I realized I was complaining about my life, which at the moment was still valuable to me, otherwise I wouldn't be running from whoever was trying to kill me. "I don't suppose this place has robes?" I asked, tossing the remote back on the bed before heading to the bathroom.

"These places barely have towels. Why?" He picked up the remote and searched the short list of channels before settling on the news.

"Well, unless you had the forethought to grab my other outfit, I just have this and I'm kind of a freak about clean clothes. Too many mornings in cheap hotels, I guess," I said as I checked the bathroom's contents. Hand soap—possibly used—two bath towels, a hand towel, a shower cap, and that was it. I shook my head in awe of the shower cap. They hadn't provided shampoo or conditioner. Instead they provided you with the option of just not washing your hair. Since no one ever used them it was probably a few years old.

"The robe wouldn't do you much good anyway," Layne called after me. "They don't have washing machines here either. This is as low rent as you can get, but it is a no-questions-asked type of place, and right now that's what we need."

I stepped out of the bathroom and looked around the room again. Bed, television, dresser, end tables, and that was it. The place smelled like so many horrible things. The rug looked like someone could have died on it, and probably had. I had officially entered territory I never thought I would reach. I couldn't wait until Deja was back in control.

"Hey," Layne whispered and I looked up at his concerned face. "You don't look so good."

I frowned and wrung my hands together. "Do you mind if *I* sleep in the bathtub?"

11

A half hour later we pulled into an outlet mall somewhere outside of Flagstaff. Layne had suggested we purchase a few more outfits for me. I wondered if he would have offered the option to Deja or if he just felt sorry for me.

I stepped out of the fitting room with a couple more jeans, two shirts, and a workout outfit that would double as pajamas and laundry apparel if we got the chance to wash clothes. I stepped up to the register with my purchases. Layne arrived behind me with a canvas bag to hold it all and another set of underwear and socks which I would have forgotten.

I flushed at seeing his choices. The socks were standard white but the underwear was black and lacy with little pink bows. He glanced over at me, looking a little uncomfortable. He cleared his throat. "It was all they had," he mumbled.

"It's fine," I murmured back.

I pulled out my credit card, prepared to add yet another load of debt to my pile. I was thankful that my low income allowed me an interest cap on the sum, otherwise bankruptcy would be in my future. As it was, I wasn't sure if the card limit had been reached at the gas station.

"I can get it," Layne offered, pulling out his wallet.

"That's okay, you've done enough," I insisted since he had paid for my lunch and the motel room.

He grabbed my hand before I could transfer the card to the cashier. She looked over the scene like she was witnessing a domestic dispute about to unfurl. I glared at him for the manhandling. I expected him to be apologetic, but he stared at me with wide eyes. He was irritated at me for wanting to pay. What foreign land of male dominance had I wandered into?

"No, really." He put on a fake smile as he pulled my hand down. "I would like to pay." His finger caressed my hand and I looked down at the intimate little touch. His finger moved from my skin and tapped the plastic card in my hand.

My eyes darted back up to his, shocked and apologetic, not to mention embarrassed for my stupidity. "Thank you." I shoved my credit card back in my purse like it might start emanating a homing beacon to my hitmen if I didn't.

"I hope you don't mind cash," Layne asked the cashier as he pulled five hundred-dollar bills out of his wallet.

"No problem." The cashier counted the hundreds again. "Did you need change for this? It's only $356." She slid one of the bills back at him.

"So it is." He took the hundred and folded it in half and half again. "I don't suppose you keep an in-house surveillance system, do you?"

The cashier blanched as she made our change. "Why?"

"No reason. I just happen to be a little bit famous,

or at least I will be pretty soon. Oscar, here I come." He grimaced and crossed his fingers. "Anyway, this all happens to be coinciding with my divorce and I would hate for the missus to track down footage of me purchasing underwear for another woman." The cashier looked to me and I smiled shyly. "I don't suppose you could do an edit on that footage before it gets uploaded into the central surveillance records?"

"I would imagine that would be possible, but I make minimum wage and that hundred bucks isn't going to do much for the utilities I'm late on." The cashier pushed his change over to him and perked her brow. She was good.

"Oh, perish the thought. Let me see what funds I have available." Layne flipped through his wallet. He had at least a dozen hundred-dollar bills there, but he hissed pretending like he was struggling to find what he wanted. I knew he must keep a lot of money on him for this purpose, but it still seemed like a lot of cash for anyone to have.

"I like that necklace you're wearing." He looked at the cashier from under his brow. I couldn't see what he was referring to. The thin gold chain was attractive, but the pendant had slipped beneath her blouse.

"It's worthless, except for its sentimental value, of course."

"Of course." Layne was flirting and negotiating. "How about I purchase the necklace and the aforementioned procedure, for..." Layne threw the hundred he was holding back out with the change and added two more to it. The cashier took the money, handed him the necklace, and proceeded to the back room to delete the last hour of footage for us. The only guarantee in the matter was that she wouldn't want her boss to see her taking bribes.

12

As we drove away from the mall, back toward the hotel, I remembered I needed shampoo, conditioner, and soap, since our fancy accommodations were above such luxuries. Layne sighed like I was asking for new sheets and a throw rug to spice up the joint.

"Come on, Layne, I'm not asking for lip gloss and hairspray. Clean hair makes me much easier to live with."

"I know, but there's a reason these cheap motels work to hide out in. They can't afford the surveillance equipment. Every stop we make is another chance to be recorded. These guys are entrenched in the system. Hell, the system was built around them from the ground up. Security functions just fine, unless they don't want it to. One whisper and the cover-up happens—quite literally with the click of a mouse."

"You mean they have guys on the inside?"

"I mean they have guys built into the mortar and stone that separate the inside from the outside. It's old-school mob stuff. There's no money in security if everything is secure. The only way to profit is through bribes. The..." He glanced over at me. I was listening intently so I didn't understand why he stopped.

"What? Why'd you stop?"

"Deja hates when I talk about this stuff. I wasn't

sure if you were just being polite by staying awake."

I chuckled. "Even if I wasn't interested, the fact that she isn't would make me interested. Go on, please."

"Okay, well, let's start with the traffic violations. There are enough violations to keep the system running, but not profitable. Public service at its best, right? Personal properties and businesses pay in a substantial amount, but there's a flaw to that system." He glanced at me; I wasn't sure if he was waiting for my question, or just checking again to see if I was still awake.

"The security systems work too well. Crime is virtually impossible to get away with. It might still happen, but the police can track anyone. Someone says they were robbed in a park? All they need is a rough description and they'll have a dozen cameras with deposited footage to find the perp, and a dozen more to track him home. Crime literally doesn't pay anymore.

"This all sounds great, but the big business drug dealers and car thieves still want to make money, so when this system really started gaining clout they started recruiting men and women to get employed by the police departments and the surveillance depots. Naturally, they get a wage for their day-to-day job, but the bosses also siphon in a little extra income, like a retainer for duties to be performed."

"No shortage of people willing to take extra money."

"Not just that, but it's way easier doing a menial labor job when you know you're part of something bigger. It's like pretending to be poor when you're really rich."

"So whenever they need to do a big job, they just call their depot contact and say delete the footage for this. Why can't you catch the employees?" I asked.

"There are just too many people with access. It's too much data. Most of the depot's job *is* to delete footage. They are supposed to go through the data in minute increments to determine usefulness, but that doesn't happen. Most of the footage gets deleted in hourly blocks. Even if we could pinpoint which employee did it, we wouldn't know for sure if the deletion was intentional or just the typical disregard for the rules. Besides, it wouldn't solve the issue, which is the crime bosses behind them."

"And that's where you come in?"

"Yeah, me and a select trusted few who have chosen to work privately. We can do things the police can't get away with. We monitor activity and when necessary intervene."

"Was it necessary to intervene for me... for us?"

Layne glanced over. "No, it wasn't."

I held my breath, waiting for an explanation to accompany that sentence, but he didn't offer one. I felt my stomach clench as I started to realize what he was saying. "I was right before, wasn't I? You were content to just monitor me, and see who my killers were so you could interrogate them. The only reason you're even doing this is because Deja figured you out and asked for help."

"That's putting it a little simply again. I obviously would have tried to stop them from killing you. But no, I never intended to get this involved. I think Deja thought *I* was the one trying to kill her at first. She spotted me after one of the attacks and approached me. I tried to play it off as coincidence, but she had me pegged from the get go. She must have realized that the attempts on her life weren't going to stop and she asked me to help watch over you while she was away."

"But why are they doing this?"

"That's one of many questions I am hoping to answer by including you in this mess."

"You think *I* know why we're being targeted?" I was still reeling from his willingness to watch me die. Now he wanted me to answer his why questions, when my list was just as long as his. "Layne, I just got thrown into this *today*. Up until this minute, I was still running under the assumption that you gave a damn about us."

Layne sighed and gripped the steering wheel a little harder. After a few more miles of silence, he pulled onto an off ramp exiting to a fuel station. He pulled behind the building and parked with the engine still running. He turned to me and pointed a finger in my face.

"I need you to stay here, out of view of any cameras. Damn, I should have bought you a hat. Just don't get out, okay?"

"Okay," I said obediently. He held my gaze for another second like he couldn't believe I'd agreed. He mumbled something about yin and yang before he was out of audible range, but I couldn't understand it.

A few minutes later he returned with a bag of shampoo, conditioner, body wash, and deodorant, toothbrushes and toothpaste, which I would have forgotten had I gone in myself. "Happy?" he asked gruffly as he shifted into gear.

"That's difficult to manage in this situation, but it makes me feel less like a kidnap victim." He looked me over before settling on my face.

"You're so different." He deepened his brow at the observation. "I knew you would be, but I just didn't think it would matter that much." He looked away, peeling out of the lot faster than necessary. As the force pressed me back into my seat, I wondered if knowing Deja from the outside was easier or if she put up just as many walls for him.

"Look, Elise, I don't want to start thinking about what would have been if I hadn't intervened. I did. I'm glad that I did. I'm also not going anywhere. We've got another day left together, and I would prefer if you didn't start second-guessing my motives again." He looked me square-on and I could see a little guilt still lurking behind his eyes. "I'm going to keep you alive. How and why are for me to mull over, not you."

It wasn't really the consoling "I do care about you" that I was fishing for, but that was a lot to expect on what was technically our first day together. At least he agreed to help Deja despite the lack of money. That showed some chivalrous character. Plus, one couldn't overlook the care of a man concerned about a girl's hygiene.

13

Back at the motel, I succumbed to the temptation of a hot shower. Disregarding the bathroom's shortcomings, I scrubbed off every last dead skin cell that had been witness to this horrible day. I mostly just wanted to cry under the sterilizing heat of the water, but Layne had asked me to keep the door open, in case someone knocked down the door and we needed a quick escape through the window. It sounded a little far-fetched, but my reservations were met with a gentle but stern suggestion that I let him do his job. Consequently, instead of letting him hear me weeping like a child to relieve my stress, I just took my OCD to a new level and made raw skin my new badge of courage.

I shut the door part-way while I dressed and kept Layne's feet in view. He seemed to be a gentleman, but he had already seen me naked once today, and it would take more than our Chinese take-out dinner to get him a second show. Not that he was interested, since I was a twin soul.

I stepped out of the bathroom wearing my jogging suit and socks to protect my feet from the filth that would never be washed out of the carpet. Layne was asleep on the bed with the remote control in his hand. I smiled at his glasses sitting cock-eyed on his face. I resisted the maternal urge that demanded I remove them and place them on the nightstand. Instead, I tiptoed over to my purse and pulled out my cell. I pressed it in my ear and slipped outside for some privacy.

The common balcony that provided access to the second-level rooms overlooked the parking lot. I couldn't see the sunset from this angle, but the residual purple smears across the cloud coverage was still attractive enough to gaze out at. I glanced around to see if I was alone. The only sounds of life, besides Layne's news channel, was the ice machine somewhere below me, struggling to catch up after a hot Arizona day.

Content with my privacy, I pressed the button on my cellular earpiece. "Memo." The device's computer voice spoke into my ear to confirm that it was ready to receive my message. "I know you hate voice messages. It *is* a little weird hearing yourself update yourself on… yourself. I just needed to talk out loud. Say something that couldn't be read by our caretaker. I'm probably going to write you a horrible nasty note, and I'm not going to apologize, because you deserve it.

"I don't understand anything that's going on. I'm just trying to keep up and not look like a complete princess. I know you tried to keep this from me. To protect me. And in my note, I'll rip your ass every which way for doing it, but… thank you. I don't want Layne to know this, but you were right. I'm scared as hell, and I'm not dealing with all this very well. I'm holding it together at least, but I kind of wish I could just fade out and let you take over for a while." I snorted. "Bet you didn't think Miss Control Freak would ever say that."

I paused to articulate the words I really needed to say to Deja. The words I owed her.

"I know you're mad about the research, but it isn't what it looks like. I would never try to hurt you just to have full control. I thought there might be a way to just separate us. Clearly that's the stupidest thing in the world, because there isn't another body to go into if one of us left. All that came of that research was the same story over and over. The only way one of us can have full control is for the other to be… How did they put it? Disembodied. That loosely translates to dead or forever in limbo, which is worse.

"It's all a lot of mumbo-jumbo that I'm not even sure I believe anymore. After the first dozen shamans I just gave up. I never had any intention of denying you your existence. I just thought… Maybe there was a better way. It was stupid and I'm sorry. I hope you can forgive me." I brushed away a tear. "I need you to forgive me." I hadn't realized until I said it how much I needed her forgiveness. The bond between us, as strange and divided as it was… I couldn't stand the idea of her hating me. It was one thing for me to irritate her with our standing arguments about clothes, hair, and fried foods, but to actually hurt her feelings? That was not okay.

"Anyway, I still have tomorrow and more than a baker's dozen of questions, so I'll see where my interrogations on Layne take me before I turn them onto you."

I paused, wanting to say something to end my

monologue. Deja and I weren't friends or family, so we never said 'I love you.' Aside from our signatures, there were no goodbyes. Wishing her good luck seemed a little dark at that point. I ended the recording and saved it as an urgent message, which made the little red light on my earpiece blink.

I sneaked back inside and slipped the device back into my purse and crawled into bed beside Layne. I tugged his glasses off, causing him to stir. "You okay?" He looked around the room for danger.

"Yeah, I'm okay, go back to sleep." I folded his glasses and leaned across him to set them on his nightstand.

He watched the movement with some interest. As I withdrew he touched my arm, not quite grabbing it, but indicating that he wanted my attention. "Don't go anywhere without me. Not even the vending machine, okay?" He sounded half asleep, but he was definitely serious. I wasn't sure how he would feel about my trip out the door, but ten feet away from him in the bathroom wasn't any different.

"Okay," I said and lay down on my half of the bed. I felt a little self-conscious lying next to him. It had been a while since I had a man this close to me in a supine position. With his glasses off, his bookish look had turned to just plain cute. His curls were ruffled from his sleep, making for good bed-head hair. He was getting a five o'clock shadow that was dappled with a little gray, just like his head. He wasn't old, but if I had to predict, he would be all gray by forty-five.

I wanted to reach over and touch him, but I

reminded myself that I had just met him that morning. He was just doing his job, and I… was really tired.

55 DEJA VU

14

I woke the next day from tendrils of sunlight peeking through the ripped curtains. My headache was finally gone and I was looking forward to a boring day. Layne was out of bed. I could hear the shower creak as the water shut off. Shortly after, he emerged from the bathroom drying his hair with one towel, while the other was draped around his waist. His torso was a beautiful sight to a love-starved woman.

"Good morning, sleepy head." He grinned.

Oh God help me, he was a morning person.

"Are you hungry?" he asked cheerfully. I nodded, rubbing the sleep from my eyes. "Good, I'll get dressed and run through a drive-through."

"Yuck, can't we get real food?"

"Real food takes longer." He was still smiling, but I recognized the tone. He didn't like being deterred from his duty. It was admirable, but I couldn't help but think this was excessive. If what Layne said about the surveillance systems was true, I just needed to stay hidden. That would be easy: no credit cards, stay in the car when traveling, stay in the hotel when not. His insistence on one room, no closed doors, and minimal time apart was paranoia from too many years as a cop.

"I think I saw a diner on the way back. Breakfast doesn't take long to make." I rolled my neck, getting a few cracks out of it. The bed wasn't as bad as I expected, but the pillows were. Layne lowered his towel and gave me the same look he had when I asked for shampoo—which, by the looks of it, he appreciated as much as me. "I'll eat whatever you bring back, Layne, but just be aware that we may need to make a stop at a drug store for Pepto if you keep getting me pre-digested food."

He grimaced at my description and went back into the bathroom to dress. A few minutes later he emerged patting his hands on his legs. "I'll be back in forty minutes. Get dressed, don't shower, don't watch TV."

"Why?" I asked and he looked at me gravely. There was no doubt that he was a cop at heart. I suddenly felt a strong desire to reach for my license and registration. "I won't, but what is your reasoning?"

"You mean other than I'm protecting you?"

"Whatever. I'll just stare at the door like a dog waiting for his owner." I moved around the bed and found my stash of new clothes. I would have preferred to wash them before wearing them, but we were well beyond that luxury and then some.

"Elise," Layne said quietly and I turned back to him. "I need you to stay quiet in case someone comes. If they do, your best chance is going to be hiding under the bed. They'll assume we've left. Do you understand? Listen and hide. Don't open the door; don't go get ice; don't call the front desk. Just don't, okay?"

I could feel myself tense with the thought of having to hide under the bed like a scared child. Hiding seemed even scarier than running. "Can't I just come with you?"

Layne shook his head somberly. "No, it's too close to town, too many locals, too many cameras. Just sit tight and I'll be back. Forty minutes." He started to go, but I grabbed his arm.

"Just get the fast food."

He took my hand from his arm and kissed it. "Thirty minutes." He winked at me and smiled. It made me feel better, but I couldn't smile back. He let go of my hand, picked up his duffel bag, and went out the door. His shadow filtered through the curtains as he walked away from the room.

I was nervous without him there, but that was what he intended. He wanted me on edge so I didn't do something stupid. I got dressed in the room in full view of the door. I nearly had a heart attack when my shirt snagged on my stud earrings and I couldn't immediately get it past my eyes.

Dressed and ready to hide, I checked my watch. Ten measly minutes had passed. A couple passed outside laughing and talking. I froze, panicked that they might just be pretending to be a happy couple.

By twenty minutes, I was feeling a little stupid. Boredom set in and I gathered my canvas bag and purse that I had shoved under the bed to hide with me if someone came. I went to the bathroom to brush my teeth. I should have waited until after I ate, but I had neglected it last night, despite my enthusiasm at having the option.

I kept an eye on the window as I quietly brushed my teeth. Around twenty-five minutes I noticed two shadows moving across the window. The suspiciously slow movement made me freeze. They even stopped and looked around, as if they were surveying their surroundings.

I clutched my toothbrush in my teeth, lassoed my purse around my neck, and clutched the canvas bag like a teddy bear. I waited as they cleared the frame of the window. I silently wished, begged, and prayed to whatever deities were on call to let them just keep walking by.

The door handle rattled quietly. Had I not been instructed to be keep the television off, I might never have heard the knob. Thankfully it was locked, with me safely behind it.

The knob shifted again and I heard a scratching sound, as if they were putting a key into the lock. My skin lit with a burning, shivering panic as I realized that they were picking the lock. They were going to get in. They were going to kill me. I was about to die.

I looked at the bed, but it was too late. It would take me a good deal of effort to squirm under it, and I was too terrified to move, let alone *closer* to the hitmen on the other side of the door. I wanted the opposite direction, and fast.

I closed the bathroom door, but not all the way. I didn't want to confirm that I was there. I looked around for a weapon, but promptly realized that guns trumped plungers on too many levels to count.

My only other option was the window. I moved to it, and opened it. Since it was the only updated amenity in the entire motel, I was able to open it quickly and without the sound of scraping wood. Assuming I could fit through the damn thing, I had a shot at hiding outside.

I crawled through fast and soundless. My adrenaline would get to take the credit for that acrobatic accomplishment. Since I was one floor up, I had to steady myself on the cement ledge outside. The panic I had been feeling inside the room was gone. I was no longer motivated entirely by the fear of guns and death. I was now running from monsters under the bed and people under the stairs. My fear was blooming to irrational proportions. It was all I could do to keep from squealing and curling into a ball.

My eyes watered as I heard the door slam open. They were only seconds from pushing open the bathroom door and seeing my head bobbing outside the window, but I had to close it behind me. They needed to believe I was already gone. Miles and miles away.

As I clicked the pane into place, I heard shots inside the room. Through the crack in the door and the mirror's reflection, I could see a puff of fluff flying in the air from the pillow-top mattress. The mattress I might have hidden underneath had I allowed myself the time.

I saw movement again and I crouched down just as I heard the bathroom door slam open. I grabbed the ledge beneath me and dropped my feet down. I reeled my legs in so I didn't kick the building and announce my location. I heard the window slide open and I dropped. My landing coincided with the pane hitting its maximum height.

I tucked back against the building under the ledge I had only seconds earlier been standing on. The building had a warbled wall design, offering incremental indentations—just big enough to tuck myself into. Between that and the protruding ledge, I was hidden. If the man leaned out the window even a foot, though, he would see me.

I resisted the urge to run. Running now was a guarantee of death. Instead I took the only other option beyond fight or flight. The one that never worked in the wild.

I froze.

I sensed the search taking place above me. I was beyond terrified, nearly ready to pass out. I wasn't even sure that I was breathing anymore. All I knew was that I needed to stay impossibly quiet. I was never more thankful for the distant toot of a train and the whisking sound of speeding traffic.

There was a scuffle of movement above, and the window slammed. There was a short conversation, but it was too muffled to interpret. I could tell they were unhappy with the results of their search. I, however, was overjoyed. I continued to listen as the sounds above me dissipated. I thought I heard a car drive away from the hotel, but I had no way of knowing who was in it. Even when the longevity of silence told me that it was safe to move, I didn't.

It might have been five more minutes like Layne had promised, but I was there an hour if I was there for another minute. Even when I heard Layne's voice calling my name, I didn't move. I was at peace with my complete and utter cowardice. I was content to make my home right there under that window and never leave. It was, in my mind, the only safe place in the entire world.

Layne must have realized I wasn't under the bed. The window opened and he craned out, hissing my name like he wasn't sure if the enemy was still lurking about. I still didn't move. I was afraid. It didn't matter that Layne was there to rescue me. Rational thought was too much to ask. Verbal skills were so far down the list of possible actions, I couldn't even be sure what words were anymore.

He must have seen me, or at least suspected that this was my path. He jumped down from above, landing adeptly with a spring in his knees. He caught sight of me huddled as flat as I could manage, breathing slowly, shallowly, quietly.

At some point, I had started to tremble, but I couldn't be sure if it was before or after he embraced me. He pressed the back of my head against his shoulder and I sucked in a few consoling breaths before I wet his shirt with tears. I tried to keep some of it in, but the hiccupping, grunted sobs were all that was left of my function.

Layne took my bag and pulled me along with his arm around my back. I didn't even want to go, but my objections to leaving my hiding place were met with a stronger pull. He took me around to his car and opened the passenger-side door.

I shook my head vigorously, but I didn't even know why. He shushed me and pushed me in anyway. Once I was inside the vehicle hugging my purse and holding my breath to stop myself from wailing, I found my voice.

"I want to go home," I said as he started the engine. "I want to go home," I said again because I knew he wouldn't take me there. "I want to go home." Now I was just being a broken record. A *very* broken record.

"I know, Elise, but not just yet."

"I don't want to do this anymore. Get Deja. I don't want to be here for this. She was right. I'm too scared."

He shushed me and hugged me over the console.

"They shot the bed," I blubbered in his ear and he pulled back, cupping my face.

"Yes, but you weren't under that bed. You did everything right. You did very good." He kissed my lips innocently enough to classify as consoling. "Now we need to get the hell out of here."

I nodded in his hands. He looked me over once more and let me go so he could drive away. I looked back at the sleazy motel with newfound hatred and enlightenment. This was real. This was what Deja had protected me from. Someone was actually trying to kill us, and I hadn't the slightest clue why.

15

We drove the remainder of the morning and the early afternoon in silence. I was vaguely aware that we had passed into New Mexico, but since I had been anticipating more arid desert, I didn't recognize the forested landscape. We stopped in a small town that prided itself on being an alien encounter hotspot and rented a cabin.

The A-frame cabin wasn't much bigger than a studio apartment, but the height of its triangular roof made it seem huge, especially in comparison to our last dump. Layne opened the door wide for me to go inside, and I immediately headed to the bed. I crawled on top of the covers and coiled into a ball with no intention of ever moving again. Layne watched me from just inside the entrance. His face was marred with guilt and the type of pity that only came from watching someone fall apart. I hated being this way, but the least he could do was not watch me. It was making *me* feel guilty.

"Deja will be back soon," I said when he didn't stop staring at me. It was the only consolatory response I could think of to make him feel better.

"Yeah," he said, as if he didn't know how else to respond to the statement. He set down his duffel bag and disappeared into the short hall of the entrance. I half expected him to leave, but I didn't hear the door open. "What's it like when you change or switch?" he finally asked.

I shifted to see what he was doing. He was at the door, staring out the horizontal windows on either side of it. His legs were parted and his hands were tucked into his pockets. He was standing guard, and by the looks of it he was prepared to stand there for a while.

"Didn't Deja ever tell you?"

"No, she doesn't remember. She says she's usually asleep or passed out when it happens."

I snorted. I knew that was a lie, but perhaps it had been a while since she'd experienced the change while awake and sober. "It's like someone is hugging you. It's not painful—unless you fight it."

"You can fight it?" He turned back to me, unable to hide his curiosity.

"Yeah, it's a defense mechanism. If you were hanging from the edge of a cliff, you could fight the change until you could get yourself to safety. In heightened states of adrenaline the change is usually delayed, unless the situation involves immediate bodily harm."

"What happens if it involves immediate bodily harm?" he asked me when I didn't elaborate.

"Secondary—"

A knock at the door sent him reeling around with his gun in hand to peer out the window. He took in a breath and opened the door, keeping the gun behind it so he didn't scare whoever was outside.

I heard a young Hispanic woman offer him a welcome basket courtesy of management. Layne inquired if everyone got one upon arriving, and she said yes. He thanked her and closed the door with the welcome basket in hand. It was a cute little basket with lots of cellophane and ribbons, but beyond that it looked to be advertising for the local businesses.

He chuckled as he tossed the pink and green blob onto the dresser next to the television. He turned to me and let out an exasperated breath. "I need a drink." He looked me over. "And so do you."

16

I stared down at my fuzzy navel. It was sweet, sour, and dangerous. I hadn't had a real drink in years. After so many hangovers I didn't even want one. Then again, I hadn't been hunted by hitmen throughout those years. This proximity to death was liable to make even the most reserved women turn to the bottle.

Layne pushed the drink closer to me. "Drink it, you could use it." He sipped on his gin and tonic, swirling the ice chunks between swallows.

"I'm not sure we should be drinking," I said, but still leaned in to draw the first sip of my sweet drink through the straw. It tasted even better than I remembered, or perhaps the bartender was just good at her job. More juice, less booze.

"Don't worry, I'll switch to water after this one." Layne jingled the ice in his drink so he could get one more swallow out of it. "I don't understand how they tracked us down to begin with. That salesgirl had no idea where we were staying. That was just too fast."

Layne lounged back in his high-backed bar chair and scanned the room, which should have made me feel safer, but it made me more wary. Anyone could be a hitman, or perhaps there was a hit-woman. I turned and looked around the nearly vacant bar myself. Layne had already determined that this was a camera-free zone.

Most low-end bars didn't keep cameras. It deterred profits more than it deterred crimes. There were a few burly men—truckers, I thought—drinking alone and watching the television like they were at home on their couch. It was too early for loud music and hard drinking. Not without a chip to show for it later. "What is today, Thursday?" I asked.

"Yeah."

"Damn," I whispered.

"What?"

"She gets the weekend this time. It's so depressing to fall asleep Thursday night and wake up on Sunday morning." Layne smiled, though I wasn't sure he was even listening. He was staring at the television on the far wall, with the rest of the barely cognizant men. "I'm sorry."

"For what?" He continued to stare at the football highlights.

"For not understanding how serious this was. I should have been more careful."

He looked back at me, his eyes fluttering over me before dropping away. "It's not your fault. I shouldn't have left you alone. I got… comfortable." I wasn't sure what that meant, but I assumed it meant that he wasn't keeping the professional distance from me that he wanted to. Transitioning from an observant private eye to full-time bodyguard was no doubt waning his indifference to me. "I meant what I said." He pinned me with his gaze. "You did everything right. You really impressed me."

I smiled at the compliment and sipped on my drink.

The straw crackled as I reach the tail end of the liquid. I furrowed my brow and looked down at the empty glass. The ice had cleverly nullified the glass's true capacity. The bartender *was* good.

I set down the glass and Layne signaled for two more fuzzy navels. He pulled out his wallet, and took a twenty from amongst the hundreds. "I feel bad that you're paying for everything," I said. He shook his head as if he had no concept of the currency he was flashing. "You know I don't have any way of paying you back, right?"

"Don't worry about it. My expenses don't come out of my pocket." He took a sip of his drink, which was just melted ice with residual gin. "Mmm, that reminds me." He reached into his left front pants pocket and pulled out the necklace he had purchased from the salesgirl. "I bought this for you. Well, actually I swindled it for you, but…"

He dangled the necklace and I placed my hand under it to catch it. The gold chain held a yin yang pendulum in silver and gold. "You got this for me?"

He nodded. "I remembered what you said about you and Deja being yin and yang. I couldn't help myself."

"Thank you. I suppose I should try to refuse it for the appearance of propriety, but…" I looked over the silver as it glinted even in the dark bar. Instead of two dots of silver and gold contrasting the halves, there were two diamonds; zirconium, no doubt, but still beautiful.

"But?" He smirked.

"But I really like it." I frowned, thinking of how

sweet the gesture was while he probably didn't give it a second thought.

"I wasn't trying to make you sad," Layne said.

"I know. It's just been a while since someone's given me a gift. I guess I'm just out of practice."

"Here, let me put it on you." Layne took the necklace back and moved behind me to clasp it around my neck—yet another simple gesture that floored my lonely heart.

As he came around to admire it, he must have noticed that it had twisted. He dipped his fingers under the thin strand of gold, grazing my chest as he followed it down to the yin yang. He was nearly into my cleavage, before the pendant flipped, and my heart was nearly into my throat. I looked up at him, searching for some sign that his intentions were flirtatious and not just incidental. Layne caught me eyeing him and he released the necklace.

I turned my attention back to my fuzzy navels while he settled back onto his barstool. I needed to stop thinking about him in any capacity other than my bodyguard or this whole situation was going to get ugly... and painful.

After a moment of silence, he cleared his throat. "I know you don't like talking about your past, but would you mind if I ask when you were put into foster care?"

I stared at him, feeling exposed in more ways than one. I might have assumed that Deja had mentioned our foster care. Or perhaps he had done a background check. However, he also could have just guessed. Children afflicted by twin souls were often put into mental institutions or foster care at an early age. I was fortunate enough to avoid the asylum, but I considered my foster homes to be madhouses anyway.

I drank down the remainder of my second fuzzy navel and began my backstory.

"The diagnosis was, and still is, dissociative identity disorder. The medical community doesn't recognize the existence of twin minds."

"Which is bullshit," Layne said as he dragged a complimentary bowl of peanuts closer to him. "You were born this way. You weren't traumatized into it."

"Exactly," I agreed. "But still, I can empathize with my parents. They could have handled two identical children, but one child with two different personalities? They relinquished their rights and put us into the system at age seven. I think they thought they couldn't help us. They thought we would be better off with strangers." I rubbed my face and shifted in my chair. I downed the third fuzzy navel to stymie the bitterness my memories were conjuring.

"You don't have to talk about this." Layne put his hand on my leg and gave it a squeeze. "I was just being nosy. Occupational hazard."

"I don't mind. I never get to talk about this stuff. I might as well get it out of my system while I have a captive audience. We'll call it free therapy."

He smiled and nodded to my empty glasses. "Do you want one more, or will that put you in the toilet?"

"A couple more, if you don't mind," I said. He ordered two more and a glass of water.

"At first I thought they were right," I continued.

"Half my life was not my own and I didn't know why. It was all I ever knew, but yet it was wrong, because everyone else had memories of seven days a week and I only had three or four. My teachers would get so mad, because I wouldn't know the lessons from the previous days. That's when I started reading ahead in the lessons. I would take notes on what I learned in class."

I paused, thinking back to those days. The days when I was just blanking out the other days. When it was still just a medical condition, a challenging disease that I just had to surmount with preparation and determination.

"Then one day I flipped open my notebook and I found new notes. Notes for the days I had missed. It was unreal. It wasn't my handwriting. It was barely legible and unorganized, but it was enough to get me through the day without embarrassing myself."

I drank down half of my drink when it arrived. I was starting to feel woozy, and I was pretty sure the other one and a half fuzzies were a bad idea. I glanced around the bar, which was starting to fill in. People were getting off work and starting to trickle in for food and drinks.

"Go on," Layne urged. He was fixated on me, waiting for the rest of the story. I wasn't sure the details mattered since he already knew the outcome, but I was more than happy to have his attention and I didn't want to lose it.

"The notes started to get more specific. Not just the lessons, but the students. She would write about a joke she told. I would write about a secret someone told me.

Eventually, the notes became like a diary. I would just tell her about my day, and she would do the same."

"Sounds like you were friends back then."

"Things change," I amended before he could get caught up in the charm of adolescent naivety. "Deja wasn't doing so well in school, and our grades were slipping. I started requesting that I take my tests over on certain days. She started taking an interest in boys, and I had to deal with the fallout of relationship issues. We tried dating after high school, but... Well, I think you can imagine what different tastes we have in men. I had the grades for college, but no money. Even if I wanted to rack up a debt with financial aid, Deja just didn't want to continue with her education. It was all I could do to convince her to stay in until we graduated high school.

"We got low-paying jobs that we both hated. I had to write down everything that I expected her to do while I was gone, or it wouldn't get done. She started drinking, sleeping around, gambling. It just never got better. One day, I went to the doctor and asked for shock therapy. I wanted to un-split my personality. He did a whole slew of tests and my blood results came back with two different types in the same sample. He tested it again, but it was the same. The doctor called it chimera DNA, but that only explained some of our physical irregularities.

"That's when I started to figure it out. The differences are so subtle, impossible, of course... at least by medical standards. Our eye color is slightly different. She's lactose intolerant. I'm red-green colorblind. She has better hearing than me. She's allergic to penn—"

A giant man leaned over the bar between us to give the bartender his order. The beefy biker had plenty of space two seats down to get his order in, but he chose to interrupt us instead. "Yo, asshole," I heard Layne gripe from the other side of the man mountain. "You're blocking my view of the lady."

He looked over to Layne with a confused grunt. He wasn't being rude, just a drunken louse. He had no idea what Layne was talking about. When he finally figured out I was there, he exhibited his long-in-the-tooth smile for me. "Hey, pretty lady. Didn't see you there." He shifted to lean on his side so he could face me. "What are you drinking?"

I glanced at the fuzzy navels. "I'm doing okay on drinks. Thanks though," I said with a congenial smile. It probably wasn't a good idea, since all he saw was me smiling, and all he heard was, "blah, blah, blah, thanks." His tongue darted out of his mouth as he looked me over. I grimaced, less than enthused about the thoughts that were probably rattling around in his head.

Rather than attempt to manhandle the lug out of his path, Layne just moved to the stool behind me and slid into it. He twisted my chair to face him and stared over my shoulder at the biker. I was used to Layne's disciplinary expressions, but he cranked his intensity up to "fuck off" for this guy. Had I been on the receiving end of it, I was certain I wouldn't have stuck around. The biker, however, took his sweet time to collect his drinks and shuffle back to his table.

Layne's face softened and he looked at me again. "Sorry about that. It's a yokel thing. Normally I would just flash my gun, but I think that might draw a little too much attention to us." I nodded and looked down at my empty glass. One more fuzzy to go and I was already smearing the line between tipsy and the deep end of woozy. "You were saying something before he interrupted."

"I don't know. I guess I should get to the part where I started researching twin souls."

"I take it you thought there was a way for you to separate."

"Yeah." I dove into the last glass despite my intentions of remaining out of the toilet. Tolerance to alcohol was yet another thing that didn't carry over from Deja. "Up to that point, medical science was failing to offer an explanation. I researched and found that there was a quiet sect of twin souls living around the country, trying to deal with the same issues I was.

There were people claiming they had been cured, but every shaman, guru, or religious healer I went to said the same thing." I downed the other half of my drink. "One body, one soul."

"Removing her would be essentially killing her?" Layne asked.

"Yeah, and no matter what a pain in the ass she is, I'm not willing to do that. I started the research a long time ago. I had all but given up. Occasionally, I would find another guru to contact, but I never expected a different answer. I just kept checking. I never wanted

Deja to find out. Not unless it was really a cure." I stared down at my hands, feeling guilty. I shouldn't have hid it from her. She may have hid the events of the last two weeks from me, but I was hiding a potentially new life from her. That wasn't fair.

"We should probably get back to the room. It's getting pretty crowded in here."

I looked around the room and saw the increasing population of the bar growing more animated with the permission of the evening hours. Layne was being generous in suggesting the transition, when really it would have been dangerous for us to stay.

"I'll use the restroom and then we can go." I slipped off the bar stool and headed toward the neon sign that read "Pit Stop." Before entering the hallway I glanced back and saw Layne watching me. On any other day it might have been intrusive, but today it was comforting.

17

The restroom turned out to be the type that was retrofitted with stalls to accommodate double capacity. Translation: it was too damn small. One stall door opened inward, hitting the toilet. The second opened outward, potentially tangling with the restroom door.

After alleviating my burden of four—no wait, five —fuzzy navels, I washed up and checked my face in the mirror. Deja always kept a few items of makeup in the purse. I pulled out the blemish stick and dabbed a little under my eyes to hide the dark circles. I swiped on a little lipstick, but stopped there so I didn't make my transformation look like more than just a touch-up.

I pulled the purse strap over my shoulder and headed out the door. I caught sight of our conversation-interrupting biker leaving the men's bathroom directly across from me. It was a stupid setup for bathrooms, especially since I had a clear shot of the urinals without even trying.

Our eyes met and he grinned. I glanced down the hall, but Layne was not in view from this angle. The biker advanced and I stepped back into the bathroom and pulled the stall door open to brace it against the door knob. The door locked six inches open despite him pressing heavily on it.

"Hey there, cupcake." His purpose may have been

to drawl the words seductively, but it came out slurred.

"Hey, big guy," I mumbled. "Making a pit stop?"

His eyes glazed as the meaning of my statement dawned on him. He chuckled. "That's funny." It wasn't funny. His eyes crawled over my body in slow motion. It was no doubt supposed to be surreptitious, but he probably wouldn't have been capable of that without eight beers in his bloodstream. "What's wrong with this door?"

He pressed on the door hard, trying to get in. He settled on peering through the crack behind the door. He checked the hallway for intervening strangers. I wanted to say something to distract him, but I already knew we were beyond that. I could have yelled, and eventually someone would have heard, but the music was too loud to assume they would reach me before the man had a chance to violate me in one way or another.

Instead, I just waited for him to get in. Given my adventure that morning, I should have been terrified, but I wasn't. Guns struck fear in my heart, but drunken brutes didn't faze me.

Biker Man gave the door the gruff push it needed to break the brass doorknob and release its restrictive angle. He forced the door open and came at me. He was faster than I expected, but it didn't matter. I was ready. I pushed my hands out in a gentle shove, but the result was anything but. The impact of my hands on his chest felt electric and hot.

He flew back out the door, across the hallway, and back into the men's restroom. A man just finishing up at the urinal gawked at the biker, then at me. I shrugged and stepped out of my bathroom. Layne was stopped in the hallway, frozen from action. He looked just as stunned as the man at the urinal.

"Did you do that?" he asked with a tinge of fear in his voice.

"What the hell is this?" A man in similar biker paraphernalia asked as he came up behind Layne. He looked over the scene of his downed comrade, with Layne and me standing over him. Naturally, he assumed Layne was at fault. "You son of a bitch!" The man threw a punch at his face, but Layne ducked out of his path.

He dropped his duffel bag and jumped onto the man's back, trying to pin his arms in a full nelson. "Easy, bud," he tried to calm him, but to no avail. The biker backed him into a wall, smashing him between wood paneling and black leather.

Layne kicked at his calves, knocking him to his knees. The man hissed as his heavy frame hit the hard floor.

"Hey!" A third biker arrived in the small hallway, just in time to see Layne wrestling his one friend to floor, while his other friend lay unconscious in front of me. "You son of a bitch!" the third man wailed with little to no originality.

I started to move forward to intercept the third one, but Layne pulled his gun and pointed it at him. The man froze and raised his hands. "This is a misunderstanding," Layne explained. "Your friend was getting fresh with my girl. It escalated, but now I'm deescalating it. Are you cool with that?"

"Yeah, man. No need to get bloody," the third man agreed and took a step back.

"What about you?" Layne asked the second biker, who was snorting feverishly below him.

"Yeah, just get the fuck off me," he griped. Layne released him, and the man grunted as he maneuvered into a genuflect.

Layne holstered his gun and put out a hand to assist the man's rise. He was obviously too old to be brawling, but since biker code allowed for nothing less, his knees would just have to be bruised for a while. The man glared at Layne's offer, but took it anyway.

Once he was upright, Layne started to retract his hand, but the biker pulled him back in. I barely noticed the knife until it was at Layne's throat. "Listen here, you little cocksucker. You lay another hand on me or my guys, you will be eating through a straw for the rest of your days."

"Likewise," I said and punched him in the face. The movement was quick, concise, and to the untrained eye almost gentle, but once again the result was the biker flying back into the wall. His shoulder even cracked the wood paneling before he slid down in a heap on the floor.

I looked down the hall at the third biker. "What about you? You like straws?"

The man stared at me, awestruck. Even if he watched it ten more times, he still wouldn't believe that I had done it. Even if I had been some bad-ass muscle girl, the power I got from such a small effort would still make the mind deny the eyes.

The third biker shook his head and stumbled out of the hallway. I looked over at Layne to see if he was okay. There was a small cut on his neck, but nothing to worry about. His vacant stare, however, was a little more concerning to me.

I could already see his ego deflating at the prospect of a woman capable of knocking out heavy bikers with one punch. I wouldn't dare mention that I hadn't been trying that hard.

"The benefit of having two people in one body." I shrugged it off like it should have been common knowledge, but it wasn't. It was rare to find anyone who "believed" in my condition, and rarer still for them to witness the one phenomenon that made it kind of cool.

Layne just stared back at me, trying to piece together his two impressions of me. The weeping catatonic wuss, and the herculean heroine. I would have preferred to be somewhere in between, but the truth was, both images were pretty accurate. Sometimes I was as fickle alone as Deja and I were combined.

I stepped over the first biker's legs and intentionally wavered like I might fall over. Layne reacted as I had hoped he would, reaching an arm around my waist to support me. "Sorry, that took a lot out of me," I lied and smiled coyly. The truth was, it took very little energy. It wasn't a feat of strength so much as a spark of energy. I assumed that if I repeated the performance multiple times, I would eventually feel some fatigue from it, but thankfully I had never been in that much danger. Not yet, anyway.

"Come on. Let's get you out of here," Layne said as

he tugged me down the hall. I was pleased to see the testosterone re-inflating his ego.

18

I stumbled through the door to the cabin, but this time I wasn't feigning to get Layne's attention. My adrenaline rush had worn off, and in its wake were still five fuzzy-wuzzy navels. Walking back from the bar, I quickly determined that I was just plain blitzed.

I wasn't opposed to playing up my feminine vulnerabilities to take his mind off the bathroom incident, but sloppy drunk was about as sexy as the vomit that followed it. Not to mention I had no desire to fall into the same category as Deja.

Layne latched the door behind us and peered out the windows to make sure our bar brawl wasn't going to bring more problems to our doorstep. I was on my own to steer my controlled fall toward the queen bed. I didn't exactly hit the target as planned, but I did manage not to face-plant.

"Easy girl, the floor isn't nearly as forgiving the day after," Layne said when he saw me perched over the corner of the bed, half kneeling, half hanging.

I laughed raucously at that. He was preaching to the choir. I was more than familiar with the aftermath of drunken stupors, more so than with the actual stupors. "Deja's going to think I did this to get back at her." I dragged the remainder of my body onto the mattress.

"Are you?" he asked, setting his constant

companion duffel bag on the dresser beside the television. I assumed he kept his extra ammo in there, but I wondered why he didn't just lock it in the room. These weren't the type of places to have safes, but surely stashed in a drawer was better than carrying the bag around like a man-purse.

"No—not the first three, at least. You can just tell her you were trying to get me drunk." I smiled and he gave me a smile in return, which made me happy until I questioned whether or not that might have been true. I lost my smile. "Were you?" The first drink was medicinal on all accounts, and the last two were just me finishing what I started, but the two in between... I couldn't remember whose idea that was.

"Tipsy maybe, to relax you, but I'm pretty sure you're a grown woman. You know where your cutoff is better than me," he said, making it sound like a reprimand. I was annoyed that he was scolding me for enjoying myself, but then I realized that I had just insulted his integrity by asking him if he was trying to get me drunk. Considering he had spent last night in my bed and not made any inappropriate moves, it was a rather low blow.

I shook my head, trying to wave off my drunken dizziness. "I'm sorry," I said. He leaned against the dresser and crossed his arms. The look on his face told me that he was not accepting my apology that easily. I had hit a hot nerve. "I'm sorry," I said more vehemently. "You're helping me and I really want to trust you, but that little voice in my head keeps doubting you."

"Why?" he asked with a cold edge in his voice.

"Because I've never…" I bit back a sudden onset of emotion that I didn't even know was there. "I've never trusted anybody. I can't even trust myself, because half the time I'm not me." I rubbed my face and stood up, shaking off more of my intoxication. "I don't have friends, Layne. Neither does Deja. We don't get close to people. We don't talk about our past with people. We don't tell people about our other selves. As far as the world knows, Deja and I are one person: Elise Welch. And she's crap-ass crazy."

"And that's how you want it?" he asked, penetrating me with his gaze. I wasn't sure what he was asking. *Do I like being alone?*

"No, but…" I turned away from him. He was breaking down some very old emotional walls and I wasn't ready for them to fall. I probably would never be ready for that. My kingdom of emotional solitude was my home and my sanity. It was why I usually didn't have one-night stands. My heart couldn't take being with someone that didn't know me, and my defenses refused to lower long enough to let anyone in to become more than that. "I need to protect myself."

"From what?" He was interrogating me now. The cop part of him was stern with just a hint of sympathy, like a stranger that wasn't invested, but still wanted to have a good honest conversation.

"From Deja." I stepped into the bathroom, which only had a standing shower, sink, and toilet. I didn't shut the door, per Layne's preference, despite my desire to have privacy. I lifted the toilet seat and crouched down beside it. I reached into my throat to help the process along rather than wait for the abrupt surprise later.

"What are you doing?" Layne leaned on the doorway.

I pulled my hand out of my mouth and glared at him for following me. "I'm already drunk, the remainder is unnecessary. Besides, you don't want me puking orange juice on your…" The thought of the specific flavor of my upheaval was enough to wrench my throat into a heave. Thankfully I was already in position for the occasion and made the transition from talking to puking almost seamless.

The process of vomiting made me feel worse, but when the stomach contractions stopped and I flushed away the evidence, I started to recover. I moved to the sink and rinsed my mouth out. Layne touched my back and it felt good, but I shook his hand off rudely. I didn't want to be a bitch, but I needed to keep myself from getting caught up in his kindness. I was letting my personal needs get ahead of my emotional ones and that was dangerous. I was smarter than that.

"Elise," he said with a sigh. I looked back and found him holding my toothbrush preloaded with toothpaste. He looked mad again. He was once again just trying to help me, and I was thwarting his efforts. I took the toothbrush and he left the bathroom before I could stammer another lame apology.

I brushed my teeth, washed my face, and stripped out of my shirt and jeans. They were far from soiled, but their proximity to my unloading had tainted them. I stepped out of the bathroom without regard to my bra and panty attire.

Layne was on the edge of the bed, taking off his shoes. "Do you want me to—?" He caught sight of my partial nudity. I didn't look at him. I knew I was tempting him, but I also knew that he wouldn't take advantage of my drunken audacity, and no matter what my love-starved libido thought, that was for the best. "Should I call the front desk and see if they have a cot?"

I glanced back at him, but he was busying himself with his socks. One would have thought he had OCD with the attention he paid to folding them and refolding them on his knee. "I don't think that's necessary." I wanted him to look at me again, but he didn't.

He stood up and headed for the bathroom. He stopped at the door, but didn't turn to look at me even though I was clearly taking my time getting my pajamas on. Damn him for being a gentleman. Always when you don't want them to be.

"Why do you think you need to protect yourself from Deja?"

I paused, trying to think where the question had come from. The previous topic surfaced in my mind and I slipped my pants on. I grabbed my top and put it on just as fast. He finally looked at me, still searching for the answer. I didn't want to give it, but he wasn't going to let it die.

I looked around the room. "Do you know how many motels I've woken up in? At least once a month, I wake up next to some guy I don't know. Sometimes I wake up alone, which oddly seems worse, since it vouches for what kind of a guy she chose. How am I supposed to…?" I shrugged. "Imagine trying to explain to your boyfriend that your other self is not going to be monogamous."

"Are you sure her philandering is causing you to be celibate?" I perked my brow with a *no duh* look. "Maybe your celibacy is causing her philandering."

"What's that supposed to mean?"

"You said you're protecting yourself by not getting close to anyone. What do you think Deja is doing?"

"Deja gets plenty close to people," I scoffed.

"Oh, right, cause one-night stands are how you connect with people." He narrowed his eyes. "She's doing the same thing you are, just in a different way. You're protecting each other and you're both miserable."

I didn't like this conversation, I didn't like him telling me about Deja, and I certainly didn't like him assessing me. "You don't know me *or* her."

His mouth twisted into a smile and he snickered. "You'd be surprised how well I know you from my observations. And let me remind you that you've never been in the same room as Deja."

"She is a *part* of me!" I defended. I couldn't believe he was staking claim to knowing her better than me.

"Bullshit! You treat her like a parasite!" he yelled back at me. "She's not some idiot slut!" The vehemence of his argument shocked me. Not only was he claiming to know her better than me, but he was actually defending her! "Just because she's not as literate as—"

He cut himself off and shook his head in frustration. "I'm sorry. This is what I wanted to avoid with you two. This isn't my relationship; you two can figure this shit out for yourselves. I'm going to take a shower."

With a dismissive wave he disappeared into the bathroom. He closed the door just enough to give himself privacy, but not enough that he couldn't hear me if there was trouble.

I sat down on the bed and replayed the argument in my mind. I was still struck by how he berated me in defense of Deja. Did he actually like her? Most men generally liked Deja, but not for much longer than a night or two. It hadn't occurred to me that over the course of their time together, Layne might have gotten attached to her. Actually, it hadn't occurred to me that anyone *could* get close enough to Deja to become attached.

Although I genuinely liked the idea of Deja growing up and getting a real boyfriend—especially if it was someone as normal as Layne—I couldn't help but think how that relationship would affect me.

19

I finished writing my letter to Deja and wrapped it up in a pair of panties at the top of my bag. I didn't want to have any more public conversations, and said as much in my letter. In fact, I spent the better part of it reminding her how I expect her to behave in regards to our shared life. She was going to love that.

I heard the water shut off and Layne stepping out of the shower. I quickly crawled into bed and turned on the television to discourage any further conversations or arguments. Less than twenty minutes earlier, while I was still reeling from intoxication, I had considered seducing Layne. I wanted to embrace this newfound and rare connection, but I wasn't sure there was a connection anymore. At least not with me, anyway. Whatever I thought had developed between Layne and me was just my imagination trying to turn an otherwise uncomfortable situation into something romantic. Damn you, Harlequin!

I sat back against my pillow, easing myself into the tired tipsiness of alcohol consumption. Layne finally stepped out of the bathroom with a towel wrapped around his waist. His naturally amber skin made him look tan even though he probably rarely saw the sun. His sopping wet curls had tightened into what looked like a fresh perm. I wondered how many times he had to run his fingers through the determined locks before they would give in and relax on his scalp.

He moved to the dresser and dug through his duffel bag. He pulled out his toothbrush and toothpaste before heading back to the bathroom to wet his brush. To pass the time while he brushed, he braced himself in the bathroom door and watched the sitcom I had selected. It wasn't something I normally followed, but it was easy humor, so it didn't matter.

Layne didn't look at me once the entire time. Considering I was the one trying to avoid conversation, it shouldn't have bothered me, but it did. What he had said about Deja was still bothering me too. I didn't like anyone telling me anything about her, because in a very weird, disconnected way it was as if they were telling me about myself. It shouldn't have mattered, since we were theoretically different people, but it always felt like a violation. At times, it was just my territorial instincts—she was sharing my body, after all—but this time it was more.

Layne wasn't just making a blanket statement about what he saw her do or heard her say. He had made a prediction about her sexual motivations based on his interactions with her, observations that had taken place over the last few weeks. No matter how much I wanted to deny it, Layne was getting a better view of Deja, and her personality, than I ever would.

It had never occurred to me that she might be lonely, just like me. Her endless string of men might have just been her way of getting what she needed without letting it impact our lives long-term. If she was looking for a relationship, then perhaps Layne was it. Maybe there was more going on between them than he was admitting to me. And if so...

"Why did you kiss me this morning?" I blurted out without planned recourse.

"What?" He spoke over his toothbrush with wide eyes. He honestly didn't remember.

"This morning, when I was freaking out, you kissed me. I was just curious what you were thinking when you did that." I shrugged. "Were you even aware of doing it?"

He nodded, but his forehead was still wrought with confusion. He moved back into the bathroom to spit and rinse his brush off. He came back out with both his brush and paste in hand and looked at me. "I just wanted to distract you. You were about to start hyperventilating."

"Is that all it was?"

He looked away and cleared his throat. "Look, Elise... You're great, but—"

"Are you in love with her?"

"What?" He was even more surprised by this question, if that were possible. "Who? Deja?"

"It's okay if you are. I can't imagine any man that wouldn't be drawn in by her. She's fun, rebellious, and easy—to get along with." I added the last part in case he was going to be insulted by my honesty.

He chuckled and shook his head before putting away his toiletries. "You two really need to meet," he grumbled.

"Does she feel the same way?" I probed further. "If

she does, you don't have to hide it from me. I don't want to stand in the way. I just never thought she would find anyone that could put up with her shit." He opened his mouth to presumably object, but I cut him off to compensate for my insult. "Don't get me wrong, I really think she deserves to have someone special. I mean… I want her to have someone special."

Layne quieted and leaned against the dresser, listening to me rant. I knew I was talking too much, but I just wanted him to understand that I understood. "I just think we should talk about it. Like you said, getting involved with a twin mind is difficult. It's like a really weird threesome, although probably the only kind of threesome that might actually work."

"Elise," he stated calmly to interrupt me as he came over to the bed.

"Oh, but no! I didn't mean to imply that you and I had to be a couple also." He sat down beside me like he needed to console me. "That certainly isn't mandatory, and in some cases it's just a bad idea. Deja and I are so different. I wouldn't even begin to expect that you would be interested in someone like me *and* someone like her."

He grabbed my face and kissed me. In my confusion, I thought he was just going to give me a tender consolatory kiss again, but his tongue pushed into my mouth and I felt an instant shockwave of desire pierce my groin and blow the dust off a far too underutilized section of my body.

For a moment, all thoughts of Deja left my mind and I selfishly wallowed in the tactile experience of his lips against mine. I let out a moan that was half desire and half relief. For so long, I had conditioned myself not to get close to people, but this was different. Layne already knew my dirty little secret, and so what if he was in a relationship with Deja? Our paths were obviously never going to cross. If he was going to be hanging around, I might as well enjoy him as well.

With Deja's permission, of course.

Which I didn't have, but was still sucking face with her boyfriend.

Oh, shit!

Before I could do the moral thing and pull away, Layne did it for me. I opened my mouth to speak, but his eyes widened. "Seriously, that didn't throw your little locomotive mouth off the tracks?" I glared and pulled back away from him. I started to speak again, but he raised his hand to my mouth and let out a corrective utterance that should have been restricted to dog training. "Let me talk for a little bit, okay? You just threw a curveball at me, and before I had a chance to answer, you started a whole new ball game. Christ, you've got Deja and me married with 2.5 kids and I've never even kissed her."

"You haven't?" I couldn't help but ask.

"No. I have now kissed you twice *and* seen you naked. To be honest, I think the first contact I've had with *this* body was just hands, and that was you too."

"Why—?"

"Shhhh." He pressed his finger to my lips. "No, more questions, please. I've got to back us out of this web of conclusions you've drawn. Unfortunately, now I feel like I'm breaking up with you, so I have to find the right words."

I sank a little deeper into my pillow. I was already feeling stupid. The kiss might have been fun, but I knew that in a few minutes I was going to wish he hadn't done it.

I glanced down, noting the gap in his towel. The exposed taut muscles of his inner thigh were just torturing me now. He caught my intrusive observation and moved off the bed. "First off, I am not in love with Deja," he said as he grabbed his duffel bag. "And she..." He let out a breathy chuckle. "...is not in love with me."

He pulled a pair of underwear and a rolled-up pair of khakis from his bag. Since he was still wearing his outfit from the first day, I was glad to see he had another set. He slipped them on under the veil of his towel, giving me only a glimpse of the backs of his thighs as he did. I wasn't above watching the display since the wall behind the television had a picture of a horse instead of the usual mirror.

He turned back to face me and tossed his wet towel on the floor near the bathroom. His chest was beautifully bare and I couldn't help but admire it. He tucked his hands in his pants pockets and leaned against the dresser. I wondered if he did it to hide what he was about to verbally deny me.

"Deja is just my employer. We aren't even technically friends, but I know her pretty well from my own observations. However, I didn't quite get the full picture until I met her. Meeting you has clarified a lot of things too." He paused as he stared at me. "It's also confusing a lot of things." He pushed his fingers back through his wet hair. "But I'm here to do a job, not find a girlfriend." His voice was back in cop mode again. He was somehow reprimanding me for tempting him, even though he was the one that kept getting his lips involved. Granted, I was usually the one without clothes on, but still.

"I like you, Elise, more than I thought I would."

"What does that mean?" I interjected. "Did she say something about me to make you think you wouldn't?"

He frowned and shook his head. "Can we focus on this moment right now? I really need to express something here."

"Sorry." I wilted back to let him finish his breakup speech.

"Aside from all the running and attempted murder, it would be really stupid for us to get involved right now." I leaned my head back, letting it hit the headboard-less wall behind me. I was apparently being *stupid* to think that I could play Deja for a night.

"I guess I'll have to raise my intelligence with a cold shower." I sighed and rolled over on my side. I tossed the remote over to his side. "Watch whatever you want."

"Elise, please don't be like that." I could feel the bed dip as he knelt on the opposite side. "I'm trying to make the responsible choice. You and Deja know nothing about each other. If I—"

I whipped back around to face him and shoved my hand against his chest. He flew off the bed and landed against the outer wall of the bathroom. He gawked at me from the floor as I held the finger of my shaking hand out at him.

"You tell me that one more time and I will put you through a wall! No matter how bad I'll feel about it afterwards. You understand, Layne?"

He stared me down, watching my not-so-badass facade degrade with my stray tears. He no doubt wanted to ask a hundred questions, but he didn't. He nodded, letting the shock leave his face. "I understand."

I rolled back over, unable to disguise my sobs as anything less than blubbering. I wasn't even sure what I was crying about: my nonexistent relationship with him or Deja. The overhead light shut off and the room filled with the blue glow of the television. I felt Layne crawl in beside me and the volume on the television turned down.

His hand touched my back and I resisted the urge to slough him off as I had before. I rolled over to look at him in case it was important. He was perched up on his pillows, prepared to finish out the night with the television. He looked at me somberly.

"I'm sorry," he whispered, matching the shift in tone to the room. "I keep belittling your connection with her and I don't mean to. I promise I won't do it again."

I glanced at the wall and back at him. "Did I hurt you?" I asked. He paused, as if he wasn't sure what answer would make me happy.

He shrugged. "Just my ego." He squeezed my shoulder. "You okay?"

I nodded. "I'm sorry if I'm giving you mixed signals. I'm kind of all over the map right now."

"It's understandable. It's not every day that you have a brush with death."

"That, but also… us. I don't I know how to act around you. I need a frame of reference and I just don't have one. I haven't been alone with a man…" I laughed and looked at the television. "I haven't been alone with anyone but myself in a very long time. And believe it or not, I'm not much of a talker with myself."

He smiled. "You don't have to be anyone for me, Elise. I know you're used to playing a certain part to disguise your condition. I can't imagine how difficult it is to live your life with huge chunks of time missing, but you can let go of that with me. I know exactly where Deja ends and you begin."

"I guess that's the problem. I don't think *I* do anymore."

He looked me over and extended his arm. "Come here," he whispered and dipped his hand under my back to usher me closer to him. I rolled over, meeting his body. He resituated a little lower and gently pressed my head to his chest. It took me a moment to find the right configuration for my hands, but eventually I just tucked one between us, and laid the other across his chest. He wrapped his arm around my back, caressing my shoulder with his thumb. "You want to watch the late show?" he asked. I nodded against his chest even though my eyes were already closing.

It was my intention to say a few more things to him before I left. It was also my intention to trace my hand over his chest to feel his soft skin. Unfortunately, the last two days had taken their toll and I was asleep before I knew it and gone before I woke.

20

I woke the next morning, alone in the hotel bed. The smell of cigarettes wafted in through the front door along with the cool morning air. I groaned and got up. I found my duffel bag—already opened—and pulled a clean t-shirt from it. I assumed Deja had recently rummaged through it to find her cigarettes. She knew Elise would throw them away, so she left them in my bag. I slipped on the sturdy gray cotton shirt and headed out to the front stoop.

I found Deja sitting on a rock outside, reading Elise's letter. I wasn't even sure she had written one, but I presumed she intended to keep it private. Deja gave me a chin up nod as she flicked her cigarette and continued to read the letter. Her face was marred with too many emotions to translate, but given the tone of most of Elise's letters I couldn't imagine that this one was any less reprimanding than the others.

I leaned against the door jamb and looked over the parking lot while she finished. At the end she scoffed and handed me the letter. She finished smoking her cigarette while I read it.

Dear Deja,

I can't even begin to express how angry I am. Just to give you a reference point to start from, I woke up in yet another hotel room, hung over—worst ever, by the way—and aching from a flipping tramp stamp on my back. I can't believe you would do something so childish.

Blah, blah, blah.

I skimmed over the long paragraph on the trust that comes with sharing bodies.

Layne! Who the hell is this guy? Where did you meet? When did you meet him? You should have told me about him. You should have told me everything. People are trying to kill us. I have no idea why. Layne seems to think I can help with that, but I have no clue.

I can't help but think that this is because of something you have done. A gambling debt gone wrong? Sleeping with the wrong man? I won't presume to imagine crimes that I don't have firsthand knowledge of, but I am well aware that you do possess a few items that are beyond our means. Please, Deja, if you can't tell me, tell Layne. He seems genuinely concerned for our safety.

In regards to my research, I have conveyed my sincerest apologies and contentions on this topic to Layne. I hope you can forgive me. I am mortified that anything in my past behavior toward you would make you think I could willingly harm you.

P.S. Please don't leave your letters with Layne. I consider everything I tell you a private conversation, and I would like you to do likewise.

I smirked at the postscript. Even if Deja cared about such things as propriety, she would have let me read the letter just to spite Elise. It was strange to see so much ire between two people that had never met. They were like roommates that worked different shifts. All they could do was leave angry notes about not drinking all the milk and remembering to take the trash out.

"How did it go?" she asked when I finished reading. "Did she flip out?"

"A little. She ran from me the first morning."

"No shit?" She crushed out her cigarette.

I couldn't help but smile thinking back to my first conversation with Elise. I hadn't anticipated that she would run away from me, let alone so abruptly. When I first indicated I had been watching her, she hit the door as if it was a dine and dash. By the time I made it to the door to call after her, she was down two flights of stairs. When I realized she had no intention of stopping or listening to my explanation, she was already in her car and flipping me off. A feat that, even now, I would have credited to Deja more than her, but she was full of surprises.

"Yeah, I had to call in a few dozen favors to have the local PD pick her up. After that I thought she was on board, but she ran again."

"How the fuck did you lose her twice?" She looked me over as if she was searching for my broken leg and/or lack of testicles.

"Shut up, she's fast. Anyway, I think we're done with all that." I waved the letter. "She understands that I'm here to help."

"She'd better. I'm not paying you to play cat to her mouse. She's already got a few too many cats after her and they aren't playing." I nodded in agreement, thinking about how close she had come yesterday to getting killed. It was a mistake I wasn't proud of, and one I didn't really want to share. "What?" Deja asked sharply, narrowing her eyes on me. She could see the guilt on my face.

I considered not telling her, since Elise had neglected to mention it in her letter. I was actually surprised she hadn't told, but apparently Deja wasn't the only one that left out big gaps of her life to protect her other half.

"Don't pussyfoot around me, Layne. Just say what you gotta say," Deja scolded.

"We had another attempt."

"What do you mean another attempt?" -Deja snapped. "How the hell did they find you?"

"I don't know," I said. Deja and I had gone to great lengths to stay out of sight when we left Colorado. As long as we stayed away from high-traffic cameras, we should have been safe, which we did. "We were only there for one night. We went shopping in one store, but I bribed the register gal. We should have been fine."

"I assume from the lack of gunshots in my body that you successfully protected her."

"Actually, she protected herself." I sighed. "I made a mistake."

Deja stood and planted herself in front of me, arms akimbo as she stared me down. Hours earlier I had been holding this tearful body in my arms. Now she was a force to be reckoned with. She had an implacable personality with no room for tears in her life, let alone comforting.

"I wanted to avoid cameras so I went out to fetch

breakfast alone. They came by after I left. She got out through a bathroom window and hid, but they took some shots at the bed, which was where I stupidly suggested she hide if something happened. Anyway, she was pretty upset about the whole thing."

"No shit she was upset! What were you thinking? Put her in a fucking hat, go through a drive-through, and move on to the next motel. What is this, day one for cops?" she condescended unapologetically.

"I underestimated them or I missed something. It won't happen again," I said sternly. I didn't like being lectured to, especially about something I was already chastising myself about.

"You're damn right it won't happen again. You're here to watch my back, which just so happens to be Elise's front, so get it right. I'd like to live through this."

"You will," I ground out. She glared back at me, obviously wanting to say more, but she couldn't without repeating herself or making her concern for Elise too obvious. She liked to play it down, but I knew she was more worried about Elise than herself, which in the grand scheme of things didn't make sense, since her getting hurt would hurt them both. We faced off for a moment before I made a concession to my attitude. "You hungry?"

"Yeah."

21

I waited while Deja stepped into the bathroom to change her clothes. Despite my previously voiced objections, she shut the door all the way. I had already given up on guarding her the same way as Elise. Deja didn't consider me her protector. She considered me her employee and that was it. In her eyes, I was just hanging out until Elise came back. The mounting list of interrupted murder attempts made no difference to her.

Deja opened the bathroom door and stepped out pinching the yin yang necklace I had given to Elise. "What's this? Don't tell me she's buying accessories."

I looked at the necklace like I hadn't seen it before. I wasn't sure I wanted to tell her that I bought it specifically for Elise. It was an impulsive thing to do. Probably romantic, by most standards, but since I was trying to avoid that situation, it was just an unnecessary expense. "Someone left it in the last motel. I guess she liked it."

Deja looked over the necklace discerningly. She pursed her lips and gave up looking for an excuse to take it off. Instead, she tucked it in her shirt where no one would see it and went back into the bathroom to apply a layer of mascara and lipstick from the makeup stash in her purse.

When she returned her hair was up to show off the

big hoop earrings she preferred to Elise's small studs. In lieu of a proper teeth-brushing, she was chewing a piece of gum. I considered offering her the toothpaste from my bag, but decided that we weren't ready for the intimacy of shared toiletries yet.

A half hour later, we were receiving platters of pancakes and eggs at a diner a few miles away. The waitress left the bill and I tucked a couple of twenties in it before I began eating. Instead of attacking the food with her usual culinary appreciation, Deja stared down at it, unmoving.

"I thought you were hungry."

"Yeah," she said without looking at me. She made the effort to pour syrup on her pancakes, but they remained on her plate uneaten, sponging up the sticky sweetness with each passing minute.

"What is it?" I asked, surprised that anything would curb her appetite, especially since Elise hadn't eaten much of anything the days prior.

"Where are we again?" She hadn't taken her eyes off the plate, but she wasn't really looking at it.

"Lower half of New Mexico. Why?"

"What do you suppose the chances are that we can make it over the border without being spotted?"

"Zero. Why would you consider leaving the country? Even if we could get out, we'd never get back in again. The feds will take blood and prints before they'll let us back in." She didn't respond. "You don't *want* to get back in?"

"No, of course I want back in. Where else but in the

USA do I have the freedom to get a parking ticket thirty seconds after parking illegally, but yet have five murder attempts go unnoticed by anyone because the people trying to kill us own the fucking police?"

I dropped my fork and pushed my plate away. I agreed with her, but I didn't like to be reminded of it. "Some of us are trying to change that."

She nodded. "Yeah, I know. It just sucks that the police are only useful if unimportant people are trying to kill you."

"You should really eat. She didn't eat much yesterday."

"No appetite? Can't imagine why," she mumbled.

"Are you going to keep throwing that in my face? Cause I really don't need you adding to my guilt."

"Tell me what happened last night. I woke up on your chest with cottonmouth and a headache, but judging by the amount of clothes we were both wearing, I doubt you took care of your secondary duties."

"I never accepted getting Elise laid as a secondary duty."

"You're right, it should be your primary duty. So what happened?"

I rolled my eyes at her, but it was futile to fight with her. She never gave in, even when she was wrong. "We had a few drinks to take the edge off the day. She had a few more than me. We talked." I decided to leave out the part where I let Elise get out of sight and she had to fend off a biker by herself. Not that she had any trouble with it, but I didn't know that at the time. "We went back to the cabin. More talking, some arguing, we made amends, and she fell asleep on me."

Deja rolled her eyes. "Fuck me, you're gay."

"What?"

"She hasn't gotten laid in over a year, she almost died, and she was drunk. At what point was she going to get any riper for the plucking?"

"I wasn't going to take advantage her. Besides, this is already complicated. I don't want to add to it."

"There's nothing complicated about it, Layne. Just stick your dick in and push until she groans really loud." I leaned back in the booth, looking around to see if anyone was listening. Deja had a way of drawing attention with the honesty of her dialogue.

"Deja, I'm not your pimp."

"Technically, you would be my whore. *I* would be *your* pimp and Elise would be my client, but since this would be a freebie, you don't have to feel dirty. Unless you want to." Deja winked, but I couldn't find it in me to enjoy her humor. I had at one time, but knowing Elise made the jokes seem less funny.

Elise wasn't just a stick-in-the-mud, antisocial prude. She was lonely, but too scared of getting hurt to reach out to anyone. I hadn't told her last night, but another reason I didn't want to get involved with her was because I didn't want to be responsible for hurting her. She had a lot of anxious energy put into keeping her half-life in order. Even if she didn't realize it, a relationship by any definition would probably give her a nervous breakdown.

"Look, I'll protect Elise like we agreed, but

anything else that happens is between her and me."

Deja looked me over inquisitively. "You like her, don't you?" I glared at her for the loaded question. "You do." She tipped her head to one side. "Why?"

"Why do *you* like her?"

She chuckled. "Who said I did?"

"She's your backboard. She's the one that keeps you in line. She annoys the crap out of you, but I see how much you respect her for trying to hold things together, even when you're tearing them apart."

I expected Deja to object to the statement. Instead she smirked and nodded slowly. "I suppose I do." She continued to look me over, searching for the gap in my armor. "I think we both know that she severely underestimates my abilities, though." She raised an eyebrow, looking for my agreement. I couldn't deny her that.

"Yes, I think she does underestimate you, but you've never given her reason not to. Your notes are lewd, dismissive, and lacking in detail. You haven't been straightforward with her about a lot of things, and I think she just assumes that you are responsible for every bad thing that's ever happened to her, because you won't back her up."

Deja continued to look me over, but not as an introspective observer. She looked more and more predatory the longer I spoke. I had once again put my opinion about Elise and Deja's relationship right out in the open air, and Deja wasn't any happier about my assessment than Elise was. Given my understanding of their hidden strength, I was already regretting the statement.

"Look, I'm not trying to create any friction here. I just see some misinterpretations of character that I want to correct, even though I know you would rather I leave it alone."

"You're right. Elise does misinterpret me sometimes, but you're running under the assumption that I don't want it that way. So, yes, I would rather you leave it alone." Her cold stare made me regret getting involved with the whole situation.

"Fine." I picked up my duffel and slid out of the booth. "But just for the record, I wasn't just talking about *her* misinterpretations." I walked away before she could aim another hard stare at me.

22

I gunned the dual-fuel engine in my upgraded Camaro to ninety and headed south to Juarez, Mexico. It was a stupid plan. I didn't want to leave the country since I didn't have any contacts there, but there was no arguing with Deja. The only upside was that we would be off the radar, literally.

Deja rolled down the passenger window and dug through her purse for the pack of cigarettes she had transferred from my bag. Her brow furrowed as she looked inside. She looked to me and I waited for her to ask the question burning in her mind. "I think I know why they found you."

"What? How?" Deja pulled out her cellular earpiece which was blinking red. "Son of a bitch! I had no idea she used it."

"She left me a message. We never leave each other verbal messages, except appointment reminders." She pushed the phone in her ear, pressed the button and requested playback.

I waited for her to finish listening before I spoke. I expected her eyes to start lolling back, but her face softened and all at once she pulled the earpiece out and threw it in the purse in exchange for a cigarette, which she lit up without regard to my freshly detailed car interior.

"Well, what did she say?" I asked.

Deja rolled the window down a little further and leaned against the door. She took a few leisurely puffs of smoke before she spoke. "She recorded that the night before last. The message input record must have saved it with the service. That means they tracked you down within 12 hours. Whoever it was, they were in or around Boulder, but now they know we skipped town, so they'll be watching surveillance like mad. Mexico may be our only option now."

"Is that the only reason we're going there?" I asked.

I wasn't privy to all of Elise's research, but one crumpled paper had managed to make its way into my hand. I knew that one particular name on the list of so-called shamans lived just outside of Juarez. It couldn't have been a coincidence. I wasn't sure what would possess her to seek him out, since she was so outraged by Elise's research, but I wasn't about to be blunt enough to ask.

She didn't bother responding to the question. She just sucked in hard on her cigarette and blew the smoke in my face. I rolled down my window to help air out the smoke. "You know that you can't keep running forever," I said with mild concern.

"Why not?" She shrugged and perked an eyebrow like she was double-dog-daring me to enlighten her on her capabilities.

"What are you going to do, live in Mexico under the cover of anti-surveillance laws?"

"Why not? That's what the rest of the rebellious Americans do. Besides, everybody in Mexico is poor;

we'll practically be rich by comparison."

"What about Elise?"

"What about Elise?" Deja put her foot up on the seat, streaking my leather with her crappy tennis shoes.

"Do you think she'll be happy living in the crime lap of the Americas?"

"I don't care what she wants. She'll be alive. She can be thankful for that."

"She won't be any safer in Mexico. Not with that high of a price on your head. Sooner or later we are going to have to figure out who it is and why they are coming after you." Deja looked instantly tired. We had had a dozen conversations about this already, so it was reasonable that she was getting tired of them, but I was surprised that she was refusing to see the bigger picture. For her it was Mexico or bust, but I knew that was only a temporary solution. At least for me it was. I had no intention of staying there.

"I presume given your rocky start with Elise that you didn't get much out of her," she said, changing the subject.

"No, but she didn't have any immediate thoughts. She seems to think that this is your fault."

"Probably," she mumbled. "Why now though? I've been out of debt for a while. I don't owe anyone anything. I already gave you the names of all the people I've pissed off, fucked over, and just plain fucked. I'm being so honest my pussy's having flashbacks."

"I don't think your angry wife list is to blame for high-level hitmen."

"Not unless they have very rich daddies, but then

again, they would probably just off their husbands instead of me," she amended.

"I've already run all the names. The closest you've come to pissing off the mob was racking Arthur Devitti, and from what I understand, his father doesn't even like him. He's not going to send out a heavy-handed hit just to preserve his son's overinflated ego."

"Maybe it has something to do with—"

"Are you going to tell me why we're going to Mexico?" I asked, trying to get her back on topic. Deja liked to keep her information flow on a slow drip, but given the danger we were in and how fast things were progressing, I was getting tired of waiting for the deluge.

"There's a festival I want to go to."

"There's a festival every weekend in Juarez."

She turned and cocked her head at me. "Yeah, and we are going to go check it out."

23

Deja was a mix of deep-seated passions with no particular focus for it. She felt compelled to protect Elise, but still took delight in making her unhappy. Even though she was furious that I had put her in danger, she was the one bringing her into the mouth of crime country.

Shortly after America's public monitoring went through the roof, Mexico passed an anti-surveillance law to *protect* its citizens from unlawful privacy invasion. Every city within a hundred miles of the US border turned into a tourist sanctuary for overindulgence. It wasn't just sex and drugs either; there was a black-market operation for everything illegal and illicit, including body disposal.

Almost overnight, seventy percent of Juarez's commerce shifted into criminal operations. There was barely a business left that didn't have some connection to a smuggling or bootlegging operation. The mortuaries started offering "don't ask, don't tell" policies on burial services and cremations—assuming you had the proper funding, of course. Restaurants started to offer coke as a beverage *and* an appetizer. The hotels doubled as strip joints and brothels; they even occasionally had beds for you to *sleep* in.

Vegas had nothing on Juarez.

This was where Deja wanted us to go. This was where she wanted me to keep Elise safe.

I parked my Camaro inside a chain-link fenced lot and eyed the two men that were supposedly going to watch it for me. The cocky, once-over look they gave me before window-shopping my precious beauty told me they weren't interested in the usual five-dollar tip that I offered valets. I tipped them each one hundred and told them that if the car was in good shape when I got it out again, I would be doubly appreciative.

They smiled and nodded, pretending to be grateful for the tip even though they could get just as much for selling the tires. Deja came up beside me and kicked one of them in the balls. The other guffawed at her gall, but covered his crotch when she turned her attention to him.

"And if it's not in good shape, I will be *doubly* annoyed." The man wisely nodded and slunk away.

I couldn't help but smile at the display. It was the best good-cop-bad-cop routine ever.

Deja slipped her arm around my waist as we walked out of the chain-link enclosure to the busy sidewalk. "Buy me a drink?" she asked with a sly smile.

"Of course." I smirked down at her and put my arm over her shoulders, which I was surprised she allowed. She either wanted us to look like a couple or she just wanted to have access to my gun. "I wouldn't dare refuse."

"Good man."

"Why didn't you tell me about your super strength?"

"I assumed you knew. You seem rather familiar with twin minds."

"So it had nothing to do with keeping the upper hand."

Deja glanced at me. "You know how guys pick on other guys, because they are smaller or weaker?"

"Sure."

"You know how those same guys won't pick on someone bigger than them?"

"Uh-huh."

"And what happens when they see someone that claims to be stronger than them, but is significantly smaller?"

"I guess they see it as a challenge."

"Those same SOBs that wouldn't think of picking a fight with a 300-pound man, will come back time and again to fight a guy that weighs half that. Because even if that scrawny little twerp beats the shit out of them, their eyes will not let them believe he is stronger."

"I see." I nodded at her logic. Logic that I assumed had come from first-hand experience. I could see how her power could ultimately attract violence more than deter it. Curiosity was often the best motivator. Add to that a pretty face with a cute body and it would attract a very unsavory kind of challenger. "And you thought I was in some way comparable to that type of guy."

"No, I didn't. I thought you were a real good guy." She slowed to a stop and I released my arm to look at her straight on. "I just knew you would protect her better if you thought she was completely vulnerable."

I blinked at her, trying to find an argument against

that subtle accusation, but there wasn't one. It was human nature to do the bare minimum. Even if I claimed to be above it, some part of me might not have been as careful if I thought I wasn't needed.

"Let's get that drink." Deja nodded to the bar behind me. The sign on the front read "El Pollo Loco."

We stepped inside the Crazy Chicken, which looked to be a pretty standard south-of-the-border dive. It was clean enough, but since the air conditioning consisted of nothing more than ceiling fans and open windows, it was a dive to me.

Deja slid into a booth halfway through the galley establishment. She sat with her back to the wall and one foot braced on the seat so she could see the patrons at the bar. I sat opposite her, staying close to the edge of the seat in case I needed to get out fast. The waitress spotted us immediately and took our order, after which she left a small nearly empty salt shaker on the table—a sample of their product.

Deja eyed the small container like she was debating on trying it. She wasn't above anything. "You know who it is, don't you?" I asked to distract her. I had wanted to ask her for a while, but I hadn't had the aspiration to deal with the fallout. Somehow, being in this hellhole made me bolder. It just didn't make any sense to me that Elise could be responsible for inciting the lethal acrimony of the three most powerful men in America. She had to be hiding something.

She looked up from the salt shaker and tipped her head, like she was considering breaking my neck rather than answering. "Are you asking or verifying?"

"Verifying, I suppose. You seem more interested in running than finding a way to stop them."

"That's because I can't stop them." She perked her brow. "And neither can you," she added.

"We can get the police involved. If we know who —"

"Don't make me smack you. You can't be that ignorant. The police are involved in this as much as the killers are."

"There are some good men left."

"Yeah, but they're called vigilantes and private eyes now. The truth is, none of you have any real power. You can call in a few favors, get me out of my parking tickets, but not the real stuff. People like Devitti, Elliot, Moreau, they can make people disappear. They can erase criminal records like it was written in pencil. Your questions, Elise's questions—they don't matter anymore, because there is no solution. Just do your fucking job and keep her alive, that's all I need from you, understand?"

I should have shut up and let it drop, but I couldn't help but prod her. "For how long?"

"As long as necessary." She glared.

"If there is no solution, we'll be running forever. How much longer do you expect me to hang around? I mean, I'm not the one being hunted. You're off the grid here. You can defend yourself. Elise sure as hell can. You don't need me anymore. Buy a gun, go south and live in the crime candy-land. Pimping suits you well enough. You can pimp out Elise for two days at a time."

I knew I was over the line, and I had partially done

it to get a rise out of her. Force her to start thinking proactively. I didn't realize how volatile the comment was until my face erupted in a stinging heat. The impact nearly tipped me out of the booth, but it was the unnatural heat, burning through my cheek and making my teeth hurt, that took me by surprise.

I looked back at Deja. She was centered in the booth. Her left hand trembled on the table next to her stilled right hand. Her jaw was set tight and I could see her nostrils flare with each breath. She wanted to hit me again and I got the feeling that she could make it hurt worse.

The waitress set down our drinks and I didn't take my eyes off Deja when I handed her a ten. She repeated the total sarcastically and I handed her another ten. She walked away satisfied.

I downed my warm gin and tonic without the hindrance of ice cubes, which, like the air conditioning, were rarely provided. I dropped a five on the table for a tip, despite the fact that I may have already given one, and walked out with my duffel bag in hand. I needed a little space to figure out what my next move was, and if it even involved Deja.

24

I had no idea what the hell I was doing, but I was certain that I had overstayed my welcome by about three weeks. Deja was a hard woman to protect, but it was getting unreasonable. She obviously knew who was after her. Or at least *why* they were after her. She didn't have any trouble defending herself physically, and I could reasonably assume she wasn't afraid of using a gun. The only purpose I served was to babysit her other half when she couldn't.

My solution of going south armed with a gun was a legitimate option for them—minus the pimping, of course. Assuming Deja could be honest with Elise, they could be safe on their own. As far as I was concerned, my services did not extend to international territory. I wanted nothing more to do with Mexico or twin souls.

However, I felt bad for Elise, especially since this was the kind of abandonment that she was trying to avoid by not getting close to people. I knew the only reason I was considering staying was because of one damn kiss, or maybe it had more to do with the memory of her standing in the middle of that hotel room, buck-naked and wet. I could blame my bad decisions for the next month on that little treat. In the end, the real reason I couldn't bring myself to abandon her was because I liked her.

Elise was a sweet girl, the type that needed and deserved to be saved.

Not like Deja. If anything, she needed a good hard smack on the ass, but since that would likely result in death for the offending disciplinarian who would even try.

There was no amount of money worth putting up with Deja's shit, but for Elise... her I would be willing to help for free.

Rather than throw in the towel right in a fit of anger, I decided to check into a hotel and sleep on it. Even if I could commit to walking out on Deja, I technically had all her money. I needed to give her the opportunity to get it back before I left, or risk her taking creative measures to get more.

I was directed to a room on the top floor overlooking the street below. The concierge, who smelled like perfume—no doubt from dabbling in the hotel's other on-site amenities—informed me that I would have an excellent view of the parade that night. I asked him what the festival was celebrating and he smiled broadly and said, "Mexico," as if that should have been obvious.

I immediately started the air conditioner in my room by opening the window. Since there was no hope of it cooling down, I climbed out onto the balcony—aka the fire escape—and watched the people meandering on the sidewalks below. I kept an eye out for Deja, hoping to catch her searching for me, but after an hour I gave up and went back in to order room service.

The room service arrived in the hands of a pale

blonde dressed in a French maid's outfit. I opened the door wide for her and she sashayed passed me. She carried her shiny silver tray over to the coffee table and set it down. She held the bent-over position a moment longer than necessary to entice me with her ruffled rumpus. I remained at the door holding out the payment for my lunch. Despite the look of my lopsided sandwich, I provided a tip as well.

The French maid took my payment and stuffed it down her cleavage. Before she left, she offered me a few things not on the menu, as well as a complimentary sample of her dessert specials. As generous and talented as she was, I turned her down. I just wasn't that kind of guy.

Even if my moral judgment on prostitution hadn't given me the motivation to send her away, there were a few other things to consider. For one, Deja might interrupt and I would never hear the end of it. Two, I wasn't a big fan of STDs. And three, the sticker shock: I was sure the French maid was a very gifted young lady, but I preferred my sex free and without contractual time limits.

Around three o'clock I lay down for my siesta and didn't wake until five. That was when the smell of cigarettes permeated my veiled senses. I expected to see Deja at the foot of my bed, but instead I found two large men staring at me. I reached for my gun, but it wasn't in the holster. I patted the mattress beneath me in case it slipped out and was just haphazardly lying on the bed.

The men smirked at my efforts. The smoking one

took in a long drag of his Camel before flicking the butt at me. The ember burned my arm before landing on the covers. I picked it up and smashed it out on the edge of the nightstand.

I looked back at the two no-name thugs, trying to determine how much danger I was in. They had guns in hand, but were resting them at their sides with seemingly no interest in shooting me. Which made sense, since they weren't being paid to kill me. The unknown code of the hitman was that unless you were defending yourself or getting paid, you didn't pull the trigger. It was a strange twist of morality, but one I fully intended to take advantage of.

"You know who we are?" the smoker asked. His Russian accent brought to mind a droopy-eared fur hat, but for obvious reasons it wasn't included in his wardrobe. His austere features were blanketed with a thin layer of black hair from his head all the way down to his exposed chest. The quizzical look on his face didn't inspire immediate fear, but even a thoughtful man was dangerous with a gun.

"Not specifically, but I understand your career path." I eased myself up on my elbows.

"That's funny, I like that," Russia said and even smiled at his partner. The balding muscle-man looked to be a good deal older than him, but his deep laugh lines certainly didn't come from his sense of humor. On the contrary, his "fuck off" face was poised for a nonverbal battle. "You know who we are looking for?"

"Yes. How did you find me?"

Russia clicked his tongue and waved his finger at

me. "I'll be asking the questions," he drawled as if he had all the time in the world. "You know where she is?"

"Right now, no. She's here in Juarez," I admitted the obvious, hoping I would get credit for the honesty. They glanced at each other and shook their heads in disagreement. "Yeah, she is. She came here with me."

"In the Camaro?" Russia clarified.

"Yes, but I don't know where she went after we split up."

"It's a nice car. The iridescent blue is beautiful," Russia added as if the compliment was necessary to maintain the casual nature of the interrogation. "I like the way it sparkles in the sunlight."

"Yeah, I'm a sucker for a pretty girl with a hot engine. Speaking of hot rods, why don't you scamper off to search the city for Deja and leave me to my nap?"

Russia shook his head slowly. "She is no longer here. We saw her leaving the parking lot in the pretty blue car. We tried to—"

"She took my car?" I sat up straight, my anger flaring anew. "That bitch!"

"Yes, quite so," Russia agreed. "She drove off like bat in hell. Nearly ran us over. Rather than causing a scene, we decided to find you. You are helping her, correct?"

"I'm not helping her anymore. I quit. I told her to get a gun and go south."

Russia smiled and nodded to my empty holster. "Looks like she took your advice."

I glanced at it and back at them. "No. No. You mean *you* didn't take my gun?" Both men pursed their lips to contain their laughter. "My duffel bag?" I squirmed on the bed to look around them. The dresser, which had the oldest functioning television known to man on it, no longer held my black duffel bag. "Shit!" I flew off the bed and started putting my shoes on. "She must have snuck in when I was sleeping. Son of a bitch!"

As serious as the situation was with two goons pumping me for information, I was more concerned about what I was going to have to do to get back home. I had hung out specifically so I didn't leave Deja stranded, and she turned around and stranded me.

"You have no idea where she went?" Russia asked.

"Believe me, boys, if I knew, right now, I would probably tell you." I stood up and the two men raised their guns to my chest. "Whoa!" I raised my hands. "I'm not involved anymore. You guys can find her and kill her as far as I'm concerned."

"We will, but there is a small price on your head that we can collect while we are here."

"What?" I shook my head.

"Layne Cantry?" Russia verified. "Devitti put a price on you."

"You've got to be kidding me."

"Oh, don't worry, he wants you alive. We would be more than happy to let you stay conscious for the journey if you are willing to behave." I looked down at the guns and around the empty room. I was really regretting not getting the dessert special.

25

"So do you guys work for Devitti exclusively, or just whoever the bids come in from?" I asked behind the cage of the retired police car that Russia and the quiet one used to deliver their bounties. By the looks of the plastic lining the back seat, that including the recently deceased ones. We were close to the border and I wasn't sure I had enough time to talk my way out of trouble. If Deja hadn't snagged the money, I might have been able to buy my freedom. After all, the highest bidder always wins.

"My loyalties side with Mr. Divitti when he needs me, but I occasionally dabble with independent contractors." Russia motioned to his partner, who had taken on the duty of driving. I had determined that the Russian's friendliness was genuine, and apart from the fact that he was about to hand me over to my killer in approximately twelve hours, I rather liked him. "I can take whatever jobs I want, so long as the hit isn't for one of Mr. Devitti's inner circle. Unless, of course, Devitti himself wants one of his men dead, but those jobs are generally taken care of in-house. Public bids are for small potatoes, outsiders—nosy reporters, nuisance cops... and private investigators." He smiled back at me.

"So how does that work?" I asked, searching the

backseat for anything that might help me. Of course there was nothing, not even carpet on the floorboards. "I mean, what happens if two guys go after the same bid. Do you have a gentleman's code or is it first come, first serve?"

"Mostly it is first come, first *kill*." Russia turned and winked at me. "We have a system, but from time to time there is some miscommunication. If we run into a conflict, we can either split the bounty, or if the target is elusive, we will just see which one gets the kill shot. Sometimes we let the other guy go first, in case the target is armed. No sense taking a bullet if we don't have to."

I chuckled. "That sounds reasonable. Damn smart, too. So you don't really have any loyalties to these small bids, you just go where the money is?"

"Money talks."

"Theoretically, if the bid was small and the target had enough money to, say, pay you off, you would probably take the cash and run?"

Russia smiled and nodded. "That is, of course, if the target had his money. It wouldn't make the bid go away though. It would just mean that another contractor would take the job. It would only buy a little time."

"I see. But ultimately the money would be your primary focus?"

Russia shrugged. "The economy is a desperate and bitchy mistress."

"What if I wanted more than just my head off a platter? What if I wanted information?"

Russia shook his head. "We don't talk about our

previous jobs. Once we collect, our mouths are cemented shut."

"Sure, sure, but what about current bids? I know why I have a bid out, but what about Elise Welch? What's her deal? How much is on her head and why are you guys traveling a thousand miles to get to her?"

Russia glanced at his quiet partner, who pursed his lips and shook his head. He obviously had no loyalties, but giving away information didn't appeal to him either.

"You don't have anything to offer us," Russia said.

"I have some money, but it's not what I had in mind to offer you."

"What *did* you have in mind?"

I nodded to the upcoming checkpoint. "I'll tell you after we're through the border. I don't want to get stranded in Mexico if you don't like my offer. You know how hard it is to get through, especially on foot."

Russia narrowed his eyes at me, but didn't question me. He stashed his gun in the glove compartment along with his partner's gun. As the line moved through the gates, motorists offered their IDs and pinprick blood samples or fingerprints. Despite the detail of the procedure, the line moved fairly quickly. Naturally, my captors chose the computer line since they didn't want me to alert the authorities.

We pulled up to the double-sided automated system and the driver rolled down the windows for the three of us. Each of us had a computer pad available to swipe our IDs and offer our fingerprints. If the fingerprints were unidentifiable, a guard would be sent to do a manual blood draw.

I didn't bother trying to screw up my fingerprint since it was virtually impossible with the gel pads, but I was able to type in my ID number instead of swipe it, since the magnetic strips often got damaged. The computer readily accepted my twelve-digit alphanumerical code of HELP-ME-GUNS, despite the fact that it was abnormally long.

I sat back and waited. The driver rolled up our windows and shifted into drive. When the bars didn't immediately rise, the thugs looked at each other. Out of seemingly nowhere, ten guards strapped with riot gear surrounded the car. Rifles and handguns locked onto each of us.

The underutilized border patrol officers were practically frothing with the excitement over the bust. Without regard to the current level of threat, they screamed and cussed at us variations of "don't move" and "get out of the car."

Russia looked back at me, his squinting eyes now bulging from their sockets. "What did you do?"

"As I was saying, I do have something to offer you."

26

A few phone calls later and I was in the office of the Guard Commissioner having coffee—and not just the crap they put in the detainment area. I took another sip of the dark earthy warmth before leaning back in my chair. I glanced over the petite desk that was swarming with stacks of paperwork. I didn't think anyone in this day and age could have so many tangible records and correspondences. The government jobs always seemed to be the last to upgrade.

"You used to work in Vegas?" The Guard Commissioner asked, putting his feet up on the desk like only a man being paid big bucks could do.

"Actually, I did six years with the SDR police academy. I trained half the workforce in southern Nevada and Utah, so I have a lot of names to drop. Before that I was in homicide, but when it became clear computers were becoming the new police... I became a P.I. when they stopped letting me do my job."

The Commissioner nodded. "That's why I'm here behind this desk. Can't stand being out on that line. Watching trucks go through that I know are strapped down with enough drugs to kill a whale." His jaw twisted as he reflected on that. "I can't even stop them, because the codes they use make them untouchable. They have more clearance than I do." He dropped his feet and leaned forward over his desk. "I've worked here for sixteen years and I can't leave this facility without offering my fingerprint."

"That's insane." I shook my head at the despicable state of the world we were all living in. It was a conversation as ubiquitous as the weather to most Americans. We wanted safety, but how could we achieve it without sacrifice? Everyone was in agreement that we had taken it too far, but no one could agree on where to draw the line. So it just kept getting moved forward. Of course, the real crime was that the surveillance didn't even provide the safety it claimed to. All the additional cameras did was reduce petty crimes. The major crime syndicates were doing just fine with the technological climate changes. The Commissioner knew just as well as I did that they had more power than him, and he was just as pissed off about it. "Listen, I hate to ask for more favors."

"Oh, right, your car. Stolen you said."

"Well… borrowed without permission." I chuckled. "It's a female friend of mine."

"Oh," he said with a knowing smile. "Say no more. I'll make a call to the authorities down in Juarez to see if they can find it for you. Would you like the woman arrested?"

"Depends what day it is," I mumbled.

"How's that?"

"Just have them call me at the hotel with her location and I'll go from there. What about my other request?"

His mouth opened but for a moment he didn't say

anything. "It's a little unusual," he said with a frown.

"It's an unusual situation."

"What the hell. It's no skin off my paycheck." The Commissioner stood and led me out of his office to an adjacent room where they were holding my new Russian friend. I could see his muscular partner through the window of the next room down. He still wasn't talking and I started to wonder if he was even physically capable of speech.

I pushed through the door to Russia's room and pulled out the chair across from him at the table. I sat down with my delicious coffee still in hand and took a sip of it. The Commissioner stood against the back wall to monitor the conversation, which didn't bother me. Despite his high paygrade, I knew he wasn't intrinsically part of this corrupt system, just circumstantially.

"Hey Vladimir," I said and Russia glared at the nickname. "My friends are going to detain you for a while. The whole gun thing is pretty weak since you have licenses for them, but taking me against my will is kind of a big deal. However, I could suddenly remember that I volunteered to get a ride with you if you answer some questions for me."

"Blackmail." He scoffed. "Typical."

"Hey, I didn't say you were going to like my offer. I just said I had one."

"What do you want to know?"

"I just want to know why you guys are tromping all the way into Mexico after Elise Welch. Why is the contract so valuable? What did she steal?"

"She is not thief. She is ex-employee. She has knowledge. Nobody likes employees with knowledge quitting. It is… bad for business."

"No shit. What was her job?"

Russia raised his hands in surrender. "That I cannot help you with."

"Who's the employer?"

"The contract is anonymous. I would be paid by bank deposit after drop-off is made."

"Where were you supposed to drop her off?"

"Depends on where I would…"—Russia looked to the Commissioner—"…find her. I get details after I call."

"You have the number?"

"Yes, but it will be untraceable. Disposable phones for disposal services." I glared at him and he raised his hand in surrender. "Sorry, bad joke."

"How many more are on this contract?"

"Independent contracts usually keep things simple. They want to stay anonymous. It is up to the bidders to decide the details. We have a system of sorts. First come, first—" He glanced at the Commissioner. "You remember. I am the second in line for the bid."

"Who was the first?"

"Don't know, don't care, but if it helps, it was not a familiar name. Sometimes we get amateurs on the circuit. Think they can make money with big guns and small *yaytsa*. Since they were not able to complete the task in the time allotted, I am next in line. However, I only have one more day to complete the task. After that someone else will take the job and finish it. Most people don't even make it to the third in line. Your lady has either been very lucky, or very smart." I nodded, thinking that it was probably a little bit of both. "You should know, comrade, it is customary for the price of the bid to double with the second attempt. If the bid stays open still, then the price is tripled, and a third-stringer will be utilized. That will dramatically change the game for you and the lady."

"I assume that means the new guy will be less discreet."

Russia shrugged. "He certainly won't be as friendly." He looked around and leaned forward. "Since we are being so honest with each other, I think you should also know that a bid of that level tends to disintegrate the gentlemanly code of conduct for my ilk."

"Are you saying that there might be more than one person competing for the bid, now that the payout is so high?"

"Correct."

"Great. Tell me something. How did you track us after we crossed the border?"

"A call was made from her cellphone."

Whatever enjoyment I was getting from the conversation was gone. "She made a phone call?"

"Yes, not too long after you crossed. We were already on our way, so we headed straight there."

"She dragged me into Mexico, set me up to get caught, and ran off with my paycheck." I couldn't believe the words, but there was no way not to. "I knew she was a double-crossing bitch, but I didn't think she would put my life in danger."

"Women are full of surprises. Perhaps she just needed a distraction so she could get away." He raised a finger to mark his change in thought. "Or perhaps she just doesn't like you very much."

I leaned back on the chair and sighed. "How right you are, my friend. How right you are."

27

My options were few and decidedly black and white. I could stay in Mexico and go back to help and/or strangle Deja, or I could go back home and forget about finding out why the esoteric crime bosses wanted such a random woman dead. At that point I was willing to assume that anyone who met Deja would want to kill her.

However, the thought of Elise waking up in Mexico alone, with only a note explaining that she could never go home again, made my heart ache. I at least needed to go back and see that she understood what was going on. I also wanted some answers from Deja about my new information and her betrayal. If she was working for these people in some capacity, then all of this was her fault. She must have been doing something pretty underhanded if she was hiding it from me.

The Commissioner was generous enough to loan me one of his employees to drive me back to Juarez. By the time I arrived, it was dark and the festival celebrating Mexico was in full swing. I shifted my wallet from my back pocket to my crotch. Short of being groped, no one was getting it—and there were no guarantees on that either.

The street was alight with the brightly colored outfits of jugglers, contortionists, fire eaters, and all manner of dancers. Feathered and fruited hats bobbed above me as I made my way through the parade that was no more mobile than honey in a freezer. I could see a figure in the window of my hotel room. The orange coal of a cigarette burned against the backdrop of darkness. Rather than try to yell obscenities over the music, I headed up to my hotel room to join my guest.

The lights were off and Deja was sitting in the window without a hint of surprise on her face at my arrival. The parade's chaotic drumming was muted, but would easily cover the argument I was about to instigate.

"Where have you been?" she asked me without any ire in her tone. She kept her eyes locked on the activity outside. I didn't answer right away. I wasn't entirely sure how I wanted to approach her. Starting with my hands around her throat seemed a little misanthropic. Instead I stepped over to the coffee table and dug my gun out of the duffel bag to place it in my shoulder holster where it belonged. "I thought maybe you'd gone back to the States."

"How the fuck would I do that without my car?" I jingled the keys which were lying beside the bag on the coffee table.

She looked back at me. "I had some errands to run. You weren't using it. I assumed you were spending the night so I took some liberties."

"Liberties! You took my car, my money, and my gun!"

"I borrowed the car, I borrowed the gun, and frankly I wasn't sure that the money was still yours. I mean, you quit, didn't you? That was what that whole display was about this afternoon."

"I haven't quit. Yet. I was just reassessing my options."

"So was I." She snuffed out her cigarette and came back inside.

"What is that supposed to mean? Are you replacing me?"

"No, that's not what I mean." She stepped toward the door and I blocked her. She smiled and drew closer to me so she had to arch her neck to look me in the eye. It shouldn't have been intimidating, but it had occurred to me that afternoon that I still didn't know the full extent of her strength.

"Do you really want to have this fight?"

"Yeah, I really do. I just got kidnapped by the thugs that came after Elise yesterday. Thanks to your *liberties*, I had no gun to defend myself, and almost got handed over to Devitti."

"Devitti?" She narrowed her eyes on me. "Why would Devitti want you?"

"You know what, I never even got the chance to ask. I was too busy interrogating them about the reason behind the bid out on your life. And do you know what I found out?" Her eyes went wide for a moment. "I found out that you are a two-timing bitch!" I pushed her away from me.

She recovered and stared back me, eyes blazing with indignation. She came back at me ready to slap me, or shove me, but I grabbed her before her taloned fingers could reach me. I clasped her wrists and pulled them behind her. She fell against me chest to chest and I hugged her uncomfortably tight, keeping her hands locked behind her. Her nostrils flared as she glared up at me. "You stupid son of a—"

"Enough of this, Deja! How could you set me up like that? I'm trying to protect you! *Both* of you!" Her struggle ceased and her expression changed to a mixture of disgust and confusion.

"Set you up?" she hissed. "What the hell are you talking about?"

"Your phone call! Don't tell me you forgot that they would trace it the minute you used it."

"I haven't made any phone calls." She jerked against me. "I'm telling you the truth. I hung around the bar and ate lunch. When I found you, you were out cold. I took your stuff and I went on my merry way. I talked to some people in person, but I never made a call on my cell."

"Prove it." I let her go, giving her a shove to get some distance between us in case she decided to swing. "Show me the usage history." She rolled her eyes and shook her head, but she went to the coffee table and yanked open her purse. She dug through it for a moment but didn't bring it out.

"I can't find—"

Before she could finish, I yanked the purse from her grasp and dumped it on the table. She stood by while I rummaged through the endless list of feminine un-necessities, along with the necessary ones. I ignored the long strip of condoms and birth control compact that had "DON'T FORGET" written on it in big red letters.

There was every manner of hair tie, lip gloss, and gum flavor known to man, but no phone.

I straightened up and looked her over. "Where is it?"

"Where the fuck do you think it is?" she snapped and reached for the cigarettes in the pile. "This is Jaur-fucking-ez! It was stolen. Probably right under my nose. Whoever took it is probably making long-distance phone calls to Puerto Rico and jacking off to phone sex operators."

She started to light her cigarette, but I ripped it out of her mouth. "She doesn't want you to smoke!"

"Fuck her! Fuck *you*! Since when are you two so buddy-buddy?" She pulled out another cigarette and lit it.

"Since you asked me to protect her." I moved to the bed while she went back to the window. "You do remember that, don't you?"

"Are you intentionally being condescending or is that a segue?"

I sat on the bed and leaned over my knees. I needed answers, but I knew that if I pushed her too hard she would just slip out the window and disappear down the fire escape into the crowd. "This afternoon, I asked you if you knew who was trying to kill you. You didn't answer. Was it because you don't know, or because you never knew who he was to begin with?"

Deja didn't react much. Her only tell was the speed at which she took her next drag. She intentionally slowed to give the impression that she was relaxed, but I was starting to see through her bravado.

I knew she was scared, but would never admit it. I also knew that if she could have found a way to protect Elise without involving me, she would have. She hated asking for help. Elise left her no choice because she was the weak one. The one that couldn't be trusted to keep herself alive. That alone was enough for Deja to hate her, like Elise said she did, but she didn't.

She wanted to hate her, but she couldn't. Elise accepted being the responsible one. She was the motherly one watching out for both of them; fixing everything that went wrong; putting every bit of herself into getting them through this strange life together. Deja, no doubt, found her motherly doting condescending and smothering, which only exacerbated her childish rebellion.

Unfortunately, Deja was in unfamiliar territory. She now had to take care of Elise and she was scared that she might not be able to do it. Rightly so, since it could cost both of them their lives.

"Deja," I murmured. "I know trust is a lot to ask. Elise has the same reservations, but you have to let me help you. Yesterday's goons will be out of the running by tomorrow night. We'll have new guys coming after us—Elise and me. They won't stop at the border. They won't give up. The bounty is too high."

"How high?"

"High enough that if I weren't such a stand-up guy, I'd be tempted." She looked at me, trying to see if I was as serious as I sounded. "I know you were employed by him, Deja. You quit. Apparently they aren't the type of employers that accept two weeks' notice. What happened? What were you doing for them? How did it go bad?"

"It wasn't me," she whispered. "It was Elise."

28

"Elise would have mentioned if she had a disgruntled former employer."

Deja smiled, enjoying my ignorance while it was still mine. "She didn't know." She huffed out her last breath of smoke and flicked her butt down the fire escape. She came back inside, but stayed by the window to watch the party outside. "Elise wanted to be a computer programmer or some shit like that. She wanted to go to college, but the thought of four more years of taking notes on shit I would never understand was unbearable."

She drifted away from the window and flopped down on the bed behind me. Her eyes glazed, entranced by the ceiling. "She didn't need a degree to do it though. She usually just moonlights as a web designer. Nothing illegal, unless she has to help me. She hacked the local police department and deleted one of my DUIs and three of our parking tickets. She never got in trouble for it, but someone took notice.

"Six months ago I was pulled aside by a suit and given an envelope with a phone in it. I was instructed to call the only number on it at my convenience. I did. Mr. Mysterious-o offered me—Elise—a job hacking into some low-level government websites. They wanted to manipulate some numbers. No big deal." She smiled and turned to look at me.

"Famous last words." I smiled back.

"I honestly didn't think twice about it. I just left Elise the details and left out the seedy nature of the request."

"You left out the part about the payment as well."

"Yeah." Her mouth quirked up in a sly smile. "I have a pretty high finder's fee. The next thing I know, I'm getting more calls and messages. Elise was pleased with the token jobs. She was suspicious of how I was getting them, but when rent was getting paid and the fridge was full of groceries, she looked the other way."

"What changed?"

"We got a job for something high-level. Hacking into a governor's email to copy some dirt on his expenses was one thing. Downloading home security videos from a senator's home was another. She started asking me a bunch of questions. Questions that I couldn't answer. No surprise to me, she refused to do the job. It was all well and good, no hard feelings. The next job that came up was a minor one, but Elise wouldn't do that one either. She told me she was done."

"And he didn't like that."

"Nope. He strongly suggested that I comply. Then he outright demanded. Then he threatened."

"That's when the hit was put out on you." She nodded somberly. "And Elise doesn't know any of this?"

"No, I've been keeping her distracted with hangovers and cleaning up after me, so she didn't wander too far from home and work. When the second attempt on my life came, I realized that I had no way to protect her. Not from guns. That's where you came in."

I sighed and lay down on the bed to look at the ceiling with her. "Why didn't you tell her? I'm not condoning the hacking on principle, but wouldn't she have continued to do it if you explained her life depended on it?"

"No, she would have gone to the police. We both know how that would have ended."

I frowned at that. I hated the way she viewed the police. I hated more that there was good reason for her to feel that way. "You realize it's entirely possible that this bid didn't come down from the crime bosses? The ax-wielder could be from inside the system. Possibly even a political figure."

"Yeah, I've actually thought about that a lot."

"Shit." I felt the exhaustion of my heroic quest bear down on me.

"You want a drink now?"

"Yeah."

29

"I'm sorry I suspected you," I hollered over the music. The dance party downstairs was in full swing, visible from our balcony seating. The strobe lights ricocheting off every shiny metal surface, made me feel dizzy on top of the liquor.

I poured Deja another shot of tequila from the bottle that cost me more than my rent. Juarez was a fun place to hang out if money was no object, but for me, it was. We would need to get out of town soon, or our budget would be ripped to shreds.

I shifted my duffel bag a little further under my leg. Pickpocketing was rampant, so leaving it in the hotel was not an option, but I also couldn't draw too much attention to it, or someone might outright mug me for it. The fact that I was openly wearing a gun was not nearly the deterrent that one might have expected it to be.

"I would have suspected me too," Deja said, downing the shot. I probably shouldn't have been encouraging her to drink more, but this hangover would still be hers. "We should consider leaving Juarez in the morning."

I looked down at my shot glass as I twisted it on the high-top table. "I've been meaning to talk to you about that. At some point we do need to discuss a long-term plan. As much fun as this is, I can't stay in Mexico forever."

Deja glared at me from across the small table. I could see the subtle variation in her eye color that Elise had mentioned. I expected her to snap at me for my potential abandonment, but she just nodded and looked away. After a long moment, she turned back to me. "You would be good for her, you know."

"Are we back to my debatable secondary duties?"

"No, but that would be good for her too." She shoved her shot glass over and shifted to face me straight on. "She needs someone like you to take care of her. Someone to lift the burden of living a half-life. Fill in the missing pieces and be a constant for her to focus on."

I smiled. "Just her?"

I expected her to glare, but instead she frowned. "She has a good heart, and she deserves to be happy."

I chuckled and sighed. "Just her?" I asked again, since it was still appropriate.

"This bounty won't go away, but if we can stay off the radar long enough then we'll just be a cold case."

"That would involve staying out of the US for… the rest of your lives." I poured her another shot and shoved it back over.

"Mexico is pretty country. So is South America. Elise is smart; she'll learn the language in no time. She'll teach you."

I furrowed my brow. "Deja, don't be ridiculous. You can't ask me to run away with you."

She downed the shot and gripped my hand as I reached to take the glass again. "She won't be able to do it without help. I mean, I could threaten her with the cold truth to get her to stay, but she won't be happy. She needs someone to take care of and someone to take care of her. You have to stay."

I pulled my hand away. This wasn't so much the maternal side of Deja, but more the desperate side. She was seeing her options running out before her eyes and she was panicking. She had screwed up big time, and was just now starting to figure it out.

"Deja, you're asking me to leave behind everything to be with two women I barely know. One of which I'm convinced barely trusts me, and one that definitely doesn't."

"I'm leaving tomorrow morning. You can decide how long you want to hang around, but the money is coming with me." Deja took the bottle and left. I grumbled and followed her out.

30

"Do you know what her research is about?" Deja asked beside me on the bed. I had assumed she was already passed out, but when I opened my eyes, I saw her glassy eyes staring at the ceiling.

"Not really. Not specifically."

"It's about separating our minds." She inhaled deeply. "There's only one way. One must die."

"She said she would never do that," I insisted. I sat up and leaned over her. "Deja, she was mortified when she found out you saw all that. She practically put claw marks in my arms, begging me to make you understand she wouldn't hurt you. I thought you understood that already or I would have discussed it with you."

"I do understand that. I'm just not sure she shouldn't consider it."

"Consider…what, killing one of you?"

"I went to see that shaman today."

"You did?"

"I wasn't going to, but then... I just wanted to hear it for myself."

"And what did he say?"

She shook her head. "She said that twin minds are either together by choice, or by necessity."

"How is that possible?"

"The souls choose." She closed her eyes and took a

slow breath. "She said that we could separate, but only if both of us choose it."

"I thought that whoever left would essentially die, though."

She nodded. "One of the legends says that if you strangle one mind, right before the other takes over, the incoming mind will survive, while the outgoing one will die."

"I guess that makes sense. At least as much as any of it."

"Another version of separation involves drowning. Bleeding out was listed, but that one sounded risky. There was even varying methods of stopping the heart, but you have to be careful not to damage it since it's a shared organ. They all have the same premise though: death must occur, just before the change. It's fascinating, isn't it?"

I stared at her, slack-jawed. I couldn't believe the cavalier attitude she was taking at one of their potential deaths. "Why are you telling me this?"

"I just want you to know what your options are."

"My options? *My* options? What, like I might just pick which one of you I like better and get rid of the other?"

"I'm not suggesting that, but if things go bad, you just need to know whoever dies while in control of the body is the one that doesn't come back."

"Deja, I'm not going to let anything happen to either of you," I reassured her, but she didn't seem to be impressed by my heroic talk.

"I'm tired."

I lay back down and took my turn to stare at the ceiling. I wasn't sure what that conversation was about, but I was just going to have to assume that it was her blunted way of offering advice for a worst-case scenario. I hoped that it didn't come to that.

31

Deja shot three bullets out of the side of the car while I sped down what was laughably considered a road. I hadn't anticipated that the new bounty hunters would be on us the very minute they clocked in for the third round. They were on our scent when we left the hotel and had no qualms about starting a firefight in the middle of a public "road." Although, since Deja was the one to start the shooting, they might have originally intended to follow us to keep tabs on us until they could dispatch us more cleanly.

The car jolted as a pothole realigned my wheels along with my spine. My poor, beautiful creation was going to need an overhaul when we were done with our cat-and-mouse game. As if she hadn't suffered enough, they responded to Deja's bullets in kind.

The pelting sound of punctured metal made me grit my teeth, but I focused on driving so we didn't both die in a fiery car crash. At the very least, we needed to die honorably, face to face with our murderers so we could spit in their faces.

Deja grunted and withdrew from the window. She panted and reloaded the gun with a shaking hand. "Can you drive any faster?" she asked.

"I can't, this road is falling apart."

"Okay." She reached out the window again and

fired off a few more shots. I caught a glimpse of the blood soaking through the right arm of her cardigan.

"Deja?"

"Just drive," she said as she fired one last shot. She flopped back into her seat. "I got the tire. They won't be following much longer."

I checked the rearview mirror just in time to see the dust plume envelop the car where they spun off the road. "Good job," I said and glanced at her. She didn't look at me, which meant she was in a lot of pain. "We need a doctor."

"Yeah right, maybe in Juarez, but I'm not going to a doctor out here. It's a flesh wound, it can wait. Besides, those goons will change that tire in ten flat and be back on our trail again. We need to get off this road, fuel up, and get into the mountains."

"The mountains?"

"Head to Durango. We can stop there for the night and you can patch me up properly." I shook my head, but didn't object. "We're probably going to need to sell this car too," she added.

I didn't even bother looking over at her. I could sense the small satisfaction she got in saying that out loud. I was fairly certain at that moment that I would have preferred to leave her in Juarez. There was still a fading guilt about leaving Elise on her own, but the longer I spent with Deja, the less it seemed to bother me.

32

"Are you done yet?" Deja griped as she took another swig from her water bottle. She had taken to drinking water since I refused to let her leave Elise hung over on top of waking up in a foreign country with a gunshot wound. She probably would have fought me on it more, but I implied that the situation we were in was entirely of her making and she gave up the fight.

"Almost." I pulled the thread through the skin on her arm for another tiny stitch. Deja was right that her injury was just a flesh wound, but it was pretty deep, and I had no intention of letting it get infected. "This is going to be a nasty scar."

"Good luck explaining it to her," she mumbled.

"You can explain it to her, in a well-thought-out letter. Right along with why she is in Mexico, and why she can never go home."

"Yeah, right."

"Listen, Deja, I'm here for one reason only. Because my opportunities to leave keep passing me by. If you expect me to hang out and help Elise when she comes back, you are going to have to own up to your shit."

"Yeah, yeah."

"No," I clipped the thread and swiveled the desk chair so she was forced to look at me. She had removed her shirt for the surgery, but for whatever reason I hadn't blinked at the revealing pink bra. Yet, when Elise was traipsing around in her underthings, I had to restrain myself from gawking at her like a hormonal teenager. "Not yeah, yeah, yeah." I scooted back a little on the bed so I wasn't in her face for the reprimand.

"You need to do this for her. She deserves to get a proper apology." I could see her eyes glazing. "And you deserve the right to defend yourself." She furrowed her brow at that.

"I thought I was the fuck-up in all this."

"You are, but that doesn't mean you can't defend yourself."

"She'll hate me for this, like she does everything else I do wrong."

"She might hate what you did, but the least you can do is earn her respect by owning up to it for once in your life."

"Wow, are those your words? Or did you suddenly link minds with her?"

"Deja, you aren't dimwitted. I don't know why you insist on letting her think you are."

She looked away from me. "Elise needs someone to take care of. I give her that."

"By lying to her and putting her in situations that make her resent you. How is that giving her someone to take care of? That's just giving her someone to clean up after."

"Is there a difference?"

"Yes, there is, and you know it. You're just too stubborn to do anything that someone else expects of you."

Deja's mouth tipped into a slight smile. I knew from experience it was brought on by the type of humor that only she found amusing.

She stood and moved to the two tall slender doors that led out onto the balcony. The hotel room was far fancier than anything we had stayed in north of the border: queen bed, table, desk, and a flat-screen television. The expense was another heated debate, but one that I had won by implying that Elise deserved to wake up in a warm bed, free of strange men and strange smells. As stubborn as Deja was, her guilt was making her a little easier to control.

She opened the doors and stepped into the frame. She tugged her flattened pack of cigarettes from her back pocket and lit one. A horn honked outside, and I heard someone yell, "Take it off!" No doubt in response to her exposed pink bra.

Deja exhaled her drag and offered the leering driver her middle finger. After another drag, she looked back at me. "How did you come to be who you are, Layne?"

"What do you mean?"

"The decisions that led you to be a cop, and then a private investigator. Who made those decisions for you?"

"I did." I sighed, already knowing where this conversation was going.

"What about your clothes?" she asked. "Who decided that you should dress like an undercover cop?"

I frowned and looked down at my clothes. "I did."

Deja tossed away the remaining half of her cigarette and stepped back inside. She exhaled her last breath of smoke as she moved to the end of the bed.

"What about sex?" she asked as she knelt on the edge of the bed. "Who tells you who you can fuck?"

I frowned as she crawled up the mattress toward me. I wasn't so much intrigued as concerned for my safety. As sensual as the action was, I knew she was pissed and she wanted to make a point. "I do."

She touched my leg, and dragged her hand up to my crotch. I moved my hand to intercept hers and shook my head.

"Who decides how you cut your hair? Who decides if you have a pet?" Deja narrowed her eyes and dragged my hand forward, and me with it. I sat up, literally nose to nose with her. "I wake up every other morning of my life, with my choices being disregarded. *I* have to think about every step I make from the perspective of two people.

What's my name?" Deja shoved me back, knocking my head against the headboard. She straddled me and pinned my arms back. I struggled against the subjugation, but the warm tingling sensation pumping through her hands was making her immobile despite our significant weight difference. "What's my name!" She shoved her face in mine when I didn't answer.

"Deja!"

"Wrong! It's Elise Welch! Just like her!" She sat back, giving me space to breathe. "I know she's the cute one. The smart one. And damn if she isn't right most of the fucking time, but it's hard to live in the shadow of someone else. Especially when you *are* the fucking shadow."

Deja shifted off me and sat on the edge of the bed. "You think I'm stubborn because I'm rebellious. The truth is, I'm stubborn so that I can keep some part of me alive, while Elise runs my life however she sees fit for us... for her."

"Have you ever told her this?" I asked after she had settled a moment.

She shook her head somberly. "It's no use, Layne. We can't have two different lives." She looked over at me. "Right?"

I stared into her eyes, seeing a pain that I hadn't expected. I wanted to offer her some kind of silver lining, but she was right. One person couldn't live two different lives.

Then again...

33

I had lain awake that night thinking about what Deja had said. I knew that if Elise understood what Deja was feeling, she would want to do something to fix it. How to fix it was the problem, though. It was one thing to want to dress differently, or wear their hair differently, but what about bigger issues? Jobs, homes, boyfriends... kids. How did you live two different lives when you shared everything, including a uterus?

I heard Deja groan beside me. She rolled slightly, then gasped and sat up straight in bed. She panted and looked around, landing her eyes on me. The room was dark, but the moonlight was enough for us to see each other. "What's wrong?" I touched her back.

Her face crumpled as she looked at me. "Layne?" she whispered. "You're still here."

I sat up and looked at her bewildered eyes. "Elise? Is that you?" I asked.

She nodded. "I fell asleep next to you." She swallowed hard. "And you're still here."

"Yeah," I whispered and moved my hand to push back her hair. "I'm still here." I instantly felt a pang of guilt, since I had almost left her behind.

She touched her hand to my face as if she had to prove that I was real. Her chest rose higher with each breath. She leaned forward and I debated stopping her, but I was just as happy to celebrate her return.

She gave me a gentle kiss, then looked at me, seeking permission to do more. I once again considered my options, but they were out the window as fast as I considered them.

I wrapped her in my arms and pulled her on top of me. We weren't so much kissing as devouring each other. I knew I shouldn't, but I had never wanted a woman more in my life.

I rolled over on top of her and she grappled with my pants. I pressed myself against her, cloth to cloth, forcing myself to keep control even if the situation was well beyond my power.

I kissed her neck, listening to her pant and moan. She groaned and her movement changed from gripping to pushing. I raised myself up to give her some space.

She saw my face and frowned. "Layne?"

"What is it? I have a condom," I offered.

Her eyes widened and she looked down at our intimate position. I shook my head even as I saw the anger rise in her eyes. She shoved her hands forward into my chest. I was launched off the bed and landed on the dresser with the television.

I grunted, struggling to inflate my lungs. I toppled off the bureau and spotted Elise getting dressed. She slipped on her pants and starting searching for the remainder of her wardrobe. "Wait," I rasped over my vacant airways. Paying no heed to my objection, she threw her purse over her shoulder, grabbed her shoes, and bolted out the door. "Elise!" I yelled after her. "Son of a bitch," I griped. I battled through the ache in my back to find my own pants, before going after her.

My previous contemplations about Elise and Deja living separate lives diminished, right along with my erection. There was only one certainty with Siamese minds: They were always more trouble than they were worth.

34

I awakened to a pressure. I couldn't breathe. I felt lips trailing down my neck and I cringed. One of Deja's leftover idiots was an all-nighter. I pressed on him, but a pain in my arm forced me to stop.

He pulled back and looked down at me. The face I saw was familiar. "Layne?" I wasn't sure it could really be him. My grasp on the timeline faltered as I tried to figure out *when* I was as much as where I was.

"What is it? I have a condom," he said.

I looked down at our precarious position. His erection pressing out hard against his underwear. This wasn't the one-night stand I thought I was interrupting. This was Layne and Deja's nightly tryst—a relationship that he had outright lied to me about. Talk about walking in on something.

I shoved him off, using more strength than necessary. He landed on the other side of the room, destroying the television right along with the room deposit. I ignored my guilt over the violent reaction and jumped off the bed. I wanted nothing to do with Deja's love nest, or Layne Cantry and his two-faced lies.

I happily found my jeans on the floor at the foot of the bed and slipped them on in a hurry. "Wait," Lane grunted as he tried to maneuver his bruised muscles off the television. With my purse and tennis shoes in hand,

I jetted out the door. "Elise!" I heard Layne cuss after me, but I couldn't stop.

I jumped into the elevator, since I didn't know how tall the building was. I pressed the button for the main floor and pressed my feet into my tennis shoes. I noted the throbbing pain in my arm and the bandage around it, but I didn't have time to explore it. I waited for ten floors to ping by. All the while, my thoughts turned back to Layne and the two days we had spent together. It was nothing, of course. I was just his job, and he was just my bodyguard. But then why did it hurt so much?

I let go of the delusions I was trying to sell myself and I started to cry. I had only spent two days with Layne, but it was already too much. I had let my guard down and in my desperation to connect to someone, I invited him into my heart. I had wanted it to be so much more than it was, and even when he had told me it couldn't be, I witlessly allowed myself to hope.

I thought he would different. I thought he would understand, but no one did. Hell, Deja didn't even understand. Not really.

The elevator door opened and I stepped out. I almost expected Layne to be there to intercept me, but ten floors was a lot of stairs. I put on my happy face, hiding my emotional damage as I whisked past the front desk.

I pushed through the front doors and stepped out onto the sidewalk. I froze, watching the car lights pass by. It was late, or very, very early. I usually didn't wake directly after the change, so I never really knew night to night when I took over.

In addition to the question mark on the time, I had no idea *where* I was. I crossed the street and started darting around until I was at least lost enough to be considered safe. Whatever that was.

"Elise!" I heard Layne somewhere behind me. I looked back, but I couldn't see him. I suspected that he was at least a block away. He hadn't seen me, he was just haphazardly calling me like a runaway dog.

I turned back around, prepared to jog a little longer. I barely made the turn, before running into a stack of boxes that seemingly appeared out of nowhere. The top box crashed to the sidewalk. The bottles within shattered, spilling their brown liquid on the cement.

A man popped out from the side door of a delivery van and looked over the mess. Another one came out of the brick building I was walking along side of. The two men converged on the mess with frowns.

"Oh, I'm sorry," I groaned. I looked back for Layne. Still not there.

The shorter man, who had apparently been delivering the boxes, made a comment in Spanish. The bigger man, presumably the vendor of said product, glared at him and said something back in Spanish. The shorter man shook his head and loaded up his two-wheel cart. There was another series of cryptic objections from the vendor, but the delivery man gave a firm, compendious "no." He just closed up his truck and left.

The vendor turned away from the distancing truck and looked at me. "You." He pointed at me. "You just cost me a grand."

I looked down at the broken box. "That cost a grand?"

"That's how much I would have made off it. Shots aren't cheap, you know."

I glanced at the open door behind him. With the rumble of the truck gone I could hear the music thumping inside. "I tell you what." I glanced back for Layne. Where was he when I needed a crapload of cash? "I only have a little cash, but maybe..." I searched my purse for my wallet, but I couldn't find it. Even my phone was gone. "...or not."

"How about we do a fair trade instead?" he suggested.

I frowned and rolled my eyes. "I am not blowing you over some spilled liquor."

He chuckled and shook his head. "Your lips aren't worth that much, sweetheart. You're in pretty good shape though. Maybe you come inside and shake your tits a while, and we'll call it even."

"No, thank you."

"I'm not really asking, sweetheart." He leaned over the boxes to glare at me. "This isn't the type of establishment that you can wash dishes to repay a debt."

"It was just an accident. Can't you just cut me some slack?"

"That's not how things work in Durango."

"Durango?" I looked around. I had been to Durango many times. I was surprised that Layne had taken us back to Colorado.

"That certainly isn't how things work in Mexico,"

he added.

"Mexico?" I blanched. "Oh, shit." I turned to run. I wanted no part of Mexico's version of fair trade.

The vendor's thick arm wrapped around me, dragging me back. I was about to elbow him back two blocks or so, but a gun barrel pressed into my cheek, stalling my defenses. I still couldn't beat a bullet.

"How's about we get you clocked in and into your new uniform?" He dragged me back toward the door. My heart started to race as I imagined the horrible scenario that waited for me inside that bar. I thought I saw Layne coming down the sidewalk on the other side of the street, thankfully still searching for me.

"Layne!" The metal door closed on my scream.

34

"This isn't that hard to understand, sweetheart. You shimmy, you shake, and the boys down there..." The vendor pointed to half a dozen slobbering twenty-somethings below my cage. They were having a bachelor party, but I couldn't tell which one was getting married. They all seemed to be making up for future lost time. Despite their overzealous inebriation, I was not living up to their expectations. "...give you money." He rubbed his fingers together. "Then you pay me. Then I unlock the cage." He rattled the padlock on the birdcage I was sitting in.

The scenario wasn't quite as bad as I had originally pictured it. I wasn't naked, covered in oil, or wrestling another woman in Jell-O, but still... I spat in the vendor's face to log the full extent of my objections. The bachelors beneath me hooted enthusiastically. One of them stood on his chair and hugged the cage. "Marry me!" He pushed his face into the bars and puckered his lips for a kiss that I didn't give him. "I'll let you spank me," he added enthusiastically. As if that was going to tip the scales toward matrimony.

"Easy, boys." The vendor pushed him away and turned the cage until I was facing him again. "Hey. You see those private rooms back there?" I looked over at the doors marked with neon XXXs. "Unless you want to put those lips to work, I suggest you be happy with the cage." He pulled his jacket to one side, revealing the butt of his gun. "You make up half my loss and I'll call it even. Do we have a fair trade?"

"Yes," I grumbled and pushed my hair out of my face. There was no point in arguing about money with a Mexican bar owner. I might as well have been negotiating with my hitmen for a running start.

He let go of the cage and I rotated back to face my fans. I looked down at my sparkling-blue-bikini-clad body. I wasn't comfortable being half-naked, let alone whatever this outfit was classified as. The men licked their lips and waved their money just out of my reach.

I looked around the strip club and noted the woman crawling down the runway. Her tongue was hanging out, and she was practically humping the floor.

The cage on the opposite side of the bar contained a young girl. Too young as far as I was concerned. She noticed the men groveling at my cage. She shouted something in Spanish at them and they looked over. They glanced at each other as if trying to get a consensus on whether or not to abandon me for a more entertaining bird.

Rather than endure this torture any longer than necessary, I closed my eyes and listened to the music. I wasn't a good dancer, but I wasn't sure that it mattered, so long as the interesting parts of my body jiggled a little.

I grabbed the bars of the cage and rolled my body. The men started to cheer for my movement and I couldn't help smiling at them. They were too drunk to know that I sucked.

I felt a bill being slipped into my bikini strap and I ignored the part of me that felt violated and belittled. This was a dance. Just a lewd, held-at-gunpoint dance.

I whipped my hair around, which got a few more cheers. I crouched down and ran my hands down my body, over my breasts and between my thighs. I bit my lower lip, pretending that I was getting turned on by my own touch.

I slid my hands out to my knees and forced them farther apart. I grabbed the bars once again, pumping my hips. The uproar that it caused nearly got my cage knocked down.

I opened my eyes to see who had shoved the cage, and I found several hands demanding to give me their money. I felt like a zoo animal, but also the opposite. I was the one performing in the cage, but the yahoos outside were hooting and screeching like wild creatures. I smirked at the overeager donations that would ultimately buy my freedom and I leaned forward to accept them.

I licked the finger of one of the extended hands and bit the twenty he was holding for me. "Oh, gawd, I love you," he bemoaned. I smiled, almost enjoying the unadulterated adoration. Even if it was based in alcohol, it was still flattering.

A movement behind the men caught my eye. Layne stared back at me quizzically, no doubt shocked by my salacious display. I opened my mouth to call to him and beg for help, but he raised his hand sharply and shook his head. He glanced over to the bar and made a rolling motion with his fingers. He wanted me to keep up the act.

I felt a bill slip into the cleft of my bra and I realized I was missing out on some potential bailout money. With my attention split between Layne and my bachelors, I continued to dance and offer my bikini as a coin purse.

Layne moved over to the bar and spoke with the bartender. He motioned over to me and the bartender looked in my direction. He furrowed his brow and shook his head.

The bartender motioned to the man who had imprisoned me. The vendor was sitting at the end of the bar, monitoring his employees. I wondered how many of them were being paid, and how many had been lassoed in by debt. Layne headed over to him. With introductions and handshakes aside, they started to discuss my early release. Layne paused to look at me after the conversation. He raised a finger at the man and pulled out his wallet. He held up a wad of bills and told him something before he handed it to him. The vendor counted the cash, considering the request, and nodded before pocketing it.

The vendor stood up and came back to my cage to unlocked it. The men jeered and cussed in Spanish. My biggest fan came up to him and squeezed one of his large biceps. "No, don't take her. We are going to get married and have beautiful babies."

The owner sloughed him off and dragged me across the bar. "Ouch, careful with the arm." I motioned to the bandage that he was grabbing much too close to. I still hadn't figured out the nature of the injury, but it was very tender.

Instead of releasing me to Layne's custody, he took me toward the X-rated rooms. I gasped and dragged my feet. "No, I was dancing. I made some money!" I looked around for Layne, but he wasn't at the bar. I couldn't imagine that he had just left me. What was the money for?

The vendor pushed into my space. "You do this lap dance and we are square. Got it?"

"I'm not going to jack off some asshole."

"Just brush up against him a few times, and pretend to like it. It's not rocket science, sweetheart."

"Fine," I seethed. He shoved me through a black curtain. I shoved it away and found another curtain right after it. Past that I found my way inside a small room with a mini disco ball hanging from the ceiling and a red horseshoe couch. Little speckles of light danced around the room and over the man sitting on the couch. "Layne?"

35

I started to move toward Layne, but he held up his hand and nodded to the cameras around the room. "Just make it look good and we can get out of here," he whispered.

I sighed and strutted toward him. My attempt at a sexy walk diminished as my heels nearly gave out. I caught myself, narrowly avoiding a broken ankle. I thought I saw Layne smirk, but when I looked again, he was somber, waiting patiently for my arrival.

When I reached the edge of the couch, I wasn't sure how to start. I felt ridiculous. I was more humiliated by standing in front of him than the lewd gyrations I had done for the bachelors. He raised his eyes to the cameras once more and nodded for me to proceed. I lifted my foot onto the couch next to him and slid my hands up my leg. His eyes fixated on the movement, watching intently as I reached my thigh. When I stopped moving he looked at me for an explanation. "This isn't for your enjoyment. I'm just playing the part."

"I'm just playing my part too." He shifted down in his seat. "I thought this was a *lap* dance."

I narrowed my eyes on him and clenched my jaw. Rather than fight it, I put my foot down and repositioned around his legs. Rather than delicately climb into a straddling position, I jumped, landing with my full weight near his crotch. He grunted and winced at the sudden pressure. "Careful, baby, I'm still a little black and *blue* from earlier," he purred seductively, but I could see the irritation hiding in his eyes.

"Good." I pushed my hips forward. "You deserved it."

"Did I?" he asked.

I frowned and looked away from him. I didn't want to admit to him, how much he had hurt me. Mostly because I didn't want to admit how much I liked him. It all seemed so juvenile now.

I fought back another round of tears and started to repeat my moves from the cage. "Why the hell are we in Mexico?" I whispered while I danced.

"Long story. Deja has a letter to explain everything."

"Why don't you just tell me what it says?" I rolled my head, intentionally whipped my hair in his face.

He glared at me, but didn't do anything to interrupt my performance. "I didn't read it. She hid it in that pig sty you both call a purse."

"What is wrong with my arm? It hurts like hell." Layne looked down as if he didn't want to admit how I had gotten hurt. I lifted his chin with my finger, trying to make it look seductive. "Talk."

"Deja got shot on the way out of Juarez."

"Juarez? Why would you take us to Juarez? Why would you take us to Mexico, for that matter? Aren't we trying to stay alive?"

"Deja wanted to get out of the States. There was

just nowhere else to run to without digging a hole and crawling into it."

I stopped dancing and just sat on his lap. "What happened in Juarez?"

"Ate, slept, got kidnapped, watched an orgy laughably called a parade."

"Kidnapped? Deja got kidnapped?"

"No, I did." Layne patted my leg. "Keep dancing."

I looked up at the cameras posted behind me and started undulating again. I grabbed Layne's shoulders and leaned back. I felt his hands slide up my sides, his thumbs stopping just shy of my breasts. I leaned forward again catching him ogling my chest.

"What the hell do you think you're doing?"

"Enjoying my lap dance."

"You're not supposed to touch me."

"I'm not sure this is the type of establishment that cares about that sort of thing. I paid good money for it, I should get something out of it." He brazenly tugged on my bikini top, and I slapped his hand away. "That color reminds me of my car."

"Behave yourself, or I will knock you clean through this wall."

"Sorry." He let his hands drop back down to my legs. "You're just surprisingly good at this."

"What, the stuffy head-case twin can't be sexy?" I snarled at the veiled insult.

"No, I knew you could be sexy. I just didn't know you knew."

I stared at him. A small smile tipped the corners of his mouth. He was too damn cute. Why did he have to be cute? I shook my head. "I'm not going to let you do this." I stood and resituated myself on his lap so my back was to him. I didn't want to look at his face anymore. His lying face.

I dutifully wiggled my shoulders and squirmed my butt on his legs. He let out a grunt as I did, but I was certain it wasn't due to pain. "Do what?" he asked.

"Pretend like you didn't lie to me. I flat-out asked you if you and Deja were involved."

"We aren't."

I twisted around. "Oh, that is such bullshit, Layne. I woke up with your hard-on between my legs," I seethed, trying to contain my volume.

He sighed. "Yes, between *your* legs. Elise Welch, not Deja."

"I wasn't there until halfway through."

"First of all," he said, raising a finger, "that wasn't half way through, and second, I thought you were the one instigating the act."

"What are you saying? You couldn't tell the difference between us? Come on."

"She was pretending to be you."

"Why?"

"Because she wants me to have sex with you."

"Why?"

"Because she..." Layne took in a breath. "She wanted you to have a little fun. Little did she know how difficult that is for you." He reached up and squeezed my shoulders. "Why did you run from me, Elise?"

"I wanted to get away from you."

"You didn't need four blocks of space. You weren't

in any danger."

"I don't know." He moved his hands to my legs, tickling the skin until the flesh puckered with goosebumps. "Stop that, don't touch me." I brushed away his hands, but he brought them right back.

"There's something here, Elise. Between us. I'm trying to fight it, but I'm failing. Right now I'm struggling to remember why I didn't want to get involved with you. If you want me to stop, you're going to have to remind me."

"Because I'm a twin soul. Half of me will forever be unattainable."

"I don't want your other half. I don't want Deja. I wasn't thinking about Deja when I was between your legs this morning. I was thinking about you."

I turned my head and stared at him. I had dreamed of hearing those words for years. Someone wanted me. Not Deja. Not both of us. Just *me*.

I shifted back slowly, leaning into his arms. His hand grazed my cheek and he shifted forward to meet my lips.

"Time's up, lovebirds." The vendor interrupted our interlude and tossed my clothes at me.

"Am I done?" I jumped off Layne's lap and grabbed my clothes. "Hey, where's my bra—and my underwear!"

"The bachelor bought them from me." He nodded back toward the main room.

"Eww."

"You can keep the blue sequins, but leave the stilettos. Those freaking things cost a fortune."

I ripped off the shoes and tossed them to him. He caught them and started to leave.

"So we're square? I can go?"

The vendor turned back and nodded. "Yeah, he covered your debt the minute he walked in the door. This extra bit was his idea." The vendor nodded to Layne.

"Secrets much?" Layne asked as he shifted to stand.

I didn't bother letting him explain himself. I just punched him in the jaw.

36

Layne rubbed his jaw again as we entered the elevator in the hotel. He was sore in more ways than one. "I can't believe you punched me." He finally unclenched his teeth to let words out.

"I can't believe you made me dance for you." I pushed my finger on the door close button to speed up our departure.

"You were upset when you ran out. I wanted to make sure you would listen to me."

"You wanted to have my body gyrating against yours."

Layne snorted and smiled. "I was coming over to retrieve you from the cage, but..."

"But what?" I propped my hands on my hips and glared at him.

"But you were so damn sexy in that bikini." I scoffed and turned away again. "You were beautiful," he whispered. I looked to him again and got caught up in his eyes. "I wanted you to listen to me, but... You know what, yes. I wanted your body up against me, legs wrapped around me just like they were this morning. I wanted that then, and I still want it now."

"Layne—" I started to speak, but he dove at me and kissed me. He backed me into the corner and all I could do was wrap my arms around him and hold on.

It felt so good to be kissed. To be desired in such a raw and savage way. Never mind the ramifications of tomorrow's tomorrow, I wanted to be kissed. I wanted to be touched. But, more importantly, I wanted to be the first, or the only. I wanted to be one with someone outside of myself.

The elevator dinged and Layne pulled away from me. He took my hand, linking his fingers in mine as we walked back to the room. It should have perhaps been a smooth journey with exchanges of bashful knowing glances, but the swift pace he set for us was serious and determined. When he reached the door, Layne jammed his card in and out so fast that the reader didn't take it. He did it again a little slower and the light signaled our admittance. He pushed open the door and pulled me inside.

In a singular, almost dancing movement he swung me around, kicked the door shut, and pulled me into another fervent kiss.

I could barely breathe, but his frenzy only added to my desire. My heart thundered with fear as much as anticipation. I ripped off my shirt, revealing the blue sequin bra. His eyes glittered over the material that he had admired so much, but it was off before I felt him unsnap it.

My breasts open to the air, he leaned down, suckling the flesh, devouring my nipples each in turn. I threw my head back and nearly cried over the satisfaction of having him. He caressed my back and slipped my pants down around my ankles. I giggled as he used his teeth to pull down the blue bikini bottoms.

He stood back up and backed me to the bed. He gave me a gentle shove and I bounced onto the mattress. I scooted back to give him room to join me, but he lingered at the foot of the bed to undress. I propped myself up and watched him remove his shirt, revealing the breadth of his chest and the soft dark curls at his sternum. His pants dropped away and I admired the erection that was once again pressing against the fabric of his underwear. Then that too landed on the floor.

Completely naked, and ready to take me, he crawled up the mattress, nibbling his way up my leg. I squirmed and giggled at the tickling kisses, until he reached the top.

I rasped and twisted my fingers into the sheets, allowing myself the pleasure that was missing from my life. Over the summit and back again, Layne proved to be as much, and more, than I had hoped.

37

After a nap to finish out what was technically still the evening, I awakened to light shimmering in through the balcony doors. I glanced back at Layne, but he was fast asleep. I slipped out from under his arm and crawled out of bed.

I stretched and smiled at the morning sun. I ignored the little voice in the back of my head that listed all of the things wrong with the situation. The issues that would develop when the real world started to invade my fairytale. It didn't matter. I had today and tomorrow. After that was beyond my control. As was the story of my life.

I picked up my purse where I had dropped it a few hours earlier. I sat down at the desk and searched its contents. I found a bottle of antiseptic with a note wrapped around it that said, "apply twice a day." I glanced at the bandage on my arm. I decided to leave that task to Layne. I didn't even want to look at it.

I pulled out a stale pack of cigarettes and scoffed. She would never quit. Not until we were both wheezing like an asthmatic eighty-year-old. I tossed the pack in the trash bin and dug deeper. I knew it had to be there.

I found the Tic Tac container and grabbed it. I tugged open the top and yanked the tiny folded note out of it. She must have actually wanted to keep it private this time. That was an accomplishment, at least.

I unfurled the note and frowned at the tiny legible writing. She actually had something to say, and her normally oversized scribbles were not going to cut it.

Dear Elise,

As you might have guessed already, we got into some deep shit and had to go south into Mexico. Sorry about the gunshot wound, but at least you aren't in the ground.

You might be questioning why I took us to Jaurez first. I had to hear it for myself. You were right. It's a dead end. I know you were hoping for something different, but I think it's time we both give up on that. I've made plenty of mistakes. Big ones that I can't take back. But if we make it through this alive, I will do my best to get us back on track.

I re-read the first two paragraphs. I almost couldn't believe this was Deja. It was her handwriting, but sober and honest. She was even being apologetic. Either we were in a hell of a lot of trouble, or her trip to the shaman was more illuminating than she anticipated.

According to Layne the bid on us has gotten bigger. Big enough that those bastards followed us across the border. I know you're scared and angry, but the only thing we can do is keep running. You need to go south. As deep as you can go. We need to disappear. We'll have to start over, but I think you will agree that we aren't walking away from that much.

If you are reading this out loud, stop. Layne doesn't know I'm writing this part.

I know that you like him, and for your sake I hope

that my little stunt has worked, so you can enjoy him before you have to leave him.

I frowned and glanced at Layne. He was still asleep.

Layne's gone as far with us as he can. The day before yesterday, he almost split on me. If it weren't for our abrupt car chase this morning, I think he would have dumped me at the nearest bus stop and headed home.

I know he wasn't leaving you. He was leaving me, but we don't have the luxury of technicalities. He was only meant to be temporary fix anyway.

The money in the duffel bag is ~~mine ours~~ yours. The computer hacks you were doing paid higher than I told you. After you refused to do the jobs, your employers decided that you knew too much and put a hit out on us to keep things quiet.

I moved over to the duffel bag at the end of the bed and knelt down to open it up. My mouth dropped as I took in the packs of hundred-dollar bills stuffed in amongst Layne's spare clothes.

There is only one way out of this, Elise, and it's together. I need you to get Layne's gun, the money, and your butt on a bus heading as far south as south goes. Don't sleep, don't eat, just get out of there before they find you. Don't trust anyone!

I picked up the holster lying next to the duffel bag. I pulled the surprisingly heavy weapon from it. I had never held a gun. I wasn't sure I would even know how to use it, let alone aim it. I didn't want to be responsible for firing guns. I wanted Layne to do that for me. But maybe Deja was right. If Layne couldn't stick it out with her, then, in the end, he wasn't going to be there for me. Whether we liked it or not, it was her and me forever.

"Mind telling me why you have my gun?" Layne asked from above me on the bed. He looked concerned, but his interest in me switched to the door behind me. I looked over and saw the shadow of legs just on the other side. I heard something click behind the door. "Shit," he whispered and leapt on top of me.

For a moment, everything felt like slow motion. Layne's body smashed against me, pressing me into the rug. The gun was ripped out of my hand just as a barrage of noise assaulted my eardrums. I couldn't even distinguish it. It was just really, really loud.

The wood door splintered, ejecting slivers into my legs. The plaster started to chip on the walls, filling the room with a fine dust. Light streamed in from the holes being created in the wall and door. Layne raised his gun and added several succinct reverberations to the already eardrum-popping noise—our only defense against the automatic weapons mowing down our hotel room.

38

I squealed under Layne, plugging my ears and begging for it to stop. I could feel the bullets whizzing past me, narrowly missing our flattened bodies. He reached for his bag and pulled out another clip. His singular recoils began again, but after the first few shots the noise outside stopped. A sharp ringing took its place in my eardrums.

The wall had stopped bursting in on us. The danger had passed.

I started to shift, but Layne pressed his finger to his lips. He stared out the fist-sized holes in the door, searching for movement. When nothing moved he got off me and handed me my pants. He moved carefully to his own clothes and started to dress. He kept his gun in hand and his eye on the door and the many peepholes in it.

He didn't bother to zip or even button up before looping his duffel over his shoulder and pulling me off the floor. I grabbed my purse, slipped on my shoes, and ducked low to follow him out the door.

Layne peeked down the hallway left and right. One man was dead in the hallway, but he must have suspected more because he kept volleying his gaze in both directions.

We skirted the walls until we reached the stairwell.

He peeked through the window and pushed me back. He jumped through the door, aiming his gun up and down.

When all was clear he yanked me forward and down the stairs. I didn't bother to ask any questions. The answers didn't matter as long as they involved us getting the hell out of there. Preferably without a new gunshot wound.

We made it down to the parking garage beneath the hotel and Layne gave it the same treatment. With cars everywhere, there were too many places to hide. He lay down on the floor searching for feet, but that didn't account for the ones hiding behind wheels.

We ran across the concrete to his blue Camaro. He motioned for me to get in and we split apart. I reached for the passenger-side door, but the car next to me opened its driver-side door, slamming it up against my escape path.

I shrieked, but a pair of arms and a gun were already around me, holding me captive. As I struggled against the over-muscled man, I saw Layne in conflict with a man on his side of the car. They had stifled the fight with brandished guns, one for each of their temples. They were at a standoff, both of them seconds away from a bullet in the brain.

"Layne!" I cried.

"Don't do anything, Elise. We're just figuring each other out."

"I'm good at chicken," the bald man threatened him, pushing the gun a little harder.

"Oh, you *can* talk," Layne commented. "Let the girl

go."

The bald man shook his head, not even looking at me. "She's gonna die for sure. You, I haven't decided."

"Betcha you would have already decided if my barrel wasn't in your ear."

"Yeah, I think you're right. I'll make you a deal. You put down your gun first, and I won't rape your girl before I put her down."

"You son of a bitch," Layne hissed, baring his teeth in contempt for his enemy.

I winced and began to weep. I knew we were done. I couldn't do anything to save myself before a bullet went through my brain, and Layne couldn't save himself either.

Even as I accepted the inevitable, I heard someone clear their throat beside us. We all looked over to the tiny interruption. A man with razor-short dark hair, broad shoulders, and a five o'clock shadow was nonchalantly standing with his hands folded before him. More interesting than him, though, was the gaggle of men at his back, armed with guns. Every one of their sights was aimed in our direction.

"Russia?" Layne asked. "What the hell are you doing here?"

"Excuse me, Mr. Cantry," the dark-haired man said, and in fact sounded Russian. "I'm afraid I am interrupting your negotiations."

"Stay out of this, Nikolai," the bald man warned him.

"I wish I could, my friend, but my new orders are very specific."

"Come on, Russia. You had your chance," Layne complained. "You guys have to step back. Aren't those the rules?"

"Oh, yes, they definitely are, but as I mentioned earlier, when the bid gets high, the rules start to degrade. Thus the reason for my *former* partner doing overtime." The bald man afforded him a quick glance, but didn't contest the title clarification. "Besides that, though, I have been assigned a new job."

"Oh yeah? What's that?" Layne asked.

"I have been appointed to deliver Miss Welch to Mr. Devitti himself... alive." Nikolai nodded toward me and a gunshot echoed through the underground garage, adding to the ringing in my ears. I felt something wet and warm drape my shoulder and I was pulled to the ground along with my captor. His arms fell limply away from me, freeing me to roll off him.

From that position I could see feet scuffing against the pavement on the other side of the car—Layne and his bald man struggling again. I heard a punch and Layne fell to the ground. I could see him clearly between the wheels of the Camaro. I sat up and saw the bald man through the car windows, aiming his gun to fire.

I raised my legs and kicked my feet forward into the side of the car. I put every last ounce of my shared strength into the effort. The car door dented in like it had been hit with a truck. The wheels screeched as the force of the impact pushed it to one side, ramming into the bald man and pinning him between the Camaro and the car next to it, effectively breaking his legs.

The bald man groaned and struggled against the pain. He looked around and saw me on the ground on the other side of the car. He pinched his lips back in a nasty sneer and raised his gun to shoot me. A single bullet fired and the bald man's head whipped back before flopping over the hood of Layne's Camaro. I looked to the shooter and found Nikolai still aiming his gun at his former partner.

I heard Layne groan and I ducked down to see if he was okay. He was tucked tightly beneath the undercarriage of his car and one next to it. Alive, but very cramped.

A pair of hands gripped me under my arms and yanked me from the floor brutishly. I panicked at the possibility of yet another attack. I turned around and slammed my fists into the chest with all my might. I expected nothing short of my usual superman strength, but the vibration that ricocheted me off him hummed down my body and settled into my feet.

I stared back at the eyes that matched my height. He smirked at me through his sparse goatee. "You should know better than to try to hurt your own."

I shook my head and backed away from him. He wasn't nearly as tall or muscular as his counterparts, but I got the sense that it didn't matter. "Who are you?"

I felt yet another hand on my shoulder and I yelped and whipped around to face them. "Don't touch me!" I screamed at the man.

"Easy, girl." The Russian, Nikolai, approached and shooed his man off me. "We are here to help."

"The hell you are!" I heard Layne yell. I turned just

in time to see the man with a goatee lift the car up and help him out. Layne gave the man the same twice-over I had as he watched him return the car to the concrete without so much as a grunt of effort. "Thanks," he said, when the many variations of questions had fallen from his face. He turned and walked over to Nikolai. "Three days ago you and that asshole were putting bullets in a bed you thought she was hiding under."

I looked to Nikolai to see if this was true. Was he, in fact, one of the men that had done that? He gave me an almost embarrassed shrug. "Three days ago I was moonlighting," he said and turned back to Layne. "As I said, Mr. Cantry, I follow the money. However, that assignment is now in direct opposition to my current employer, so I find myself in a rather ironic situation, as it will now be my duty to protect Ms. Welch."

"Why the hell does Devitti want her? Is he the one who put out the original bid?"

"I doubt it." Nikolai dipped his brow. "That would be counterproductive. The bid for her head is still out. There are several interested parties. Mr. Devitti has offered a substantial counteroffer in order to get her back to him alive."

"Why?" Layne glanced at me. If he was waiting for me to answer, he would be waiting for a while. I was still trying to figure out why Nikolai wasn't trying to kill me anymore.

"I don't ask questions, Mr. Cantry. I just deliver the goods." Nikolai reached for me and I took a step back.

"You aren't taking her anywhere." Layne stepped in front of me.

"Mr. Cantry, I think you and I are honorable men."

"You're a killer."

"Yes," Nikolai said with a tone that demanded a "duh" at the end of it. "But I am still an honorable man." Layne nodded in agreement. "Let's not sully what has been a rather pleasant cat-and-mouse game with things like bullets and blood. I will make you a deal. You can come with us. To make sure she is treated respectfully."

"And if you deliver me to Devitti, you can get your payment for me as well."

Nikolai made a "bah" noise and waved away the suggestion. "Your bid is tiny change compared to Miss Welch. You will be more of a nuisance than your bounty is worth, but..." Nikolai touched his shoulder. "I will take you with us to maintain our reciprocity and to keep Miss Welch more comfortable. How does that sound to you?"

Layne glanced back at me. "Is Devitti going to kill her?"

I looked to Nikolai, eager to hear the answer.

"As I said, I don't ask questions, but... I am certain that a man like Devitti would not spend this much to achieve what someone else has already fronted the money for. I suspect that Mr. Devitti just wants to know why Miss Welch has become so popular." Nikolai turned to me and brandished a debonair smile. "After all, knowledge is what saves us when arrogance has damned us."

39

I stood outside the bathroom of a fuel station in Nogales. One of my bodyguards had stepped inside to check the stalls for murdering thugs, while the other remained with me. I kept glancing at the stony gray eyes and thick umber brows that were eyeing me harder than I could return.

I had never met one of my own kind before. I wanted to ask him a thousand questions about twin souls and his experiences, but three bathroom stops later I still couldn't muster the courage. Maybe I didn't really want to know.

I looked over the horizon at the falling sun. I would barely have a half a day left in Vegas before Deja returned. I supposed that was for the best. She was better equipped for this stuff anyway. Or at least less likely to cry in the bathroom during every pit stop.

"She's pretty," the bodyguard said. I looked at him lounging against the stucco wall. He didn't seem to have a care in the world about the potential doom he was delivering me to. "Yeah, she is," he responded to his own observation. "Your name's Elise, right?" he asked.

"Yeah." I nodded.

"Mine's Britt, but everybody just calls me Deuce."

"Nice to meet—"

Britt banged on the bathroom door. "Are you taking a crap in there, Rod?"

"I'm comin'!" Rod yelled from inside.

"Hurry up, Britt's getting fresh with the bounty." Britt chuckled after his statement and shook his head at me. "Don't mind him. He isn't as virile as he once was." His face contorted into a sneer. "Fuck you, Britt," he griped... at himself.

I gaped at the transformation before me. "What is going on with you?" I asked.

Rod stepped out of the bathroom, zipping his pants on the way.

"You're up, girl." Britt pointed to the door and I stepped inside. He started to follow, but I put my hand on his chest. He looked down at it with a smirk.

"What is the point of checking the bathroom if you are going to just follow me in anyway? Just give me five minutes to change my tampon and we'll be on our way."

"Eck! Why did I have to know that?" Britt grimaced and stepped back, as I knew he would. Men were nothing if not predictable.

I went inside and took care of my business. Meanwhile I dug through my purse and found a pen. I always had pens. I pushed my pants down past my knees and continued my letter that I had not dared write on paper. Too much was happening, and I needed Deja to know everything so she didn't get us killed when she got back.

With blue indelible ink translating my day over the curves of my thighs, I pulled up my pants and stepped outside the stall. I looked in the blurry unbreakable mirror. I had since cleaned myself of my attacker's blood, but I couldn't wait to take a proper shower. I needed to rinse off the last few hours. I only wished I could wash away everything that had happened in the last week.

Hangovers, tattoos, and gunshot wounds. Hitmen, kidnappers, and mobsters. Stalker, private eye, friend, lover, and now...

Who *was* Layne to me now?

Just another in a long line of men that couldn't handle the crazy that Deja and I threw out on a daily basis. Although, with that being said, I was beginning to think that Britt might have an overstock of nuts in his cabinet. Maybe it could be worse.

I washed my hands and splashed some water on my face before leaving the restroom. Just as I left, I caught sight of Layne being ushered over to his vehicle. The Russian man, Nikolai, wouldn't let us ride together, so I hadn't had a chance to confront him about the letter Deja wrote me. However, seeing him wrench against three men to get over to me made me want to forget about her accusation.

"Let me talk to her!" Layne yelled, but the men shoved him into the black SUV and piled in after him.

"Got yourself a boyfriend, I see." Britt held my arm as he led me back to my designated vehicle. With three identical black SUVs, I wasn't sure we were creating the low profile that Nikolai wanted.

"I'm not really sure," I answered honestly. "It's complicated."

"Always is with us."

I felt his grip tighten. "Come on, you two. Let's get the hell out of Mexico." The grip loosened again. "Oh, have a heart. Why can't we just let them have a word or two? All he wants is to check if she's okay. After that he'll settle down." Britt's huff sounded more like a growl, and he turned to me. "Just tell him you're okay, so we can get the hell out of here."

"Okay," I agreed.

We veered off and Britt tapped on the window of Layne's SUV. The window rolled down partway and he signaled for it to be rolled down all the way. The men complied and Layne leaned over to look at me.

"Are you okay?"

I smiled. "You mean other than being a forced dinner guest to a mobster?"

His face fell and he nodded. "Other than that. I'm so sorry about this. I should have listened to Deja and just gotten us as far south as we could go. I just didn't want..."

"I know." I glanced back at Britt and took a step forward. "You should just ask Nikolai to drop you off once we're over the border."

Layne frowned. "No, Elise. I'm coming with you."

I stepped up to the window and glanced at the man between us. He was doing his best not to interfere with the conversation, but the closer Layne and I got to one another, the more he was becoming a third wheel.

"Are you sure you know what you're saying?" I asked. "Haven't we gotten you into enough trouble?"

"I'm not leaving you." Layne leaned all the way

over and kissed me. It wasn't a sweet, enduring kiss. It was powerful, demanding, and wanton.

"Oh, for the love of God." Britt pulled me back, breaking our connection. "Let's go."

Britt took a tight grip on me and directed me back to the middle SUV with Nikolai and Rod. After we were situated, Rod drove us toward the border.

"Nikolai," I called up to the Russian in the passenger seat.

He looked back at me. "What is it, Miss Welch?"

"When we get over the border, you should ditch Layne. He's a former cop and once he's back on American soil he will call in every favor he was ever owed to get me away from Devitti."

Nikolai smiled. "I am way ahead of you on that one, pet, but thank you for being so honest."

"You're welcome."

"You are such a sweet and polite young woman. I bet you would still be so if you weren't being held at gunpoint. I never get to experience mannerly people in my position. It pleases me that I did not complete my bid to kill you."

"That also pleases me, Nikolai." I slumped back into my seat. "Very much."

We moved into the farthest border lane and Rod pulled open the toll box on the windshield. We didn't even have to stop at the station to submit our fingerprints or IDs. We could—and were—carrying a significant amount of contraband, but the border police didn't even blink as we drove through at highway speed. It was disappointing to witness firsthand how much influence men like Devitti really had.

"Back in the good ol' USA," Rod announced as we cleared the official border. "Happy, Deuce?"

"I never much minded Mexico, but I'm sure my brother will be happy about it when he wakes up."

I looked over at Britt, trying to translate the mercurial conversation from the fuel station. "Which one are you?"

He turned his bright silvery gray eyes on me and smiled. "Britt Thatcher. I go by Britt, he goes by Thatcher, but we both go by Deuce. It's hard for everybody to keep us straight, especially when we're in at the same time."

"How do you—wait, what do you mean at the same time? You are both conscience at the same time?"

"Yeah, between every transition. Like two ships passing in the night. Only our ships stop and talk to each other for a while."

I stared at him, mouth agape. "How is that even possible? Isn't that confusing for you? For both of you?"

"No, but it sure does mess up everybody else. They still can't keep track of when we're in and out."

I glanced at the rearview mirror, catching Rod's eye as he looked back at me. "So, everybody here just knows what you are and deals with it?"

"What else can they do? I'm kind of indispensable."

"Because of the strength?"

"Well, that and the other stuff."

"Other stuff?" I twisted in my seat to face him. "What other stuff?"

His eyes danced over me. "Are you serious? All you know about is the strength?" He chuckled. "Elise, you have two souls inside your body. Do you have any idea how powerful one soul is?"

"I guess I never really thought about it."

"A soul is like a magic bean that makes all this possible." He motioned to his body. "A second soul isn't just twice as powerful. It is a soul that isn't bogged down with the daily humdrum of maintaining a human body. All that extra energy can be used to do some pretty superhuman things."

I frowned and shrugged. "I've never done anything beyond shoving drunk assholes on their butts."

"Oh, Elise, that's just the beginning. There's running and jumping and..." He leaned in closer. "Even the sex is better."

I smiled and nodded. "I guess I'll have to investigate that."

"I could help if you want."

I cleared my throat. "I don't know that you and I—"

"I meant the running and jumping, but I could certainly help with that too." He perked his brow.

My lips got away from me, turning into a goofy shy smile. I knew my face was turning bright red, but I couldn't help it. I felt guilty flirting with Britt when Layne was only a few car-lengths away from me, but I was actually considering his offer. This was the first time in all my life I had met someone like me, and I was enjoying it. He knew my affliction better than I did, and he had no reason to judge me. All logic went out the window the minute my hands ricocheted off his chest.

"I think I would like that," I said without specifying which aspect of his training was so intriguing to me.

He put his arm over the back of the seat and smirked at me. He reached for me, brushing a strand of hair behind my ear. His smile instantly faded and he looked out the front window.

"Swerve!" he yelled at Rod.

Rod did as he said, even as the SUV in front of us exploded, sending it flying up and back toward us. As we passed the fiery mess, I looked back to see if the trailing vehicle Layne was in had time to avoid it. They veered over just in time, following our path to safety.

"What the fuck was that?" Rod yelled. "Don't tell me they've installed road bombs on a public highway!"

"Missile launcher," Britt answered as he unbuckled his seatbelt and crawled into the far back.

"Missiles?" Rod looked around for the source.

"What, did they sent the military?"

"Either that or they just lent their heavy hitters a few toys," Nikolai suggested.

"Brake!" Britt yelled from the back.

Rod slammed on the brakes just in time to avoid a missile that jetted harmlessly past his radiator. It landed across the road and threw bright flames up into the sky.

"This is insane!" I shouted. "I'm just an amateur hacker! This can't all be for me!"

"Where are they even shooting from?" Rod yelled over my babbling.

"It must be the cliffs over there," Nikolai pointed out. "Deuce?"

"I'm coming, boss." Britt crawled back over the seat with a long flat case in hand. He opened it and pulled out a sniper rifle. "Excuse me, Elise, I'm just gonna need your window."

He rolled down my window and positioned the rifle on the window's edge to aim. I leaned back as best I could.

"Can you even hit anything from a moving car?" I asked.

"Let's find out." He leaned in and looked through the sight. "Don't move," he warned. I held my breath and closed my eyes.

I heard the whir of another missile and the rifle went off in front of me. I felt the explosion, but we were still racing down the road. I opened my eyes and followed Britt's gaze out the back window.

The SUV following us had tipped over on its side and was skidding to a stop. The distance was growing between us, with no sign of stopping.

"Turn around," I demanded. "We need to get Layne!"

"We've got a tail," Nikolai shouted over me.

Britt threw down his rifle and pulled a handgun from his shoulder holster. He poked his head out the window and fired on the truck that was speeding up on us from behind.

Nikolai pulled his own weapon, leaned his arm out of the passenger-side window and started firing on a van that was suddenly in front of us. "Deuce!" Nikolai yelled between shots.

"I see them," Britt yelled back.

The SUV lurched forward and Rod steered away from the truck that was trying to bump us off the road. The van ahead of us slowed down, bringing it right alongside of our vehicle. "Nikolai!" Britt yelled as he ripped my seat belt off me. The side door of the van opened and a man layered with riot gear and holding a machine gun came into view. Britt wrapped his arms around me and we rolled over the back of the seat.

The machine gun pelted the seat I was just sitting in, while we landed on the bench seat behind us. The assault shifted back, splintering the window as the surrounding metal frame thumped with the impact of the bullets. However, the vehicle's resistant construction kept us safe and free of holes.

I heard a few shots fire closer to us, and the machine gun fire stopped. Nikolai and Rod cheered. Britt peeked up through the window and smiled. He looked down at me where I was trembling and seconds from weeping.

"Two birds, one stone. Nikolai shot the driver of the van and it ended up running the truck off the road too," he said proudly. This must have been the equivalent of a field goal in hitman speak. I wasn't sure what he wanted me to do, so I just stared at him. "You okay?"

I shook my head. "No."

"Are you hurt?"

I took a moment to think about that. I couldn't really feel anything other than the pressure of his body on mine. My arm was hurting, but since that was an old injury it didn't really apply. "No."

He smiled at me. "Are you going to cry?" I nodded. "Okay, I'm going to leave you here then. Just come back up front when you are ready." Britt released his weight and climbed back over the seat. I listened to the men congratulating each other on a job well done.

After a moment to restrain my tears, I flung myself upright. I looked out the back window, but I didn't see the other SUV following us. If they were still back there, then they might still be in danger.

"We need to go back for Layne," I announced.

"You're the cargo, not Mr. Cantry," Nikolai answered.

"I am not cargo, and I am not going to Vegas without Layne!"

"You wanted me to kick him out anyway," Nikolai said. "He will just have farther to walk this way."

"What about those guys back there? What if they try to pump him for information? They'll get my location and they'll kill him."

"Layne will be fine, Elise." Britt touched my hand. "He has four highly skilled men to back him up."

Before I thought about the stupidity of my plan, I reached behind my seat and grabbed one of the guns from their overloaded stash. I pointed it at Britt. "We go back or I start firing."

"What the devil are you doing, girl?" Nikolai looked back over his seat at me.

"I need you to turn this beast around and go pick up Layne... please."

"Your good manners will not buy you any points in this argument, my dear. Deuce!" Nikolai hollered back at him.

"It's fine. She won't shoot," Britt said calmly. Nikolai waved his hand at us and turned his attention back to the road. "Will you?"

"You can't just leave him there."

"You must care for him a good deal if you are willing to risk going back into the line of fire to get him."

"I care enough not to treat him like roadkill."

"We aren't going back. It isn't even a discussion. Now hand me the gun." Britt eased forward and I tightened my grip on the gun.

"No."

Britt smiled. "I like you, Elise, but I'm going to have to get a little mean now. I'm sorry about that, but you should know that if my brother were here, you would already have a black eye."

I opened my mouth to respond, but my face exploded with pain. The gun was ripped out of my hand

and my arms restrained before I could even comprehend that Britt had moved.

"Ouch!" I felt my eye water and I looked at Britt. He was sitting beside me clamping my arms to my sides. "Did you just punch me?"

"Well, you did point a gun at me. Granted, it wasn't actually loaded, but still... kind of rude."

Rather than lament on the nosedive my heart had just taken, I shoved his hands off and punched him in the gut. This time the blow took and he coughed at the strength I had put into it.

I tried to get another hit in, but he lassoed my arms and pinned me back against his chest. I writhed and screamed, but my strength was once again useless against him. After a minute of the futile battle, I gave up and relaxed against him.

His mouth pushed closer to my ear and he whispered, "It was a good try, Elise, but you have a lot to learn about being a *dyad*."

41

Somewhere outside of Tucson, I fell asleep against Britt and didn't wake until the sun was glaring in my eyes through the bullet-riddled window above me. I pushed a heavy black vest off my chest and tipped my head back to see beyond the obtrusive morning light. I could see a fuel sign and an advertisement for slot machines. We were in Nevada, at any rate.

I heard the chirp of a cellphone followed by Britt's muffled voice. "Yeah," he answered sharply. I sat up and saw him outside, leaning against the vehicle. He was the only one around that I could see. "Where the hell are you? … Anyone hurt? … Well, shit. Yeah, get that taken care of, I'll let Nikolai know. … You're kidding! Well, I'll be damned. He's more useful than I would have given him credit for." Britt chuckled. "That doesn't surprise me. Well, do what you gotta do. … Yep, see you there."

I grabbed my purse and opened the side door. I jumped out and shut it behind me, then moved around to where Britt was leaning. He looked me over, evaluating me. I did the same to him. "Where is everyone?" I asked.

"Getting breakfast. They'll bring you back something."

I looked over the roadside fuel station backed into a

ledge of the otherwise mountainous area. The long wooden building was a station, convenience store, restaurant, and a tiny casino all in one. "Which one are you?"

"I go by Thatcher. Which one are you?"

"Still Elise."

"Still, huh? You don't cross paths, I take it."

"No, not like you and Britt."

"Must be nice to have a quiet roommate." He tapped his head. I nodded at him, but I wasn't sure it was nice. "What's the other one's name?"

"Deja. She'll be here tomorrow." I scraped my shoe in the dirt beneath me. "She's better at dealing with this kind of stuff."

"She's good at dealing with hired thugs?"

I looked up at Thatcher. He seemed to think I had misspoken. "Yeah," I answered. "She tends to get herself into trouble. Get *us* into trouble."

"I look forward to meeting her." Thatcher smirked and turned his attention to the road and an oncoming car. "Come here." He motioned me toward him and I stepped closer. "Stay behind the vehicle."

I watched the car pull into the lot and I tucked closer to Thatcher. He shifted to keep the car in his line of sight, but when it stopped, the only threat to emerge was a lesson on the hazards of Vegas.

Two girls hopped out of the four-door car, while a third propped open the back door to puke on the ground. The first two girls regaled on how awesome the night was and then laughed at their friend.

"Shut up, I'm really sick," she said.

"I need food. Stay here and feel better," one of the girls said and ushered her other friend off to the restaurant for breakfast.

"I'm gonna go to the bathroom," the sick girl hollered after them, but they were selfishly more concerned about eggs and bacon than their friend's possible alcohol poisoning. She got out of the car and wobbled around the building toward the sign marked "Restrooms." Staring after her, I realized that I also had to use the restroom. I decided to wait for the party girl to get her meals out before I joined her.

I looked back at Thatcher. He was watching me. I took the opportunity to look over his features, since I was a little closer. His eyes were still a beautiful gray, and his physique was the same. My eyes traced down his neck to a slight bit of ink peeking from under his t-shirt.

I reached for his collar and stopped to look at him for permission. He glanced down at the source of my curiosity and reached for the material himself. He dragged down the elastic trim and revealed a tattoo of two male faces on his breast. The faces were grimacing in agony as they tried unsuccessfully to rip away from one another.

It was a beautiful and terrifyingly accurate depiction of my own struggle. I smiled even as I felt tears come to my eyes. "That's beautiful."

Thatcher grumbled an agreement and reached for my necklace. He pulled it from beneath my shirt collar and tilted his head back to see the tiny pendant. He smiled and dropped it back down into my cleavage.

"Any tattoos?"

I shook my head. "Used to, but I had them removed." I looked toward another oncoming car, but it didn't even pull in.

"You sure about that?" Thatcher tickled my lower back, where my shirt had crept up.

"Hey!" I jumped back and tugged the fabric down. I remembered my most recent addition and grimaced. "Oh, yeah, I forgot about that one. That one is new."

"May I?" he asked, approaching me.

I frowned, but turned to allow him to see it. "It was not my idea."

He chuckled and lifted the back of my shirt. He tugged on my waistband and I helped him push it down a little further. "Is that an arrow?" he asked.

I twisted away from him. "Not my idea," I repeated. He smirked at me. "It's not funny and you know it."

"No, I would definitely have words with Britt if he inked me without my consent. However, that is a rather attractive design. You should consider keeping it."

"Oh, don't start that." I yanked my purse back onto my shoulder.

"Start what?"

"Taking sides."

"I wasn't taking her side, I was just admiring your backside."

I rolled my eyes at his joke and cleared my throat. "I should get my morning stuff taken care of." I pointed to the bathroom.

"Can you wait until the others are back?"

"Not really, I—"

"Say no more." Thatcher raised his hands and looked around the road. "I need to keep a watch on the road. Go fast. I'll check on you in three minutes."

I gave him a salute and jogged off to the restrooms.

The smell of the bathroom was enough to make my bladder seize, but I ventured further in. I noticed the sick girl at the counter washing out her mouth. I nodded to her and checked the first stall. "Oh, yuck!" I backed out of the stall.

"Tell me about it," the party girl said. "The last one is pretty clean."

"Thanks." I moved down to the last stall and took care of a little business, including writing an update on my thigh. I was running out of room, but I was also running out of time, so it didn't much matter.

I heard the bathroom door open and I froze. The female voices of the other party girls put me back at ease.

"Ahh, OMG!" one screamed and laughed.

"Oh, sick, what mammoth woman took that dump?" the second complained and chuckled. "Oh, is there somebody in here? Sorry! Pee on my friend."

I chuckled and finished up the details of my duties. I slung my purse over my shoulder and stepped out of the stall. The two girls were clustered by the door, giggling. I wondered if they were still drunk. So glad to see them driving.

I leaned over to wash my hands. I could see the sick girl in the reflection of the mirror. She was coming out of the stall next to mine. "Still sick, huh?" I asked.

She continued to come up behind me. She pulled out a scarf and whipped it over my head and around my neck. She yanked me backwards. My muted scream was covered up by the ruckus of the twenty-something laughter near the door.

The sick girl dragged me back into a stall and twisted me around to face the toilet. I screamed and she jammed my head into the toilet water, smothering my noise and taking away that much more of my air.

I scrambled for a moment before I found a target. I slammed my fist into her foot. I heard the bones crack and she wailed in pain.

The pressure on my back released and I stood up. She tried to stab me with a knife, but I intercepted her stabbing hand and twisted her frail wrist. After another set of bones cracked, she called for assistance from her girl pack.

I flung her over my shoulder by her broken wrist and she crashed into the toilet. The porcelain shattered under her weight, and she didn't move.

I turned to the clicking guns behind me. I knew they didn't want to use them, since it would draw the attention of my bodyguards, but I also knew they weren't likely to just let me come at them.

I grabbed the metal door on the stall and slammed it shut. It broke past the confines of its latch and hit the outstretched hands of the women.

I jumped out after the door and grabbed their heads while they were still distracted. I slammed them together parietal to parietal. I felt an awful hollow thunk as they hit.

They dropped to the floor and didn't move. Blood quickly pooled around them, as their caved-in skulls drained like faucets. I looked back at the sick girl. Her eyes were open, staring at me under the contorted position of her body.

I swallowed hard and tried not to think about the reality of three dead women. Dead by my own bare hands. I pulled my purse up over my shoulder and let the fog of adrenaline carry me through the next few steps.

I checked myself in the mirror and washed off the blood splatter from my face, along with any residual toilet water. I smoothed down my disheveled, partly wet hair and moved to the door. I pulled on the door, but it had been locked from the inside. I unlatched it and stepped out, where I noticed a blank magnetic sign on the door. I flipped it around so it said "out of order."

I walked around the building and saw Thatcher approaching me casually. "Good, you're done. Boys are done eating. We need to get moving." He stopped in front of me. "What's wrong with you?"

I licked my lips and pointed back to the restroom. "I didn't have a choice. They were going to kill me."

"What?" Thatcher tugged on the scarf that was still wrapped around my neck. He frowned, no doubt seeing the beginning of my ligature bruising. He pulled his gun and ran to the restroom I had just left. He jumped inside with his brandished weapon.

I waited for him to return. When he did, he was walking fast. He grabbed me by the arm and tugged me toward the SUV.

"I didn't mean to kill them." I started to cry.

"Oh, don't start that. It was self-defense."

"I've never hurt anyone like that before. Bruised ribs, maybe a broken nose."

As we met up with Nikolai and Rod, they looked at Thatcher's urgent grasp on me. "What did she do?" Nikolai asked.

"Triple bitch threat in the bathroom. She killed all three."

My eyes shot to Nikolai. For a moment, I thought he might be mad. He looked me over. "Are you hurt?" he asked. I shook my head. "They are getting clever. They obviously know we are working for Devitti now. They'll be waiting for us the minute we hit the city limits. We should call for a pick-up when we get closer to Vegas. Rod, you still good to drive?"

"Yup."

"Let's go then." Nikolai motioned for Thatcher to get me in the vehicle.

I started to move, but stopped. "Wait."

"There's no time, let's go," Thatcher insisted.

I ripped my arm from his grip. "Their car is available." I pointed to the four-door sedan still sitting in the lot.

Thatcher looked to it and back at me. "Nik, you wanna switch to the sedan? The girls won't need it."

Nikolai froze in the door of the vehicle. "It's not bulletproof."

"Nope, but nobody is looking for a sedan. Not to mention the bullet holes on this one are kind of giving us away."

Nikolai nodded. "Okay, let's switch the weapons and get her covered up. There's no tinting on that one either."

Rod jumped into the SUV and drove closer to the sedan. Meanwhile, Thatcher pulled the scarf from around my neck and put it over my head. "So nice of those ladies to contribute to your escape." I frowned and tears started to pour relentlessly. "Oh, damn it, Elise. You were doing so good."

"I can't do this," I sniveled. "I just want to not be scared. Is it so much to ask that I have a normal life?"

Thatcher grimaced and propped his hands on his hips. "I think you know it is." He sighed and looked around. "You're not doing so bad."

"I killed three women," I shrieked.

"Shhh!" he hissed and rubbed my arms. "That' s a good thing."

"It's *not* a good thing! I'm not like you. I'm not a killer."

"Well, it's not like I have much of a choice, do I? Job security doesn't exist for our kind. Besides, I'm mostly just a bounty hunter. Granted, not all of my bounties live beyond my delivery, but I only kill when I have to defend myself." He lifted my chin with his finger. "And there is nothing wrong with that."

I nodded, but it didn't change how I felt about killing three human beings. However, it did change how I felt about him.

$$43$$

We managed to make it into Vegas ahead of schedule, in that we arrived before Devitti was even home. I stood in the foyer of the outrageously marbled mansion, waiting for instructions from the men responsible for my delivery and the men responsible for my captivity.

"We will wait to receive our money from Devitti," Nikolai insisted.

"He won't be back until supper. I do not intend to entertain you for that long," the butler/bouncer said.

"I am not taking her out of this mansion again. She is too high risk to be seen anywhere in public," Nikolai explained.

"And I'm telling you I can't let you stay."

"Can't you just call Devitti?" I asked. Everyone looked back at me. "Phone." I wiggled my phone fingers near my ear.

"Just a minute," the butler groused and tapped the cell device that was already hanging from his ear.

Nikolai turned back to me and smiled. "I am really beginning to like you, Miss Welch. If Devitti doesn't kill you, I think I will hire you for my ops team. We need a simple mind to get us out of trouble sometimes."

"Thanks, I guess."

"I wouldn't mind having her for my undercover

team." I looked back at Thatcher, but I found a familiar sparkling-eyed smile that told me Britt was back.

"Shut up, Britt. She's been through enough today. She doesn't need you fawning all over her," Thatcher said from the same mouth. I could almost see the switch from rogue to rigid in his face. It made me smile.

"Yes, sir," the butler said into his cell. "No, I didn't know, sir. … Yes, I'll do that. … Thank you, sir." He clicked the device off and turned back to us. "Mr. Devitti extends his deepest apologies for not being here to greet you. He was unavoidably detained. He will of course offer a room to Miss Welch and the rest of you are welcome to enjoy the mansion's amenities... in full," he added with notable disdain for the concession.

"Excellent!" Nikolai raised his hands and clasped them on the butler's shoulder. "Then I suggest you fetch us a round of drinks after you've gotten Miss Welch situated. We'll be at the pool." He released the man and headed toward the back of the house.

Rod followed him. Britt swung into my path and smiled at me. "Are you still mad at me?" He motioned to my eye and frowned as his gaze lowered to my neck. He touched the bruised line on it. "Who did this? Thatcher?"

"I didn't do that," Thatcher pushed through.

"Long story," I said. "Thatcher will fill you in." I started to pull away to follow the butler, but he drew me back by my waist.

"You didn't answer me. Are we still friends?"

I took a breath and debated my answer. I wasn't a big fan of being manhandled, but since I was the one who started it, I could hardly blame him entirely. Even if I was still mad, I knew his charms would break my resolve soon enough. There was just something about him, be it Thatcher or Britt; I was just drawn in the minute I touched him.

"You really want to be my friend? Find out from Thatcher what happened to Layne." I pulled away from his grip and he watched me go with a growing smirk.

44

I sat in the shower for nearly an hour, sterilizing my skin and getting all my tears out of my system. I was careful not to ruin my note for Deja, and even added another sentence to it about my triple murder. I wasn't sure she would care, but I wanted her to know that I was officially a murderer.

After I slipped out of my private bathroom, I found a selection of clothes on my bed. I was happy to see that Mr. Devitti was prepared for me, despite the creep factor it put into my visit. I slipped on a pair of capris and a tunic before heading out to the pool.

I stepped through the patio doors into a courtyard that wasn't much different than the pool area I would expect to find in a hotel. There were several women in bikinis sunbathing. More than a few Hawaiian shirts circled it as well. I heard Nikolai yell my name from the other side of the hot tub.

I meandered to the tiki bar where my three kidnappers were sipping on the straws in their coconut drinks. "Where's your bikini?" Britt asked.

Nikolai put out his arm for me and I reluctantly moved into the sideways hug. "I have just been informed that Mr. Devitti will be returning in time for a supper meal with you."

"Goodie." I faked a smile.

"Elise, Elise, Elise." Nikolai pressed his head into mine. I could smell the liquor on his breath. "I am sorry that you are frightened, but I can promise you, Devitti is not nearly the monster that he is portrayed as."

"No, he's just the hand behind the marionette monsters."

"There are plenty of hands, my dear." He pointed his finger in my face. "I would advise you to shake the hand that isn't holding a gun."

"You mind reminding me which one that is?" I tapped my finger on the hilt of the gun in his shoulder holster.

Nikolai looked down at it and chuckled. "I do like you." He squeezed me tight. "You have a smart little mouth, but I like that. If Devitti doesn't want you, I will take you for myself."

"For the team, Nik?" Britt asked him. He gave me a wink.

"Yes, the team!" Nikolai released me and threw up his hands. "I am tired of running all over the country. We need more intelligence. People always want people dead, but what they don't understand is that people have knowledge." Nikolai tapped my forehead. "Like you. I would have just shot your pretty little face off and not thought twice about it."

"That's comforting," I murmured. Britt snorted at my sarcasm.

"But it would have been the wrong choice," Nikolai continued. "Because you have information that someone could use. Abilities that *I* could use. And you are strong... and beautiful." Nikolai's eyes glazed as they looked me over. I frowned at the attention.

Britt cleared his throat and grabbed the Russian's shoulder. "You're lettin' her get to you, Nik." He shook his shoulder forcefully.

Nikolai nodded and blinked away his googly eyes. "I'm sorry, my dear. I don't mean to be rude. The liquor is my mistress. It makes a hard mind soft." He smiled back at Britt. "And a soft man hard." Nikolai laughed uproariously at his joke. Rod and Britt joined him.

Britt released his shoulder and ushered me away from him. "Don't mind him. He's usually more civil, but between alcohol and your double aura, he's not doing so good."

"Double aura?"

Britt stopped and gawked at me. "Wow, you really know nothing about yourself." He ushered me to a pool chair. I situated myself on the plastic strips and leaned back. He sat on the edge of his and leaned over his knees to talk to me. "Haven't you ever noticed that some men—and occasionally women—are immediately enamored with you? To the point of almost being inappropriate?"

"I do tend to have a lot of admirers at bars, but I just thought that was because I was a warm body with breasts."

Britt chuckled. "That's most of it, but imagine if you could have the allure of *two* warm bodies, and *four* breasts."

"Does that work on everyone?"

"It's still based on attraction. For example, I find you very attractive, therefore I really, really want to skip the civilities of conversation and just start making out with you."

I scoffed and shook my head. "I take it this works both ways."

"Mm-hmm." Britt switched from his seat to the edge of mine. "Do you find yourself almost uncontrollably drawn to me?"

"Almost." I crossed my arms. "What did you find out about Layne?"

Britt rolled his head back and groaned. "Yeah, he's fine. They had a bit of a firefight after they crashed. Layne took up arms and saved two of Nikolai's men. Since they owed him a debt, they are going to bring him here."

"They are?" I confirmed excitedly.

"Yes, they are. Thatcher wanted me to tell you that he would have told you, but you didn't ask." Britt shifted away from me.

"Is he gone now?"

"Yes."

"How does that work with you two? I don't understand the crossover. Deja and I have never been in at the same time."

"I'm sure you never tried either." Britt dug in his pocket and pulled out a coin. He held it up for me to see. "This is you." He turned it around. "This is Deja. A coin..." He flipped the coin up in the air and caught it. He slapped it on his wrist and showed it to me. "...is either heads or tails. There really isn't much in between." He showed me the narrow edge of it. "Thatcher and I are more like the head of a statue. From the front we are just like the face of this coin. One side, one mind. But turn a statue, and you see its profile—both halves at once. Turn it again and you see only the back."

"So every time you and Thatcher change, there's a period of time when you are both inside the body."

"Yes."

"You're still separate minds, though. Who controls the body?"

"Technically we both can, but we've learned over the years to be polite. We always wait to take over full motor function until we are alone. Generally, whoever is coming in sits on the sidelines until the other is gone."

"Do you feel it? I mean, when he's in there?" I asked.

"Yes."

"Does it... feel... good?" I wrinkled my nose.

Britt chuckled and scooted closer to me. "Are you asking me if it feels good to be inside of another man?"

"No, I don't mean it like that. I just don't know if I like the idea of sharing this body with Deja, I mean at the same time."

Britt smirked and leaned across me bracing his hand on the other side of my chair. "Actually, Thatcher and I are very good at sharing. Sometimes we even share our body while we cavort with our lady friends. What's your position on threesomes?" He looked me over. "Or foursomes, for that matter?"

I tried not to smile, but I couldn't bring myself to resist. He was definitely right about being drawn to him. If it weren't for the audience around us, I might have already leaned in for a kiss. As it was, he was still inching closer to me and I wasn't exactly moving away.

A hand landed on his shoulder and we both looked up to see who was interrupting us. Layne took one swing at Britt, knocking him off my lounge chair. "Get the hell away from her."

45

"Layne!" I took in his disheveled appearance. In addition to a dirty face and burnt sleeves, he had more than a dozen cuts and bruises. "Are you okay?" He tore his eyes off Britt and looked at me. He inspected my new outfit and my casual poolside chair.

"I thought you might need me, so I talked the Russian's men into bringing me here." He looked at Britt. "Guess I was wrong." He walked away. I awkwardly maneuvered out of my deep chair and followed him.

I waited until we were inside to petition his forgiveness. "Layne, don't go."

"You obviously aren't in danger. You seem to be doing pretty well for yourself, actually. You don't need me." Layne met up with his former captors at the door where they were talking. "Give me my shit, I'm leaving."

"Leaving?" one of the men asked. "You just got here."

"Job's over, boys. The girl is safe. Give me the bag."

"Don't give him that bag," I ordered them before they could hand the duffel over to Layne. "That belongs to me."

"Excuse me?" Layne turned around to face me.

"Deja told me the money is ours. You can take what you think is fair for the job, but the rest is mine."

"I actually think the entire bag is fair at this point."

"Does that include the sex?" I asked. "I wasn't sure who was paying who for that favor."

The men started to snicker. Layne ripped the bag from their hands and dug through it. He pulled out a wad of hundreds. "That ought to cover my time." He pulled out a few more stacks. "That ought to cover my car." He dropped the bag at my feet and turned around.

"At least I get to see you walk away this time?"

He stopped and turned around. "What is that supposed to mean?"

"Deja told me that you were going to leave after we got to Mexico."

Layne shifted and looked to the men eagerly watching the argument. "Do you mind?"

"Not really," one said.

"Leave!" Layne screamed at them. They mumbled and grumbled, but left us to speak privately. After we were alone, Layne grabbed my hand. "Come on, let's go."

"What?" I tugged my hand away from him. "No."

"Yes, we need to get out of here before Devitti returns." He came at me again, but rather than waste any effort on negotiations he tackled me and flopped me over his shoulder.

"Layne! We can't go back out there. It's too dangerous!"

"Devitti is more dangerous!" He carried me to the front door and opened it. I could see a glimpse of the bright sun outside and a limousine pulling up to the front of the house. "Shit!" Layne slammed the door and turned around.

"Put me down!"

"Not until you're safe." He shuffled around searching for an exit, but as expansive as the options were, it was hard to tell which hall would lead to an exit. He went into one room, but it turned out to be only a bathroom.

"This is ridiculous, Layne. Put me down."

"You heard the girl." Nikolai's voice stalled Layne's feet. "Put her down."

Layne turned and set me on the floor. I could see the front door open and a white-suited man entered, followed by several more men that looked like tennis pros in spite of the guns holstered under their arms.

"You disappoint me, Mr. Cantry," Nikolai continued. I turned back and saw him standing with Rod, Britt, and the two men Layne had arrived with. They were poised for battle.

"What's going on here?" The man in a white suit joined us on the rear with his douchebag armada.

"Nothing to worry about, Mr. Devitti," Nikolai said.

I looked back at the man in the white suit. He looked to be thirty, maybe a little more. He wasn't who I pictured ruling half the crime in the country.

"Nothing to worry about?" Devitti asked. "There are way too many guns in this lobby. That worries me."

"We were just discussing some things with Mr. Cantry." Nikolai nodded to Layne. "And Miss Welch."

"Miss Welch?" Devitti stepped forward and looked

me over. He smiled. "I've really been looking forward to seeing you again. And this must be the legendary Layne Cantry."

"Legendary?" Layne turned to face him. "How's that?"

"Well, legendary in this area anyway. I've got half the police force in my pocket, but not a one of them is willing to trade favors if it's against you. Considering how deep my pockets go, I consider that pretty legendary."

Devitti turned to me. "And you. I have something for you."

His hand whipped across my face, sending me careening to the marble floor. I heard Layne cuss and guns cocking. By the time my stars had cleared, Devitti's suit jacket was into his throat with Layne's fist directing it there. His gun also took up a position under his jaw. Naturally, Devitti's men had raised their arms, but to my surprise Nikolai's crew had also drawn their weapons.

Devitti seethed at the offense, baring his teeth the same as Layne. The room was seconds from erupting into gunfire, and Layne and I would be the first to bleed.

"That's enough." A quiet, calm voice carried over from the front door. An older man stood at the door in a suit similar to Devitti's. I immediately noticed the similarities in their features and realized that this was the real Devitti. The father. The Godfather, for all intents and purposes. "Lower your guns." He directed his men and they slowly lowered their weapons. "You too." He pointed toward Nikolai's men. They all looked to Nikolai and he nodded.

Devitti started climbing the winding staircase leading upstairs. He stopped halfway up and looked to Layne. "Mr. Cantry, I understand that my son can be difficult to get along with, but he is still my son. I consider myself a godly man, but if you choose to kill my son in my home, in front of me, I will be seeking advice from the devil for your torture."

Layne glanced at him, but there was no denying the promise that came with his threat. He released the son and started to put his gun back in his holster. Devitti's son ripped it from his grasp and turned it back on him. He then shifted it on me.

The room tensed again, but no one dared move.

"Arthur!" Mr. Devitti yelled at his son. "If you shoot that girl, I will tie you to a chair and lock you in a room with Mr. Cantry."

Arthur yelled through clenched teeth and lowered the gun. He tossed it at Layne and stormed out.

"Miss Welch, my apologies for not staying for an official introduction, but I will see you at dinner. It will be ready at six o'clock. I'll have something brought for you to wear." I stared at him, fearful of saying anything. "If the rest of you can behave until then, you are welcome to join us." Mr. Devitti left the room just as he had entered it—with a style that had long since been bred out of the common man.

46

"No, I am not leaving," Layne argued with Nikolai at the tiki bar, while I continued to sunbathe under my beach umbrella. "Devitti has already invited me for dinner. What's the big deal?"

"Mr. Devitti is not the type of man you want to gain association with. Especially as a former cop."

"Then why are you staying?"

"Because I am a businessman."

"You are a hired gun. That hardly requires business dinners."

"You are arrogant, Mr. Cantry, and I suspect that you have another agenda by being here, but let me educate you. Being a guest of Mr. Devitti is worse than being in his employ. He doesn't trust anyone he can't pay for."

"And what about Elise? You want me to just leave her in the lion's den."

"Mr. Devitti will wine her, dine her, and then offer her a highly paid position. I guarantee it."

"And if she declines the position?"

"Then her guest pass expires. She will be back out on the street to fend for herself. And you and I both know that she won't live five feet past this driveway. As long as she is under Devitti's roof she will have a team of men keeping her alive, including mine."

Layne glanced over at me, but I pretended to be reading my magazine.

"Look, Mr. Cantry, I really do hope that your motives for coming here are purely romantic and not part of your investigations, because that will make your decision much easier."

"What do you mean?"

"I mean that Elise is already down the rabbit hole. I know you want to be the hero and save her, but it is too late. You can't just pull her out; that would get her killed. And if you hang on too tight, you might just get pulled in behind her. Is that what you want?" Nikolai leaned in closer, speaking gravely. "To be a part of this world? A world of murderers and mobsters? Make your decision now, Mr. Cantry or it will be made for you."

"I take it Arthur has already met Deja," Britt asked from beside me. He sat down across from me. "Uh-oh, that doesn't look like a good look."

"What look is that?"

"Like you're plotting someone's murder. Who's the victim?"

"I have a list. Earlier you said you could teach me." I wheeled my feet to the floor and faced him. "Can you teach me and Deja to run faster, jump higher, and whatever else you can do?"

"Sure, but it's not that simple, and besides, I know what you're thinking. It's nothing I can teach you overnight. It could take years to transition into full dyad."

"Dyad? You said that before. What do you mean by that?"

"You and Deja are still two minds, two halves to a whole, separate from each other at all times. To access the strength your souls can provide, you would have to allow your minds to start overlapping. You would transition more frequently, just as Thatcher and I do. Unless you can share the body simultaneously, you can't become a true dyad. And you won't be able to access the entire skillset available to you."

I frowned and shook my head. "Deja and I don't even like each other. I can't even imagine sharing my body with her at the same time."

"I can't speak for what you might experience, but as frustrating as it is to share an identity, I wouldn't give it up for the world. Thatcher is as much my brother as he is my friend. We bicker and disagree, but he keeps me balanced."

"Have you ever heard of a ritual that would sever a twin soul?"

Britt frowned and shook his head. "Don't go down that road, Elise." He stood up and looked down on me. "All you'll find is ghost stories." Britt walked away to refill his drink and he didn't look back.

I looked for Layne, but he wasn't around. I wasn't sure if he had taken Nikolai's advice, but I imagined that he was going to have to at least give it some thought. As if our potential relationship didn't already have too many compromises; now he had to skew his morality just to be with me.

47

I slipped on the red dress that barely hit my knees. I wasn't sure if Thatcher had revealed the location of my tattoo or if the plunging back was just coincidence. I put on a layer of makeup and threw my hair into a semi-intentional up-do.

I stared back at my reflection in the mirror. My eyes flickered over my face. Her face. Our face.

"If you were here with me, you would tell me that I'm being a chicken-shit." I smiled at the thought of my other half scolding me.

I tipped my head and narrowed my eyes at the woman in the mirror. "You're being a chicken-shit, Elise," I scolded myself. "You and I both know that when we actually put our minds to something, we can make it happen. If you want out of this, you'll find a way." I slammed my hands on the bathroom vanity. "You hear me? Stand up!" I stood up. "Now, go put your fuck-me heels on and do what you came here to do. Have dinner with the most powerful crime lord in America." I stepped away from the mirror feeling better. I knew that it was only pretense, but I knew Deja well enough to play her part. Of that I was sure.

My heels clicked against the marble floors as I made my way toward the piano music coming from the dining hall. I stepped through the open double doors and took in the long table and white linen filled to the brim with candles and crystal. Never mind that I couldn't afford the meal. I couldn't even rent my seat at the table.

Being the only woman in the room, I was bound to draw a little attention from the meandering, mingling men. However, the bright red dress with dangerously high heels made my tux-bound associates stare just a little longer at my arrival.

I took an immediate inventory of the room as I bee-lined for the man handing out Champagne. Mr. Devitti himself, Arthur, Nikolai, Rod, and the other ones. I saw Britt give me a nod, but I suspected that he was Thatcher now. It was difficult to keep track, but the personalities were getting easier to identify.

I grabbed a Champagne flute and downed a bit of it to hide my frustration at not seeing Layne. I wasn't sure how pathetic it was to be pining for a one-night stand, but I really had felt like there was something between us. We seemed a million miles apart now.

Mr. Devitti approached me and raised his hand for a handshake. His graying hair was combed back tightly on his scalp and his fitted tux showed off his muscular arms. He wasn't tall, and in my heels he was actually shorter than me, but I got the sense that his fifty-something body was not lacking for workouts. I took his hand and he squeezed it gently rather than actually shaking it.

"Hello, Miss Welch, it's nice to officially meet you. I am Edward Devitti."

"It's a pleasure to meet you, Mr. Devitti. I'd like to say that I've been looking forward to this, but as you know I was forced to come here."

"Yes, I noticed the bruise on your eye earlier. You seem to have covered it with makeup now. I hope that wasn't due to any inhumane treatment by Nikolai's men."

I glanced over at Nikolai and noticed him taking an interest in our conversation. Enough interest that he was inching closer to hear it over the music. "It was, but I actually had a gun to his face first, so..." I shrugged.

"I see. I'm glad to hear it. As far as the treatment you have received while you were here, I must apologize on behalf of my son. He is... Well, I should resist the inclination to demean my son in front of new acquaintances, but rest assured he was not raised to hurt women. I bore his mother's wrath for years and never once struck her. I consider that a feat of strength above and beyond my gentility."

"Will Mrs. Devitti be joining us tonight?"

"No, she died last year."

"I'm sorry to hear that. May I ask what took her?"

"A bullet from my gun."

I frowned at him. "You're kidding. You shot your own wife?"

"To be fair, she did shoot me first. So..." He shrugged, mimicking my previous explanation.

I swallowed hard, feeling his eyes on me. He was completely unfazed by the conversation. "Are you used to speaking to people this way, Mr. Devitti, or are you intentionally trying to scare me?"

"Not at all. I just wanted you to know that although I may be a gentleman, I do have my limits."

I took in a breath to keep control of the waver in my voice. "Yes, we all do have our limits. Boundaries that we won't cross. Moralities that we won't bend."

"Are you speaking about anything specific, Miss Welch?"

"Mr. Devitti, I'm sure that you enjoy this game of cat and mouse very much, but I prefer to skip the seduction. What do you want from me?"

"Firstly, I want to have a lovely dinner with my invited guests. I hope that your preference for no seduction doesn't include common courtesy and gratitude."

"Of course not. I am exceedingly honored to be among your guests. And since I haven't eaten anything since breakfast, my gratitude for your generosity will likely be overstated, come mealtime."

"Good, and in that case, against my preference of not talking business before a meal, I would like you to do for me what you did for your previous employer."

"You want me to hack into elected officials' private security systems?"

"Yes, I suppose that is the gist of it."

"It's not the gist though, is it? You don't just want information. You want access. You want me to make evidence disappear and crimes to be dissolved."

Devitti's eyes bore into me and he took a step closer to me. "I think you're getting ahead of yourself, Elise. May I call you Elise? You see, this is why I don't like conducting business prior to my meal. It sours the taste.

I think it would be best to continue this conversation after dinner."

"Mr. Devitti, with all due respect—"

"Miss Welch, *kroshka*." Nikolai closed in on us and grabbed my hand. He bowed and kissed it, before continuing. "My dear, you are making my heart thrum like a teenager. Must you be so beautiful?"

"I think it's the dress, Nikolai."

"I'm afraid I must disagree." He drew me forward by my hand. "You see, it is your face that has me dumbstruck."

"Have you been drinking?" I asked.

"Ahh, only a little." He glanced at Devitti. "Oh, Mr. Devitti, how rude of me. I'm interrupting your conversation."

"Not at all." Devitti continued to stare at me, not fully glaring, but only because he wouldn't dare show his hand. "Miss Welch is due for a refill. Why don't you take care of that? I'll catch up with you after dinner, Elise." Devitti walked away as calmly as he had come. He was beyond cool, but I had a sinking suspicion that he was also beyond cruel.

"Come." Nikolai wrapped his arm around me, engulfing me with the intoxicating aroma of his woody cologne. I let him lead me across the large room that could have hosted a mini ball. "I like you, Elise."

"You've said as much."

"I think you are honestly a nice young girl, with an over-developed capacity for computer jargon."

"Thank you."

"Unfortunately, you have tangled yourself in a

web."

"Deja did the tangling."

"Oh, excuse me." He released me and turned to face me. "I was under the impression that hacking generally referred to unauthorized access to data. Perhaps I am misunderstanding my English. It happens from time to time."

"Do you have a point?" I snagged an appetizer from a passing platter and stuffed it in my mouth.

"My point is that you are a hacker, and a good one, apparently. Mr. Devitti did not bring you here to dress you up and feed you caviar. He brought you here to test your usefulness."

"Are you suggesting that I play along?"

"No, I am suggesting that you stop playing. Show him what you can do, and it will save your life."

"At what cost? Who dies because I become a bad guy?"

"Bad? Good? What world do you think you are living in? This is America; the only good guys are the people without power. Ethics never survive a rise in ranks. Trust me."

"You are asking me to willfully choose a life of crime."

"No, I am asking you to willfully choose to live. I meant what I said. I like you. I don't want to be the one to have to put a bullet in the back of your head."

"Is that an option?"

"That is always an option. I am a hitman, and Mr. Devitti pays very well. Or did you forget who brought you here to begin with?"

I stared at him, disappointed that even after spending time with me he was still willing to pull the trigger. "I'm sorry to hear that, Nikolai. I was just starting to like you back."

"Take my advice, Miss Welch." Nikolai kissed my hand once more and walked away.

I moved around to the far side of the long table to avoid the banal chit-chat of the men. Cocktail hour always lasted forty-nine minutes too long for me.

I touched the marble mantel around the fireplace. It was a ridiculous inclusion for a house that was air-conditioned year round, but I was quite certain that was never taken into consideration.

"You look rather nice this evening," Thatcher said as he approached me from the other side.

"Thatcher?" I asked just to be sure.

He smiled and nodded. "You're quite good at that. Most people can't tell us apart."

"Well, you weren't leering at me, so I assumed it was you again."

"Oh, I'm leering just as much as he would be. I'm just not as overt about it."

"Well, I can hardly blame you. I think I've worn more cloth than this in a swimming pool."

"Don't feel too objectified. This is just Devitti's way of skipping the pat-down at the door. Believe you me, if he could get away with putting us in speedos and still claim to be having a classy dinner party, he would."

"Speaking of your attire." I moved to him and straightened his tie. He lifted his chin to allow it. "Does he have a tailor on retainer?"

"Thank you. No, but he does have the equivalent of a tux shop in his storeroom. He likes his parties."

"So, this is normal. All of you hanging out for dinner."

Thatcher wobbled his head. "Normal is whatever Devitti wants it to be. I suspect the impromptu invite has an ulterior motive, though."

"Ah, the seduction continues. I get tipsy on Champagne." I raised my glass to the waiter across the way. "Then he offers me a job, and I stupidly say yes because his fancy dinner has convinced me that money is more important than my peace of mind."

"I'm not quite sure it will be that simple."

I exchanged my empty glass for a full one and the waiter moved away again. I looked at Thatcher and his eyes dipped away. "What is it? What aren't you telling me?"

"More than likely Devitti invited us all to stay because he wants me to stick around."

"Because you are the only one who can keep me contained without putting a gun in my face."

"Right."

"And you'll have no problem doing it because, like everyone else in this room, when Devitti talks, you open your wallet and listen."

"I'm no one's yes-man, Elise."

"No, you're worse, because you voluntarily put the leash on. You're practically superhuman and you're taking orders from an old man."

Thatcher glared at me a moment. "I was just giving you fair warning, Elise."

"Yes, I seem to be getting an overabundance of that tonight. I'll be sure to switch you back over to the enemy column, but I think I'll keep you there this time."

Thatcher looked a little disappointed, but he didn't argue the point any longer. Much like Nikolai, he could hardly change his nature just because he was getting to know me.

I turned around and nearly collided with Layne. "Layne," I whispered and stared at him with wide eyes. We were practically in each other's arms, but I didn't correct the distance and neither did he. "I thought you had left."

"No, I just couldn't find a suit that fit." He looked me over. "You look extraordinary."

"It's the dress."

"How are you doing?"

"I'm tired of not having any friends."

"I'm your friend." He touched my arm.

"Are you, Layne?" I whispered. "Because I keep thinking how awful yesterday would have been if you left us. Whether I would even be alive."

"I feel awful about that. I was questioning my choices, but I came to my senses."

"Are you sure? Are you sure it wasn't about Deja taking you too far from your case?"

"My case?"

"Your investigation. You needed me to be a target so you could trace my murderer back to his boss."

Layne frowned and shook his head. "I don't care about all that anymore. I care about keeping you alive, and safe."

"And how do you intend to do that? I'm standing in the house of a criminal mastermind, sipping his Champagne, while an underbelly of US spies is plotting my murder."

Layne glanced around the room. "I think you should take the job."

"Even though I would be working for one of the very men you've spent your entire life trying to incriminate?"

Layne touched my face, caressing my cheek with his thumb. "I want you safe. Whatever that takes."

"When Deja wakes up and finds herself right back in the thick of things, she won't be happy."

"I know."

"She isn't going to like following orders and I get the impression that Devitti doesn't ask twice. She's the one who is going to need your protection now. Can you do that? Can you keep her from getting us both killed?"

"Yes."

"I'm trusting that, Layne. I'm trusting you. I'm not good at that."

"I know."

"After things settle down and Deja isn't fighting Devitti at every turn, if you want to go, I'll understand."

"What? What are you talking about?"

"Layne, as much as I want to fall in love with you and live happily ever after, this situation is not normal. I don't expect you to just—"

Layne stifled my words with a kiss. I wrapped my arms around him and enjoyed the moment. I heard the call for dinner, but ignored it. He continued to cradle my face, holding me captive in his lips' embrace. After a couple of throats were cleared and a snicker, he released me.

I nearly toppled onto him since my feet were still stuck in the clouds. He held me up and directed me to a seat at the table. I sat down and looked over the hardened faces at the dinner table one by one until I reached Devitti's.

He nodded politely to me and I smiled. Time to start sucking up to the boss.

48

I couldn't see the point of the six-course meal since I was full after the soup course, but an hour and half later the desserts were being chased by unforgivably bitter coffee and stale conversation about politics and sports.

"Why don't you gentlemen leave us alone?" Devitti suggested and the hum of dinner conversation turned instantly silent. The men each in turn looked to Devitti before standing and leaving. "Mr. Thatcher, you can stay."

Thatcher turned back and looked at me before returning to the table.

When Lane didn't move from his seat, Devitti turned his contemptuous gaze on him. "You may take your leave too, Mr. Cantry," he drawled.

"I prefer to stay with Elise, sir."

"I'm sure you do, but that isn't what *I* prefer." Layne took in a breath to argue his point further, but Devitti wasn't having any of it. "Mr. Cantry, your presence here is already a little suspect to me. I am more than willing to be hospitable as a means of keeping Miss Welch comfortable, but I think we can both agree that your welcome is already wearing a little thin. As is my patience."

Layne looked to me and I nodded my permission

for him to unsaddle his white horse.

There was no point in fighting it now. I had suspected that Layne would eventually be out of the picture, and that was for the best. No reason for him to be a part of all of this if he didn't have to.

After Layne was gone, Devitti stood and moved from his throne to sit next to me by the fireplace. I turned myself outward to match him and waited for him to pop the big question.

Will you be my hacker?

"You must be cold," he stated and moved to grab a remote from on top of the fireplace mantel. He pressed a button on it, lighting the gas flames in the hearth. He sat back down and smiled. "Better?"

It *was* better, actually. Sitting for nearly two hours in thin fabric had put me in goosebumps. "Yes, thank you."

"Miss Welch, I've been given to believe that you are something of a genius."

I scoffed. "I'm not a genius."

"I did some digging in your records. You tested exceptionally high on your college entrance exams, yet you never enrolled."

"Deja doesn't like studying."

"I imagine not. Tends to be that way, doesn't it?" Devitti looked behind me and I suddenly realized that Thatcher had moved around the table to stand right behind me. "One is always a little smarter. Twin minds fascinate me, but they are a pain in the ass too. No offense, Mr. Thatcher; I've grown rather fond of you."

"None taken, sir."

Devitti leaned forward, resting his arm on the table to look me over. "In truth, I wasn't sure I wanted to be in association with another one. I'm a man who appreciates order. It's hard to come by in my home life, but in my work life, I find that keeping people on task is easy with the right incentive."

"Money?" I posed sarcastically.

Devitti's lip twitched with amusement. "Yes, but that won't work on you." He took a breath and sat back. "Let me ask you a question, Miss Welch. Do you like living in the United States? Do you like having every inch of your life videotaped, logged, and deposited?"

"No, but I like being safe."

"Ahhh." Devitti leaned his head back with his realization. "That is the greatest sales pitch, isn't it? It all starts with safety. Did you feel safe when hitmen were openly trying to kill you on American soil? Where were the police? The national guard?"

"Being paid to look the other way by men like you I assume."

Devitti shook his head. "They weren't there because they were the ones who put out the hits."

"What? The police wouldn't do that."

"You think corruption is born and raised behind these walls alone?"

I gulped and looked to the fire. "How do you know it was the police?"

"Because the bid was contracted by someone in a precinct just a few blocks from where you live. It took quite a bit of digging, but I found out who it was." Devitti reached into his breast pocket and pulled out a small photograph. He handed it to me and I analyzed the young face in a police uniform. He was much younger in the picture than when I met him. "This can't be the guy. This was Deja's probation officer, Gary something. He was assigned to her after her DUIs, but that was years ago. Why would he put out a hit on me? I thought this would have come from someone higher up."

"I'm sure it did." Devitti took the photo back and placed it in his pocket. "The grunt-work always ends up on some cop's desk. A senator barks, and the chains rattle. Next thing you know a meter maid is putting a bomb in someone's car. It's all just a matter of who has control, who wants control, and who is strong enough to get it."

"I take it that you are strong enough to get control, Mr Devitti."

He nodded and chuckled. "I am one of three men who are strong enough to get control. I would prefer to be the only man strong enough to get control. Unfortunately my expertise up to this point has been relying on my connections inside of the system. However, in recent days I've been considering expanding my expertise in the field of automation. When I heard about you I decided that perhaps you might be just the person to get me there."

"Mr. Devitti, I don't think I am who you think I am. I'm just a part-time hacker. I can't even imagine the global scale that you're talking about."

Devitti nodded to Thatcher and he stepped away to retrieve something from a side cabinet along the wall.

"I don't expect you to take over the world, Miss Welch. This is an entrepreneurial endeavor. I just need to get a foothold into this world, so that I'm not completely reliant on my human connections." Thatcher set down a laptop in front of me and opened it up. He tapped the trackpad and the screen came to life. After a quick fingerprint scan the desktop emerged. "How about we give this a try? I want you to access the Las Vegas DMV—more specifically, the driver's license area."

"Is this a test?"

"Oh, yes."

"What happens if I fail?"

Mr. Devitti smiled. "I don't think you will, but on the off chance that you disappoint me... there will be consequences."

I gulped and set my fingers to the keyboard. After several minutes of getting to know the program, which was remarkably similar to the one I broke into for Deja, a screen popped up with the DMV's driver's license database. With just a click of the name, I could change the address, the number of moving violations, or even the photo. It would be excessively easy for me to punch in my own information and request a new identity. "Okay, there we are."

"What am I looking at here?"

"This is basically an alphabetized list of all the driver's license holders in Las Vegas. From here I can access anything regarding the license holder. Moving violations, accidents, points lost."

"Interesting. So you would actually be able to input a traffic violation on any one of these people so they would lose points on the license?"

"Yes. It can be disputed since there wasn't an actual written ticket, but it's a pain in the butt."

"At any rate, it would slow up the system for a while."

"Yes, definitely."

"Do it."

"Do what?"

"Input some violations on one of these names."

Mr. Devitti didn't really offer an option, so I chose a random name and started to input the information for several violations.

"Put in a few more," he instructed.

"But two more and he'll lose his license. It could take him months to get it back."

"Do it."

"But you don't even know this guy. I picked him at random."

"So neither do you. It won't affect you one way or another."

I stared at the stone cold expression that he was giving me. This was yet another non-optional request. I wasn't interested in finding out about the consequences, but I also wasn't interested in ruining a man's life at random. I punched in the last two violations, but quickly unchecked the box that demanded his license be revoked immediately. It was done in a flash and we were back to the main screen. "There," I said and sat back in my chair.

"That's very good, Miss Welch," Mr. Devitti said with a cold tone. "Not quite what I asked for, though."

He took in a long, cleansing breath; I half expected fire to come shooting out of his mouth when he finally spoke. "I think, as we've already touched on, it's not going to be possible for me to secure your devotion with monetary means. Unfortunately, your morality is a little too touchy at this point for me to expect independent devotion. So, why don't we review other methods of influence?"

Thatcher reached around me, strapping me to the chair with his strong arms. I struggled, using all my power, but I still couldn't break free. The electric energy just bounced off of Thatcher's rigid grip.

"It's always advisable to have a loyal dyad around." Mr. Devitti picked up my hand and kissed it. "I hope you understand that this is just business. I would much rather not do this."

"What are you going to do?"

"Just give you something to remember. A little proof of what I'm capable of when I don't get my way."

I panted as he started to lift my middle finger. At first it was just a stretch, then a harsh pull on the tendon as he bent my finger as far backward as the connections to the bone would allow. I screamed and cried, begging for mercy, but he held it there a moment as his face contorted into a sadistic grimace.

He released my finger. I gasped and cried as the pain continued to radiate through the tender tissues. Not quite broken, not quite dislocated, but it was going to hurt for a very long time. It was definitely something I would remember.

I lay over the table bawling into a napkin as I cradled my hand in my lap. I had anticipated violence, or at least the threat of it. What I hadn't anticipated was the demeaning method of its delivery. This man was perfectly willing to be civilized about his business, but in the end he would kick me like a dog to make sure that I stayed at his feet.

I hadn't wanted any of this. All I wanted was to go back to a normal life. I would've given anything to just be waking up in a hotel room with a stranger. Or having to search for a new job because Deja lost ours again. These were simple problems. It was something that I could deal with and have control of. In this world, I didn't have control of anything. I was more a prisoner than ever. My only satisfaction was that Deja was stuck here with me. This was all her fault and I hated her more than ever for it.

Thatcher tugged on my shoulders, trying to draw me upright. "Come on, time to go to bed."

"Fuck you," I grumbled. I looked back at him. "Is this what you are? You aren't just a hired gun, you're a hired thug."

"Don't get mad at me because you couldn't do what you were told. It's all very simple in this world. Do what you are told, get your money, and shut the hell up."

"I don't want the money. My loyalty can't be bought with paper."

Thatcher leaned down, practically putting his nose up against mine. "Then you'll be bought with a fist. Now stand up so I can take you to your room."

I didn't want to make the situation worse, but since Devitti had gone to bed already, I decided that this fight could be between me and the man indirectly responsible for my pain. I put everything I had into an uppercut punch. I heard a crack and he stumbled back grasping his face.

When he recovered he stood up tall and glared at me. He moved forward slowly and I stood to meet him. We shifted from offense to defense, each trying to anticipate the other's move. Finally Thatcher stood up straight and pointed a finger at me. "I'll give you a pass, just this once. But only because I don't want to hear about it from Britt."

I frowned, thinking that Britt would have done this damage to me as well. Neither one seemed to like the idea of hurting me, but both were more than willing to do it for the sake of their duty.

"You could be so much more," I said before I really thought about it. Somehow the idea of being able to communicate with my other self opened up the idea of a camaraderie, and a partnership in life. I wasn't sure it would make things easier, but I was pretty sure that two minds working together could certainly be more powerful than two minds working against each other.

Thatcher stared at me blankly for a moment. A cool

frown formed on his face and he straightened up, squaring his shoulders. He narrowed his eyes on me. "So could you."

I wasn't sure what he had seen in me that allowed for that evaluation. Deja and I certainly weren't the best team, but at least we weren't working for a deplorable man, doing God knows what harm to people. Then again, how far was I from that very situation? Perhaps we were both making assumptions based on the immediate circumstances in our lives. Neither one of us really new jack shit about the other one, but somehow we had both come to the same conclusion about each other: Something was lacking.

After a moment of stringent judgment shared between us, he moved forward and bowed down to pick me up. He tossed me over his shoulder despite my objections to the position. I cussed and punched his back, but I couldn't duplicate the strength I had used before. He was ready for it this time.

He carried me over to the door. I heard it open and he stopped. "Put her down." I heard Layne say.

"And who's gonna make me?" Thatcher asked.

"Just put her down," Layne said again, sounding exasperated. "She doesn't need more mistreatment tonight. Save it for the morning. I'm sure Deja will be happy to share in the misery."

Thatcher chuckled. "Yeah, I am looking forward to meeting her." He leaned down and I slipped off of his shoulder. I backed away, trying to glare at him again, but I was starting to fall apart. My strong sturdy mask was starting to slip away again. I turned around, tucking into Layne's arms as he walked me out of the room. I managed to keep most of my sniveling to a muffled level.

50

I sat on the bed, my hand trembling with belated shock. Layne returned to my room, shutting the door quietly behind him. He rushed over to me and pressed an ice pack to the back of my hand. I hissed and whimpered again. He frowned and rushed into the bathroom. He retrieved a cold glass of water and brought it back to me along with two white pills. "Here, take these."

I did as he bid and guzzled down the water. For a few moments, he stared at me. I could only imagine what he was feeling. He had wanted to leave me alone, but now he didn't have a choice. He was as much a rat in this trap as I was. And worse still, he was an expendable rat. As Devitti had said, the only reason he hadn't been kicked out upon arrival or killed was because it would've made me far less cooperative. The threat of death wasn't nearly as motivating as the threat of pain, apparently.

Layne kneeled down in front of me and touched my leg. He massaged my calf with warm hands, reminding me that I was much colder than I preferred. He opened his mouth to speak.

"Don't," I said. "I don't want any apologies. I don't want any explanations. I just want to get through this night with as little pain as possible. Deja can deal with the rest of this."

Layne squeezed my leg and nodded. "Okay." He looked down at the floor, but his eyes caught on something. He moved his hand back up my leg and pushed the skirt of my dress off my knee. "What is this?" he asked, seeing the writing on my thigh.

I gave him a thin smile. "It's my letter to Deja. It's the only way to keep it private now."

Layne chuckled and moved his hand further up my thigh. "Well it does look like a good area for something private." His playful smile dimmed and he furrowed his brow. "Do you ever worry that you won't come back?"

"I never used to, but lately yes. It used to be like falling asleep. A very long sleep. But now it's like I'm handing the keys over to a child and praying that they don't drive us both off a cliff."

"I'm not going anywhere, Elise. I want you to know that. I'll take care of you by taking care of her."

"Seems the tables have turned. Now Deja is the one that's a danger to us, not me."

"I'm not sure her personality is going to fit in well here, but I'll do my best to keep her civil."

"Good luck with that."

He smiled and squeezed my leg. "I should probably go. I mean, you'll need to get your sleep."

I nodded and he stood up to leave. "I've kind of gotten used to you sleeping beside me."

He looked back at me, evaluating me with interest. "I could stay. If you want." He glanced at my hand. "Whatever would make you more comfortable."

"I'd like you to stay."

He moved back over and caressed my cheek. "Are you inviting me into your bed, or into your arms?" I pushed my face into his palm. He raised his other hand, cupping my face and bringing it upward as he descended to my lips. He pressed a tender kiss against them.

I drew my wounded hand back to a safe distance while my other hand moved forward and grasped at his shirt. He moved toward me as I moved back, sliding along the comforter. When I stopped, he lay down against me, pressing himself between my legs.

He continued to kiss me, occasionally dragging his lips down my neck and back up again. The slow progression had me arching against him. He eventually slipped my panties off and released himself.

He pushed my dress up and watched me as he pressed inside of me. The steady rhythm he provided was different than our first time. It wasn't as urgent, but still just as commanding of my desires. I stared back at him, entranced by the power he held over me. He seemed determined not to blink, for fear of missing his view of me for even those mere seconds. I would be gone in the morning and he was going to get as much of me as he could. In more ways than one.

51

Somewhere between my dreams and awakening, I rejoiced at the feel of soft skin under my fingers. I reached forward to caress the smooth belly beneath my hand. I leaned in and kissed the delicate curve of her shoulder. I could still smell the sweet apple scent of her shampoo.

"What the fuck are you doing?"

My eyes fluttered open and I looked across the bed at Deja. The narrow, accusing eyes demanded an explanation for my familiarity. I sighed and shifted away from her. Whatever lingering memory I had of last night disintegrated in light of Deja's cool calm and critical attitude.

"Good morning, Deja," I said to her as I stared at the ceiling. "Good to see you again." I lied. Although it was partly true. Mostly because I thought Elise deserved a break.

"You mind telling me where the hell we are?"

I looked over at her and smirked. Not because there was anything funny about what had happened over the past two days, but because she definitely was due for an update. I gave her the rough cut of everything, with a strong emphasis on the details regarding our current hosts/captors.

She took it all in stride, eyeing me carefully as I

explained it all. At the end of it, she sat up and looked around the room, officially taking in her surroundings. "Are you telling me that we are inside of Devitti's home? His private estate?"

"Yes, that's exactly what I'm telling you. He wants Elise to be his private hacker. He's already done a number on her. He tested her skills last night and then tortured her when she didn't do exactly what he wanted. Nearly ripped her finger out of socket."

Deja held up her hand and looked over the swollen middle finger. "No wonder my hand hurts like hell. Son of a bitch."

"Look, now that you're back, we need to start talking about how the hell we're going to get out of here."

"Get out of here?"

"Yes. I wasn't willing to put Elise through an escape attempt after everything she'd been through, but I'm sure you can handle it."

"The way you make it sound, Moreau and Elliot want us dead about as much as Devitti wants us alive."

"I just need to get to a phone. I know a ton of cops in the Vegas PD that can help us out."

"You sure about that?" She stood up and moved toward the bathroom. "I know you got connections, but so do the mob bosses. The minute you let anybody know what our plan is, we are going to end up on the 5 o'clock news." She stepped into the bathroom before I could justify the need for an escape.

While she took care of her morning business I started to extricate myself from the bed. Last night I hadn't wanted to leave it, not for a second. The morning after, however, felt like waking up next to a complete stranger. It wasn't entirely true, but at the same time the subtle differences between Deja and Elise made it impossible for me to view them the same way.

Deja cursed from inside the bathroom. "What is it?" I asked as I heard the toilet flush and her feet scramble to the door. She ripped it open and bolted back out toward me. She shoved her hands into my chest and I vaulted through the air. I landed back on the bed. I rubbed my chest where I could still feel the heat of her hands. "What is wrong with you?" I yelled at her and sat back up. I stared at her while she continued to fume, hurling belligerent curses at me. "I have no idea why you're mad!"

Deja lifted the hem of the dress that was now being used as a nightgown. She motioned to the scribble of words across both her thighs. I frowned and shook my head. "What is it? I haven't read it," I reiterated, hoping to once and for all get a straight answer.

"She had to kill someone." Deja's voice trembled with unexpected anxiety. "She killed three women."

"What?" I eyed her legs, trying to figure out where this revelation had come from and why I was only hearing about it now. "I had no idea. I wasn't with her when that happened."

"Where the hell were you?"

"Barely surviving an attack on the road. They went on without us. Look, if she killed somebody it was for good reason. You should know that. Elise is a good person."

"Yes!" Deja shrieked. "She is a very good person. She doesn't need to be dragged down by the burden of murder, self-defense or otherwise."

"No she doesn't, but that's not the situation that we're in right now. The situation that we are in is the one where you hired out your other self to do dirty jobs for dirty people. Now, because of that, she has been kidnapped and held captive. You can't change the decisions that you've made up to this point. I certainly can't change the fact that I am now involved in this. The only thing that you and I can change is the choices that we make from here on. I need to know if you are on board for getting the hell out of here, before Elise has to endure one more day in this house."

Deja looked around the room again. She rubbed her forehead and moved over to the window to look outside. I could see her eyes probing the yard surrounding the estate. She was probably already considering the options in front of her. Laying out a plan of her own.

However, just when I thought she would agree with my plan, she turned back to me, her eyes glazed over and a guilty frown dragged down her face. "No."

The word didn't make sense to my ears. I shook my head trying to backtrack and figure out where that word connected to our conversation. "What you mean, no?"

The guilt in her eyes subsided, and her jaw tensed. "I mean no, I won't help you escape."

I narrowed my eyes and moved towards her. I dipped my head, positioning my ear that much closer to her. "You are just going to let Elise wake up in two days back in the hands of that monster?"

I expected her guilt to return, but Deja no longer seemed interested in humoring my plots. "Listen to me very carefully. I don't want Elise to get hurt. And the best way to do that is to do nothing. All they want from her is her fingers typing on that keyboard. If she just shuts her mouth and does what she's told, we can get out of this."

"No we can't. This isn't a one-time job. Devitti is going to keep her on as a goddamn pet. This isn't about money anymore, this is about power, and he needs Elise to maintain that power." Deja still didn't say anything. Her resolve had stiffened to the point of making her stone cold. "How can you do this? Are you... Are you actually afraid? Is that what this is? You're giving up?"

Her mouth dropped open. I could see her tongue probing her teeth as if she was cleaning them in preparation of a fresh ass-chewing. She stepped forward, pushing further into my face. The shimmer in her eyes was just slightly different than Elise, making them sparkle in a wild way. "I don't give up. I don't run away. That's not who I am."

"I'm confused. Isn't staying running away in this case?"

She smiled and licked her lips. "Maybe, Mr. Cantry, you should stick to what you know. In this case, that seems to be Elise." She brushed past me, knocking her shoulder against mine as she did and once again proving that she had more than twice my strength. I waited until she was in the bathroom and rubbed the spot on my shoulder she had likely bruised. I was getting tired of being pushed around. I wanted to help Elise, but it was going to be very difficult to do that if Deja was not willing to help her too.

52

I stepped out of the bedroom, nearly running into Deuce as I turned to head back to my room. He looked me over and then at the door behind me. "Good night?" He smirked.

I rolled my eyes and started to walk away.

"Wow, hold up." His voice sounded slightly deeper and I started to suspect that this was Thatcher talking. "Mr. Devitti wants to talk to you."

"About what?" I asked.

"I'm not usually let in on the details. I just deliver the message and then the product."

"Where is he?"

"I'll take you to him."

I followed Deuce downstairs and back into the same hallway leading to the ballroom, only this time we bypassed it and headed deeper into the west wing of the house. We passed by a series of archways leading into various lounging rooms, all complete with an endless amount of expensive furnishings. At the end of the hall was an expansive game room, complete with three pool tables and a line of antique slot machines. Deuce moved to the back of the room and opened a door that blended in perfectly with the wood paneling. Before he went through, he turned back to me. His eyes were once again bright and his smile a little devious. "I gotta know, is the other one here?"

"The other what?"

"Oh, come on, man. The other half. What does she call herself? Deja. Cute."

"Yes, she's back."

"You hittin' that one too?"

I tensed my jaw and cleared my throat. Naturally he assumed that having two women would be better than one. I couldn't say that I hadn't thought about it, but the thing about Siamese minds was that they were always on opposite ends of the spectrum. If you liked one, then there was a chance you would hate the other one. "No, I'm not."

Deuce smiled. "All right, I'll see if I can make any headway with her today." He pushed through the door, bringing us into a small office. The traditional masculinity of leather bond books and taxidermy animals clashed with a modern flare of black furniture and understated art. Mr. Devitti looked up from his oversized wood desk as we came in. "Cantry, sir," Deuce said in the slightly deeper voice I attributed to Thatcher.

Devitti waved us in and motioned to a black leather chair in front of his desk. I sat down, noting the textured feel of the cool fabric. Deuce, on the other hand, stayed at the back of the room, guarding the door. "So this is what it feels like to be in this chair," I said with a smile.

Devitti's brow dipped slightly. "I'm sorry, I don't catch your meaning."

"I've heard rumors about this chair."

Devitti's mouth broke a small smile. He folded his hands and leaned back in his own black leather chair. "What sort of rumors?"

"Rumors about how many times blood has been cleaned off of it."

Devitti laughed. "That is genuine stingray leather, Mr. Cantry. I may be rich, but I'm certainly not cavalier with my property."

"I'm sure you're not, but isn't stingray incredibly durable and easy to clean?"

Devitti perked his brow. "You're experienced with fine leathers? I wouldn't have guessed that."

"I'm full of surprises." I shrugged.

"I don't doubt it. I myself have a few surprises."

"Would you mind if I switched to one of those cream chairs out in the hall before you reveal them to me?"

"You are funny, Mr. Cantry. I wish I could keep up with your humor, but I'm afraid I don't always follow the nuances of comedy. Perhaps you could explain one of your jokes to me."

"Which one is that?"

"It's the one where you shot a bullet into my leg."

"Oh, that one." I hissed and shifted forward in case I needed to defend myself. "Is that why I had a bid out on me?"

"You did say that if I had any questions, you could meet with me anytime."

"Wow, your men are very communicative. That is definitely a surprise."

"With all the hullabaloo yesterday I didn't get a

chance to speak to you about it. However, since it's obvious to me now that Elise was your ultimate priority, I think I can forgive the foolish nature of your humor."

"Thank you." I glanced back at Deuce to make sure he wasn't sneaking up behind me to slit my throat. Devitti could say what he wanted about the expense of his fine leather, but I knew I was sitting on a cheap rug.

"Mr. Cantry, I didn't bring you here for retaliation. I brought you here to discuss your continued presence in my home." Devitti leaned back in his chair and knitted his hands before resting them on his chest. "This is an unusual situation, wouldn't you agree?"

I nodded. *Getting stranger by the minute.*

"You can see how I might be suspicious of a former cop residing in my home."

"I'm here to protect Elise."

"I admire chivalry, but unfortunately that streak of goodness could affect my progress."

"So could kicking me out. Elise is smart and talented, but in case you haven't noticed, she's not prepared for your world."

"Of course not, and if she judges me purely on last night's example then she will never see me as anything more than a monster. However, I think in time she will come to understand that having me for an ally and employer is not just in her best interest, but may potentially give her a very pleasant life."

"What are you going to do? Just keep her locked up in here forever?"

"Not at all, but there are a series of events that need to take place before she can freely manage her own lifestyle. For example, the first thing that needs to happen is she needs to get weaned off of you."

"I'm not leaving."

"Last time I checked this was my residence, and you are currently a guest. The minute you are no longer welcome I will remove you forcefully, if necessary. And let's be honest, I consider myself a very generous man for not shooting you on sight. I know very well who you are and the pull that you have. I also know that you would like very much to dig up enough dirt on me to put me behind bars."

"Everybody has to have a hobby."

"My ultimate goal is to gain the trust and loyalty of Miss Welch. I think part of that journey will involve playing nice with her boyfriend. However, with that being said, you will also have to behave." He leaned forward again. "If I suspect that you are taking advantage of your proximity to my home in order to spy on me, plant surveillance devices, or procure evidence against me, then I'll have to find out how easy stingray leather is to clean. Do we have an accord?"

"Yes."

Devitti turned back to his computer screen, effectively ending the conversation. Deuce tapped my shoulder and nodded for me to get out. I stood and followed behind him, but stopped in the doorway. "Mr. Devitti, I was wondering if I might be a little bold in making a request."

Devitti eyed me from his desk. "What is it?"

"Elise is now in her other personality. Deja is a little more flamboyant than her. To be perfectly blunt, she's a loudmouth bitch, but I would like you to consider her as valuable to you as Elise."

"Since they share the same body I don't imagine that will be a problem."

"You wouldn't think so, but she really is quite a handful."

"I'm sure Mr. Thatcher can keep her on her best behavior." Deuce nodded. "If not... we'll figure something out."

I grimaced, imagining what he had in mind for subduing Deja. It wasn't going to be easy, but somehow I was going to have to convince her to do a little sucking up.

53

Deja ran across the pavement, jumped, clutched her knees to her chest, and landed with an oversized splash in the pool. The ladies sunbathing across the way were none too pleased with the performance. They stood up, picked up their towels and moved a little farther from the edge.

Deja popped up and watched them go. A smug smile perched on her lips as she waded back out of the water. I couldn't blame her for wanting to scare them off. Their high-pitched giggles were enough to irritate me. When I had first arrived, I suspected the random women might be in the employ of Mr. Devitti. Spies disguised as eye candy. However, the more I observed their vain behavior, the more it became clear that they were merely parasitic social climbers. They had probably slept with Arthur at some point, and because everyone appreciated having something to ogle poolside, they kept letting them visit.

I watched Deja step out of the pool from my comfy plastic strapped chair. She was in her newly gifted bikini, the likes of which weren't leaving much to the imagination. Not that I needed one. I was now quite familiar with her body, the oddity of which was still settling in.

She caught me watching her and I looked away.

"Whatcha lookin' at, Layne?" she purred at she moved over to my chair. "Fat chance getting Elise to put one of these on."

I bit back a smile, thinking about the blue sequined number that I had ripped off of her before making love to her the first time.

A pair of wet legs straddled me, followed by a wet ass that plopping into my lap, making my crotch wet. "Deja! What the hell?"

"Oh, shut up, it's just water."

"Hey, is there enough to go around?" Deuce said from a lounge chair down the way. He hadn't wasted much time exploring the option of hooking up with her —a prospect that bothered me less and less as the day went on.

Deja looked him over. "Jealous?"

"Extremely."

"Don't worry, Douche, there's always more wet lap to go around." Deja smirked at me.

"It's Deuce," he corrected forcefully.

"Yeah, yeah." Deja all but waved him off and braced her arms on the back of my chair, putting her rainbow bikini top in my face. "I take it from our cozy position this morning that you and Elise have gotten close."

"None of your business."

"Oh, but it is." She shifted her hips, rubbing against my crotch. I quickly grabbed her thighs to stop the movement. "Did you, or did you not, fuck her?"

"Don't say it like that."

"Oh, god! *Make love*," she mocked.

"Why are you even asking me this? I thought that was my secondary duty."

"That was before you almost ran off in Mexico."

"I didn't almost run off in Mexico! Why did you even tell her that? We had an argument. I considered leaving, but I didn't."

"The circumstances forced you to stay."

"What do you want me to say, Deja? I had some doubts about getting involved in this, but I came to my senses."

"You know it never works out, right?"

"What are you talking about?"

"Boyfriends." She glared at me. "We've tried. They always get jealous, or worse, they get greedy. 'Oh, sorry, I thought you were Elise. Ha. Ha. Oh, well, since I'm already here.'" Deja playacted what I assumed was a real scenario. "It just doesn't work."

"It might work if you'd keep your legs closed more often." I motioned to her current position on my lap. I hadn't even realized how insulting the statement was until her hand slapped my face. It was the second time in our short acquaintance that I had said something to warrant her physical anger.

"Geez!" Deuce chuckled down the way, no doubt enjoying the live soap opera.

I turned back and saw the expression on her face. It wasn't the fury I had anticipated, at least not below the surface. I had actually hurt her feelings. For a moment, I considered what she had just said about the difficulty with boyfriends. How could Elise or Deja ever be in a long-term committed relationship with a man if that man wasn't willing to accept the other half as a permanent fixture in his life? This wasn't about Deja being loose. It was about me accepting her with or without that judgment.

She started to lift off of me, but I touched her arm. "Wait." She paused, but wouldn't look at me. "I'm sorry. That was a cheap shot."

She leaned back and got in my face. "Just because I enjoy the company of men doesn't make me a slut," she seethed. "You don't know anything about me." Her eyes flitted between mine.

"I know enough about you to know that you would do anything to protect Elise." Her eyes narrowed on me. "I'm not going to hurt her. I'm not going to leave like the others. I'm not going to cheat like the others."

She pulled herself off me and stood up. She grabbed her pack of cigarettes from the side table. "That's what they all tell her."

"I'm not telling her. I'm telling you. Elise and I will figure out the relationship stuff as we go. I just need you to know what my intentions are."

She scoffed and pulled a cigarette from the pack with her lips. "Are you asking my permission to date my other half?" she mumbled over the filter in her lips.

"I need it, don't I? I mean, that's the only way this works, right? Say what you want about two separate lives, but if you don't let me have her, she'll never let me either."

Deja paused and looked me over. She pulled the cigarette off her lip and tipped her head to examine me in a more dramatic way. "I'll think about it."

I smiled and let out a breathy laugh. I shouldn't have expected any less, or any more.

54

"What's your name again?" Deja asked as she leaned over the pool table to block Deuce's shot with her bikini-clad breasts. She wasn't actually playing the game, but since Deuce and I were maxed out on sunshine, we all moved indoors for a little competition.

"Deuce. Hey, don't get the table wet. Mr. Devitti is very particular about his pool tables."

"I can see that." She looked over the other two tables in the game room. "Where is he, anyway? I thought I would get to meet the legend." She jumped up on one of the many stools to observe the game with inactive boredom.

"He had some business to attend to. He won't be back until the event this evening."

"Event?" I asked.

"Another dinner party."

"How many dinner parties can one man have?"

"You'd be surprised." Deuce raised his eyebrows.

"Deuce, tell me more about dyads. What's the point?" Deja asked.

"The point is, two heads are better than one."

"But you're talking about combining them into one consciousness."

"No, that would technically be a Siamese mind. If you go that far, you're stuck permanently together, no transition whatsoever. It's virtually impossible to achieve. Dyads, on the other hand, always keep a separate consciousness, no matter how often our minds overlap. If Thatcher and I continue to advance, we will be able to jump in and out as needed."

"Yes, but by whose command? Who's in control?"

"Both."

Deja shook her head vigorously. "That would never work. It's bad enough being separate and together, but to have no control…"

"You have all the control."

"Shared control, that's not the same."

Deuce chuckled and shook his head. "I'm not sure that Thatcher and I would ever become full dyads and share our body 24/7. Judging by your reaction, though, I think you two are definitely better off being separate."

Deja glanced over at me. "We're just better people on our own. We're both too stubborn to change."

"I couldn't agree more," I said.

She frowned at me. "What about tryads?" She turned back to Deuce. "You know anything about them?"

Deuce snorted. "That's a myth."

"You sure about that?" Deja persisted. "What exactly does the myth say?"

"There's only one way that a tryad could exist."

"Oh yeah? And how's that?"

Deuce glanced around as if he didn't want to be caught gossiping about twin minds. "Something has to either go very right... or very wrong."

"Wrong with what?" I asked.

Deuce looked to me and frowned. "The ritual that created it."

"Ritual?" I chuckled. "Are we talking magic now?" I glanced at Deja to see if she was finding just as much humor in this conversation, but to my surprise she looked rather grave.

"You guys got a bathroom on this end?" she asked as she dug something out of her purse. She hopped off her chair to search for one.

Deuce cleared his throat and motioned to the office door. "You can use the one in there if you hurry. Wait." He came at her and motioned upward with his finger. "What do you have in your hand?"

Deja's brow crumpled and then she perked an eyebrow at him. "Just a little something I need to get inside of me as fast as possible." She held out the colorful pink wrapper that only a child could mistake for candy.

Deuce's face crinkled with the universal discomfort at conversations involving the female cycle. "Oh, right, that." He pushed open the door that was almost perfectly disguised as a wood panel.

"Holy crap! Secret rooms too!" Deja said with joyful mockery. "Wow, this guy really is an asshole."

"Hurry up—and hide that thing in the trash."

Deja turned around and waved the little cylinder at him. "Are you sure you don't want to come with me and help me slip it in?" I sputtered laughter as I watched Deuce's face contort in shock, abhorrence, and finally ire.

"Christ, woman! Why would I—gross! Just go do

your shit!" Deuce snarled and came back to the pool table. I could see Deja smirk, happy to have dismissed him with a simple female weapon. She even winked at me and she headed off to the small bathroom just off the office. Deja wasn't what I would have called skillful, but she certainly had a knack for getting rid of people.

I continued to chuckle as I leaned in for my shot. I was turning out to be a rather crappy competitor, but Deuce wasn't as good as he had claimed either. "I told you she was a handful."

"Yeah, I thought you meant smart-mouthed and sassy, not foul-mouthed and gross."

I chuckled again and looked over to where I could see into the office. Deja was leaning down looking at something by Devitti's desk. She caught me looking at her and pressed her finger to her lips. I didn't know what she was doing, but I knew anything resembling a covert activity while inside that room was liable to get her and me into big trouble. Deuce started to move around the table, which would put him in line to catch her. "Deuce, your shot." I pointed to the cue ball at his end, momentarily distracting him while Deja returned to the safety of the bathroom.

55

Devitti seemed to have an endless calendar of social events. Even with Nikolai and his men out of the picture, there was still a dinner party scheduled with some of the more upstanding members of the Vegas community in attendance. I wasn't sure what it was about money, but it seemed to unite people regardless of their social upbringing, basic morality, or even their theoretical position on the line of good and evil.

I was extremely surprised when I came down to the dining hall to find Mr. Elliott amongst the A-list guests. The man was yet another legend in the crime world, despite being the least powerful of the mob trio. His short stature had gained him the prestige of a Napoleon complex. From what I understood, he was actually the most violent of the men. His climb to power had less to do with money and far more to do with revenge—a private endeavor that he used his earnings to facilitate in the cruelest ways possible. The basis for his vengeance had been left to rumors and they spanned as far as the imagination could create. The death of a brother, the rape of a wife, or perhaps the rumors were true and it was all because of a kicked dog.

I never put much credence in any of the gossip, but standing before the man with a perfect smile, I wondered what it really took to earn his hatred. His black hair was slicked back, exacerbating his deep widow's peaks. His Jack Nicholson eyebrows were perpetually cocked in an angry expression. Much like the rest of the party guests, he was dressed in black tie. The only distinction between him and the rest of the men, aside from his height, was a prominent pin on his lapel. The odd pink heart stood out as if he was representing a new segment of the Susan G. Komen society.

He caught my eye as I awkwardly held at the entrance, unsure of where to stand or who to socialize with. I was at the door of the lions' den, staring at the predators. Since I had resigned myself to taking care of Elise, I was no longer the hunter, but now merely the prey.

Elliott's mouth tipped to one side, turning his already cheerful smile into a lopsided goofish smirk. He offered a single finger to the people he was talking to and moved away from them, approaching me with a confident swagger. He thrust out his hand for a handshake and I submitted to the aggressive shaking. "Allow me to introduce myself, Mr. Cantry. I am Jonathon Elliott. Although I'm sure you know that already."

"You have me at a disadvantage. I wasn't aware that you knew who I was."

Elliott laughed with delight. "You are more famous than you think you are. In fact, I'm quite a fan. I've actually been thinking about bringing you on."

"Bringing me on?"

"Yes. You seem to have this natural knack with

people. Your friends in the departments are very loyal to you. There's quite a few people that refuse to give me any dirt on you."

"I've mentored a lot of men over my years in the Academy."

"An influence that has, no doubt, helped your PI business."

"Yes, I would have to agree." I shifted a little more, uncomfortable that he knew so much about me.

"It must be strange for you coming in here, seeing us all playacting like normal businessmen. It's practically cops and robbers having tea, isn't it?"

I glanced around the room. Even as I nodded to agree with him I noticed a rather pertinent figure in the crowd. "Is that the governor?"

"Oh, you'd be surprised who shows up to these things. Funny thing about politics is that it's only a few steps away from being criminal. The funny thing about crime is that it has just as much politics as the government. In the end, it's all business, but you can't have business without friends. And you can't make friends in this business without making enemies."

I stared at Elliott's casual attitude in describing his business, which as far as I knew was a string of murders that had laid waste to four criminal families running close thirds to Devitti and Moreau. If it weren't for him, their profit margins would still be slivers. In a way, Elliott had elevated the mob game to a monopoly. A monopoly that was in competition with government control. "So, is this what you all do? Get together to congratulate yourselves on your success in undermining a system of law?"

Elliott's smile dimmed as he considered my question. "I'm not sure why you're so excited about the current system of law, but I assure you, we aren't doing anything that the government hasn't been doing for years."

"The government doesn't participate in petty crime. Larceny, arson, murder—those are the games that the mobsters play."

"I agree that some of our methods of finance are a little less direct than taxation, but if you think the government officials aren't murdering to keep control of their positions then you are far more delusional than I ever anticipated."

"And what should we do, Mr. Elliott? Should we turn our backs on the president and elect you in his stead?"

Elliott nearly spat out his drink as he took a sip. He chuckled and coughed. "Absolutely not. Me in the oval office? Wouldn't that be a funny sight. You know your problem, Layne? You have a one-sided view of right and wrong. Black and white. Up and down. What you haven't taken into consideration is that right and wrong will never be direct opposites. People always view what's right differently depending on their perspective. And what's wrong—well, it's only wrong if someone feels that it's in direct violation to what's right. The more you feel you're right, the less you view what you do as wrong. Eventually, your two-sided line has angled so many times that it's come full circle.

"What I suggest is to balance everyone's rights and

wrongs with their own set of rights and wrongs. Our government has a commitment to protecting the people from external attacks and internal detriments. They will do anything necessary to do so. However, as you well know, certain members of the government manipulate those purposes to fund or propagate other endeavors. That's where we come in: A few more sets of lines balancing out some of their bad, so that they can in turn balance out ours. You may not know it, but right now we are in a perfect state of balance."

I snorted and shook my head. "How in the hell did you come up with that idea?"

"Quite easily. The government has a baseline for right and wrong. Moreau has a slightly tilted view of right and wrong. Devitti has another tilted view—tilted in his favor, of course. And I have the final baseline, which in many ways is completely contradictory to what the government's is. However, I think mine balances out the good and evil just perfectly. So, you see, with our lines drawn in the sand, we create a perfect octagon of balance."

I stared at him a moment, trying to digest the logic of his process. "You know what octagons make, Mr. Elliott?" I leaned in a little closer, taking advantage of our difference in height to lord it over him. "Stop signs," I whispered to him and moved on. I wasn't entirely interested in hearing a criminal's logic on right and wrong. I may have been a little naïve about how deep corruption went in our government, but I still knew the difference between protection and murder.

56

Deja slipped up beside me and linked her arm through mine. I glanced over at her with the intention of asking her about the incident in the office earlier. I wanted to know why she would be so cavalier as to snoop through the personal belongings of a mob boss. Unfortunately, one look at her threw my train of thought clear off the rails. Memories of last night crept into my mind as I looked at her up-do hair, tightly fitted red dress, and the ruby lips that matched. I couldn't help smiling at her. She caught my eye, noting the interest in my gaze. "What?" she asked, immediately suspicious.

"Nothing. You look beautiful."

Her eyes glinted with delight, but she immediately rolled her eyes. "Why, because I look like Elise?"

I scanned her face as she almost pouted while looking over the crowd. Even with all her bravado in place, she was just as sensitive about her individuality as Elise was. My mouth ticked up into a smile and I shifted slowly, using a single finger to pull her chin to face me. "You are both very beautiful women. I do have to admit you have the most stunning eyes, but I think that's because you're a little more predatory than she is."

Deja smirked at me and clucked her tongue. "Are you flirting with me, Mr. Cantry?"

"Not at all. Just offering polite conversation."

"That's good, because I think she likes you."

I smiled at first, but then I frowned. "Did she say something about me in the letter?"

"No, but sometimes I can feel what she feels. In the transition, two ships passing in the water. Most of the time the waves just collide with each other and disappear, but when she's particularly angry or happy it's a stronger wave and it hits me on the way by."

"That's amazing. Almost like a psychic link."

"More empathic."

"You two really are fascinating."

"Did you hear what I said?"

"What's that?"

"She likes you, Layne. She hasn't felt that strongly about anyone ever."

"I feel pretty strongly about her. Is that what you're worried about? You still think I'm going to leave?"

"I think you *should* leave."

"But you just said—"

"I said she likes you. I didn't say that she was good for you or that you are good for her."

"Why are you doing this? Why are you trying to sabotage everything that she has? I thought I understood you. I thought you cared about her. First you want me to protect her. Then you want me to have sex with her. Now, when she needs me the most, you want me to leave her."

"She doesn't need you anymore."

"You have no idea what she needs and even less of an idea of what she wants." She squeezed my arm tightly. I could tell that she wanted to hurt me for being so presumptuous. "I've been trying very hard not to get between the two of you, but right now this isn't an issue of me getting between you. You are now getting between us."

"You don't have an us."

"No more of this bullshit, Deja. I don't care what you say, I am not letting you stand between me and the woman I love."

Deja's eyes widened at the last word. Her shock slowly faded and her gaze wilted to the floor around my feet. I opened my mouth to reel back in my professed love, but Mr. Devitti chose that moment to disrupt my retraction. "Mr. Cantry, Miss Welch, I'd like to introduce you to David Moreau." We turned to contribute a set of fake smiles and suck up to yet another mob boss.

I looked over the tightly cropped white hair and goatee that made him look militaristic. Just as his legend claimed, Moreau was nothing short of Herculean. The girth and definition of his muscles had gained him a reputation as "the The Steel Trap." The name was also attributed to the fact that his business deals were so clandestine that they bordered on being mythical. Even the police weren't actually sure what his criminal activities were.

Initially, I had suspected that Moreau was killing the witnesses to his crimes. However, in more recent months, I had come to believe that his dealings revolved around technology. He was obtaining his wealth, power, and control through hackers like Elise.

His tight-knit community of criminals were not violent subcontracted hitmen like Devitti's or Elliot's. They were backstage recluses that spent as much time at their computers as Moreau spent in the gym. His operation was definitely not the bloodiest, but it was the most lucrative. And, in many ways, he was the biggest threat of them all, because not only did he have money, he had information. Which meant it didn't require big parties to keep and maintain his contacts. All he had to do was send an email with evidence to back his blackmail.

It was a litigious operation that I had been working for years to dismantle. Unfortunately, his protégés were as loyal as mine and they all knew how to cover their tracks to keep me from finding them. I thought perhaps Elise was the key to uncovering and unraveling this operation, but it became very clear early on that she was not aware of her situation, let alone would she be able to help me track down her employer.

"Nice to meet you," I said and put out my hand to shake.

Moreau surveyed us both with stern, commanding eyes and then turned his attention to Devitti. "Is this some kind of joke? Do you really expect me to stand here and socialize with a cop?"

Devitti took a breath. "Mr. Cantry hasn't been a cop for several years. I assure you I haven't brought him here to entrap you."

Moreau's lip twitched with annoyance. "I'm not talking about Cantry." He turned and pinioned his stare on Deja, who was grinding her teeth and staring right back at him. "I'm talking about her."

57

"Damn it, Deja!" Gary griped as one of my mayo- and ketchup-slathered pickles fell onto his paperwork. He grabbed a handful of tissues and did his best to clean up the mess. "Get that outta here." He waved me away, revoking my over-the-shoulder reading privileges.

"Sorry," I said over a mouthful of burger. "I got the triple stack today. It's virtually impossible not to make a mess with these things." I plopped down in my squeaky chair and continued to devour the glorious meal.

Gary frowned at me across the expanse of our joined desks. His baby blue eyes never seemed to match his face. They should have been brown, and because they weren't, they drew a lot of attention from people. Not just women. Even men tended to stare at him for inordinate amounts of time, their minds trying to rationalize something that just didn't make sense to their eyes. It was probably because he had fuzzy low-cropped golden brown hair that had probably been contributed to his DNA by an errant African-American hookup somewhere in his white-on-white lineage. Not that the features made him unattractive, just a little different. "How can you eat that and still look the way you do?"

"And how do I look, Gary?" I baited him, because

that was always fun. Gary had had a crush on me since the day we met. Unfortunately, that was the day he was assigned to be my probation officer. Even if he had wanted to ask me out, the conflict of interest prevented it.

"I'm serious," he continued, unaffected by my attempt to make him blush. "Do you know how much crap is in those things?"

"Please don't tell me. Do you know how many articles about trans fat and high fuck-tose corn shit I have read? It doesn't matter, Elise is a health nut. She eats carrot sticks and runs like five miles a day."

Gary snickered. "Well, at least someone is watching out for your ass, and the size thereof."

"Excuse me, Mr. Vegan, do you see any fries here?" I waved to my french-fry-free zone. As much as I enjoyed a good burger, I did see Elise's point about the dangers of trans fats. Not that I would ever admit that to her.

"I'm not a vegan, I'm a vegetarian."

"What's the difference?"

"The difference is I don't give a shit about the animals, I just don't want to have an impacted colon."

"Fine, whatever. Are you finished reading the letter or not?"

"Yeah." Gary tossed Elise's letter back to me and fell back against the weak back support on his chair. "There's got to be a way to convince her to keep doing it."

"Nope," I said with certainty. "Do you see the oversized words at the bottom of the page? Those are her big girl letters. She only whips those puppies out when she's really mad."

Gary looked around the office for prying ears, but between the massive layoffs and the lunchtime hour, there was no one around to answer calls, let alone listen in on our top secret plots to uproot the increasing corruption in our midst.

It wasn't so much about taking down the bad guys for Gary as finding a way to unravel the threads that were tangling up an otherwise simple system of criminal justice. I had never been a fan of constant surveillance, but it wasn't until Gary recruited me that I realized how often it was used as a weapon instead of a defense.

"We can't make any progress on this case without some kind of connection to what's going on inside the system. Without Elise we can't get close to Moreau's people. Obviously outright infiltration isn't going to work."

"I don't know, I could give Arthur Devitti another try. There's always room for more *sexlettes* around the pool."

"You kicked him in the balls on your first date."

"That's true, but he asked for a blow job—"

"Which you were willing to give for the sake of the investigation," Gary continued the story for me. "But he asked for it before the appetizers, instead of waiting for dessert."

"Are you mocking me?"

"Of course I'm mocking you. You should have punched the guy in the throat when he told you not to wear underwear because it will just get in his way later."

I chuckled, reminiscing on how much of a bastard Arthur Devitti was. "You have to admit, though, at least you know exactly where you stand with him."

"Sure, if by stand you mean kneel."

"Too bad the senior Devitti isn't desperate enough to go on blind dates. I could probably make more progress with him."

"That dude is like 70."

"It's not the age that matters, Gary. It's how good your Viagra is."

"Gross." He rolled his eyes. "So what are we going to do about Elise?"

"Nothing. She's out, man. Short of pointing a gun to her head she isn't going to do any more work for us."

Gary leaned forward and tapped his finger on the metal top. I recognized the thoughtful expression on his face. I almost dreaded hearing the plot he was forming in his shaggy-haired head. "What if we did hold a gun to her head?"

"You aren't serious. Do you not remember the last time you got aggressive with one of us?"

"Oh come on. Are you still holding the Christmas party over my head? I was really drunk, okay? I have apologized one million times."

"Followed by hitting on me one million more. So, no, apology not accepted."

"I apologized because it was rude and uncouth, not because... never mind. Okay, look." Gary stood and moved around to plead his case on the corner of my desk. "I'm not suggesting that we actually hold a gun to her head, but metaphorically speaking, what if there was a threat? I mean, she's running under the mistaken assumption that this is some sort of corrupt operation and you're getting her into trouble. What if, by no stretch of her imagination, you actually do get her into trouble?"

I crossed my arms. "I'm listening."

"Okay, so the game up to this point has been to convince someone that we are connected to one of the mob bosses. Lure someone into our web and wheedle information out of them. Since we are already pretending to be mob bosses hiring a hacker, why don't we pretend to be a mob boss hiring a man to kill said hacker?"

"What the hell, Gary? If we put out a hit, some yahoo actually takes the job and Elise gets killed. Then I will become a ghost and kill you."

"No, no. I'll put out the hit, but then I'll claim it. It will actually validate our image as bad guys."

"If you claim it, how will she know that she's being targeted?

"A few potshots should do it."

"Potshots?"

"I'll miss."

"What if you miss missing her? Do I have to explain the paranormal murder again?"

"I know how to aim. I can't use blanks, or she won't even know I'm shooting at her."

"Okay, setting aside my sensitivity to bullets. Let's think about this from her perspective. Elise is very fight-or-flight, and 90% of the time she chooses flight. The minute there's even a whisper of an attempt on her life, she's gonna go to the police. That's going to cause more than one problem in our relationship, considering that she'll probably come down here. The station I work in."

"If we could just tell her about the job, we wouldn't even have to—"

"No!" I threw a glare at Gary and he waffled with his own irritation. It wasn't the first time the subject had come up regarding Elise's lack of knowledge about my employment. I had only been on the force a couple of years, but my exposure to violent crimes was a constant threat. I had already covered up a gunshot wound by claiming that it was a burst appendix. It took a lot of cooperation from the hospital staff to do it, a luxury that wouldn't have been afforded to me if I hadn't had a badge to back it up.

If Elise knew I was a cop, she would constantly be afraid that I was going to get us killed. I didn't want her to go to sleep every other night worried that she would never wake up. It just wasn't fair for me to foist that on her. Not when I could simply allow her her ignorance.

"She doesn't trust me any more than a complete stranger. Even if you did tell her I was a cop and that I needed her help, she wouldn't do it."

"You don't know that."

"Gary." I closed my eyes for a moment. "I don't want to have this argument again. She doesn't need to know about the job. We have to find a way to convince her that there is a hit out on her without scaring her into going to the police."

Gary paused in contemplation. His fingers tapped incessantly on my desk. "What if we got someone to watch her when you're not around?"

"A babysitter."

"A bodyguard. What if I went to her and said that I —?"

"No!"

"I haven't even explained the plan yet."

"The answer is no." I wrapped up the remainder of my burger and threw it in the trash. Gary stared at me, dumbfounded.

"Could you expand on that?"

"She doesn't like you."

"She barely knows me."

"She knows you as my former probation officer. That is all she needs to know."

"Is this about the job again? Because I won't tell her. Or is this about something else?"

I stared into those damn baby blues, trying to decide if I liked the way he looked at me or not. My wavering opinion of him aside, Gary was a nice guy. The type of guy that Elise could fall head over heels in love with. It would be happily ever after... for them. "I don't trust you with her," I admitted.

Gary's face crumpled as he looked me over. He slipped off my desk and walked around with his hands propped on his hips. When he looked back at me, I could see paragraphs lining up in his eyes, waiting to spill out his mouth. His mouth dropped open, but nothing came out.

"It doesn't matter anyway," I said, interrupting his silence before the faucet of lacerating words could pour out. I had clearly hurt his feelings, but it was also the truth. As selfish as it was, I didn't want to share Gary. We were partners. It may not have been the sexual relationship that he wanted, but it was still an important bond. At least to me. "You can't watch her for four days a week. You have a job to get to."

Gary nodded and moved back to his desk to pout properly. After a moment of staring into space his eyes perked back into his thoughtful consternation. "We need somebody to watch her who is just as interested in getting these guys as we are. I have just the guy. Layne Cantry."

"Don't know him."

"Then you are one of few. He's trained half the cops from Sacramento to Denver. He worked in the Vegas PD on homicide before that. He practically watched Devitti climb the ranks to criminal mastermind, but couldn't do a damn thing to stop it. He's even more devoted to taking down these guys than us. He spent years pushing the case at his superiors, but much like us he got shoehorned into a desk position and was basically told not to try so hard. Now he's in private investigation, but from what I understand, he's still got his eye on the prize."

"You trust this guy."

"He's the only guy I trust with this stuff. We kind of have a standing information exchange. He lets me know what he hears and I let him know what I see."

"So how does this play?"

"Okay." Gary rubbed his hands together with anticipation of his reveal. "I put up the bid, then I claim it myself. I call up Layne and let him know that there is some mysterious activity going on with a woman named Elise Welch. I give him the highlights of your misdemeanors, and express my own curiosity about the reason for your sudden rise to execution status. He'll be more than interested in following up to see who this Elise is and why she suddenly appeared on a hit list. That's where I come in. A few of those potshots we were talking about. Layne realizes the hit is real and you approach him about protecting you when you're not you."

"Whoa, whoa, whoa." I raised my hands to stop the nonsense. "Nobody said anything about him knowing my condition."

"You've got to be kidding me. He's not stupid, he'll figure it out anyway. Deja, we need him to believe that Elise is in grave danger, so *she* can believe she is in grave danger."

"If she believes that she's in grave danger she will go to the police. She actually believes we still help people."

"Then we take her out of town. Somewhere with shit cell reception and no police for miles. That will give Layne time to convince her that he can protect her, and more importantly, that she needs protection. Then when she is sufficiently freaked out, you write a letter to her explaining that you screwed up and she has to keep doing the hacks or the bad guys won't stop trying to kill her."

I pinched my brow. "I don't know. This is really risky. What he finds out I'm a cop? He's going to be pissed that you used him."

"So you'll go undercover as your pre-cop self for a while. No big deal. All we need to accomplish is getting Elise back into the game. We keep drawing Moreau's attention with increasingly bold hacks on the system, until one day she gets a little message from an anonymous benefactor. Asking for her services."

"You think he'll try to recruit her?"

"I guarantee he will. Especially after we establish that she's worth killing for."

I considered the options on my plate. I rubbed my face before leaning over my desk. "I've done a lot of shady things to Elise, the least of which is not telling her that I'm an undercover cop and that all the times she woke up in the hospital with bruised ribs and stab wounds it wasn't because of a drunken brawl. If I do this to her, manipulate her into doing my bidding, I am officially the worst person alive."

"What difference does it make if she already hates you?" I shifted back, looking at him through hooded eyes. "I just mean, if it all blows up, you'll be in the same position you always are: Trying to defend your actions. The only difference is, you'll be defending yourself with the truth instead of lies."

I didn't like the sound of that, but only because it was the truth. Rather than start another argument, I leaned back in my chair. "So how do we get Cantry to go along with this? Please don't tell me he's one of those do-gooders that will do it out of the goodness as of his heroic heart."

"Now that's the easy part. Just wave a bunch of money in his face. Guy's still gotta eat."

58

"Yeah man, no problem," Gary said into the phone. "I just thought it might be something up your alley. ... No man, just drunken recklessness and traffic violations. I don't know why her name popped up." Gary gave me a thumbs up and I smiled at him from his couch. His place was definitely a bachelor pad, but it smelled nice and the furniture was pretty expensive-looking. He wasn't the neat freak that I expected him to be, but since I could grow penicillin in my laundry pile I couldn't really complain. "Yeah, I'll let you know if I hear anything more."

Gary clicked off his phone and tossed the earpiece onto his coffee table. "We are in. Not only was he interested, he was *very* interested. I guarantee he'll be down here in a day to start watching you. I'll dress the part, so it looks like I'm watching you. A couple of misdirected bullets later and you two will be on the run to who knows where."

"Sounds good, Gary. If this works out the way you're figuring, we could find ourselves doing jobs for the big bad. Inside jobs." I grimaced, once again thinking about how dangerous this was for Elise. I was using her to gain her loyalty instead of just explaining the situation. It was low. More low than I had ever sunk before. Unfortunately, even if I wanted to call it off, it was too late. The bid was in. Layne was on his way. The show must go on.

"Look, it's going to be okay." Gary sat down on the couch beside me, folding his hands in his lap. "You keep worrying about what's going to happen to her, but you didn't take into consideration that I wouldn't do anything to put you in danger."

"I can take care of myself," I mumbled.

He frowned and nodded. He stood back up and moved away. "Either way, just keep me in the loop." He scratched his head and glanced at me.

"What is it?" I asked.

"I was just thinking that if something does go wrong, or really right, you're probably going to be done with the desk job. I just mean if the mob bosses take an interest in you, you'll be stuck in undercover mode for a long time."

"That was the ultimate goal. What's your point?"

"My point is... In a few hours we won't be able to be seen together, so this is probably goodbye. At least for a while."

"Oh don't go teary-eyed on me."

He chuckled and shook his head. "No, I won't, but I figured I'd give you one more chance."

"Chance at what?"

Gary clicked his tongue and motioned his hands over his body. "Come on, Welch, do I have to spell it out for you? We won't have another Christmas party, you know?" He smiled, letting me know that he was just kidding. He was always kidding, except that he wasn't. He really did want me, but since we worked together, it made things complicated.

"Okay," I said.

He chuckled at me, but when I didn't laugh with him, his smile died away. "What do you mean, okay?"

"I mean let's do it. Skip the eggnog, go straight to the sheets."

Gary stared at me, his mouth hanging open. "That's not nice, Deja. You know I got a thing for you. Don't tease me like that."

I stood up and moved to him. Even though I was right in front of him he didn't reach out for me. He still thought I was joking. At any other time, I might've been, but he was right; these were going to be our last few hours together, and for some reason the idea of not being able to see Gary every single day I was awake felt wrong. I couldn't think of a better way to see him off than giving him what he wanted.

I moved a little closer and put my hand around his waist. He gulped and tensed. He frowned and his eyes flickered over mine, still waiting for the trap to snap shut on his hand—or in this case, his penis.

I slipped my hand underneath his shirt, caressing his tight abdominal muscles. His chest rose and fell a little faster. I pushed my hand up to his chest, feeling the little bit of fuzz that it offered. His face pinched with anger. "You'd better not be fucking teasing me."

"Or what?" I smiled. "What will you do to me?"

He gritted his teeth together, knowing full well that he couldn't do shit to me. Not unless I allowed it.

"What's the matter, cat got your tongue?" I taunted. "Come on, Gary, I may be a bitch." I moved my hand back down again, cupping the firm length stretching the fabric of his pants. "But I'm not a tease."

I didn't have to do any more to entice him. Gary grabbed onto me for dear life and kissed me. Somewhere between heavy breathing and his grappling effort to touch every part of me at once, he picked me up, wrapped my legs around him and carried me to his bedroom.

He threw me down on the bed and ripped his shirt off. I pulled my own over my head. By the time I was out of it, his pants and boxers were already off. He reached for my pants as I unbuttoned and unzipped them. They were gone in an instant, tugged off my legs. My panties were only a memory as he dove on top of me pressing his body between my legs, threatening to impale me.

He pulled off my bra and paused to stare down at me. He looked up at me, panting and shaking. "You are so beautiful."

"Oh, don't start that shit. Just do me."

"Shut the fuck up, Welch. You are the hottest damn woman I have ever had in my bed and I'm going to enjoy every last second of it."

"Fine, just so long as you don't make me vomit."

He chuckled and shook his head. "I should have known you'd be just as much of a hard-ass in bed is out of it." He leaned down and kissed my breast. Relieved that he was done talking, I leaned my head back and enjoyed the slow progression of his lips from breast to breast and nipple to nipple. He didn't stop there though. He moved down, kissing my stomach and my thighs.

Just as I started to complain about him taking too long, he crawled back up on top of me and inserted himself. His eyelids fluttered as he groaned with pleasure. As much as I hated watching men in the act, I actually enjoyed seeing his pleasure. It was something that he had anticipated for a long time, and the fact that he was willing to prolong the occasion even after I had said yes made me wonder if I should have given him a little more credit.

Despite the soft subtle flirtation he offered with his mouth, he was far more forceful with his own pleasure. I wrapped my legs around him and rode into ecstasy right along with him.

Drained of energy, he collapsed beside me and wrapped his arms around me. The intense grip made me claustrophobic. He moved his lips to my ear and whispered, "Why the hell didn't we do that sooner?"

"Because we would never get anything done."

"You're amazing, you know that?"

"Whatever." I pushed his arm away and slipped out of bed. "I've got to get going."

"Deja, what the hell? Don't leave yet."

"I can't be seen with you, remember?"

"Bullshit, we've got hours until Cantry gets into town. Just stay here with me."

"Why?"

"Because we just had sex for the first time."

"I came, you came, we're good."

He frowned at me. "Fuck you. I can't believe how much of a stubborn pain in the ass you are, but more so why I actually like you. You treat me like garbage sometimes, Deja. And in case you haven't noticed, I'm the only person who even knows you. The real you. You think I don't get it. You think I don't understand the twin soul thing, but I do. I know that I can't have you all the time. I would be lucky to have a quarter of you, let alone half. I'm not asking for either, though, because I know you aren't ready for that. All I'm asking is that you let me have you for another hour."

I glanced around the room for an answer to my dilemma. I didn't want to get caught up in anything romantic, but he seemed to know that. It had been a long time since I had slept with someone I didn't meet in a bar. Gary wasn't just a one-night stand. He was my friend and partner. I owed him more than a bash and dash. I slipped back into bed beside him and realigned myself with this body. He reached his arm over me and kissed my cheek.

"Are we just going to lie here?"

He chuckled and tickled my side. "Just shut up, Welch."

59

"Just look for anything that looks unusual," Layne said as he freely explored my bathroom. I knew he was looking for drugs. He quickly made some assumptions about me and I was happy to let him keep them, much as I was happy to let a lot of people keep them. "Maybe somebody slipped something on you. Used you as a mule or something."

"What's the point? We never go anywhere." I left the chaos of my bedroom and went into Elise's room. We had always offered each other the respective separate space. The budget didn't really allow for two of everything but somehow we managed to make do to appease our desperation for privacy. As strange as it was, the little things made all the difference to us. The color scheme in her room was a little more drab than mine. Her devotion to soft fluffy things was an obsession that I could never match.

I ransacked her drawers pretending to look for the missing link in the mystery of our murder bid. As I reached the bottom drawer my hand bounced against the bottom panel of the drawer. The distinctly hollow sound alerted me that something was different with this drawer. I pulled the clothing out of the way and knocked on the wood. I searched the sides for a notch and found one just big enough for my pinky. I pulled up the specially made panel and lifted it out. Beneath it I found something I never expected to find.

At first it was just a mess of papers, a bunch of names and numbers along with a slew of chicken scratches. None of it made any sense until I put it all together. I noted the names that were crossed out and the one name at the bottom that wasn't. Each name coincided with a list of details explaining the ritual sacrifice required to *split* a twin soul.

I had heard about them. And everything that I had heard resulted in one of the twins dying. I never thought to pursue it. I might not have been happy as a twin soul but I certainly wasn't desperate enough to kill my other half. Nor was I miserable enough to want to kill myself, which in some cases was the result of such a forced ritual. After all, one twin was always a little stronger and one twin was always a little smarter.

I blinked at the papers. I couldn't believe it. I couldn't believe that she would do this to me. That she would even consider it. I wasn't sure what bothered me more: the idea that she hated me enough to do such a thing, or that she was so unhappy she was willing to do it.

"Did you find something?" Layne asked from the doorway. I picked up the paperwork and threw it across the room. Layne flinched at the oncoming paper cuts. He caught one of the papers and looked it over. He frowned and looked at me. "Is this what I think it is?"

"Yeah," I answered.

"I take it you didn't know about this?"

"No." I bit my lip to keep myself from breaking into

tears.

"Look, Deja, we don't really have time to deal with this. We need to get some distance before you switch again."

"Yeah, we definitely need some distance." I stormed past him and headed back out the front door of my apartment. I was so furious that I completely forgot about pretending that I was afraid of the potential bullets that might be seeking a home in my head. Gary had taken a few shots at me over the last two weeks. It was enough to convince Layne that my life was in danger. He was even the one to suggest that we hit the road and get some distance on our usual haunts.

As I stepped outside, I heard the gunshot just as my doorbell sparked beside me. I had barely connected the two before I was leveled to the ground with Layne on top of me. Two more shots fired, plinking off the endless stone planters around the complex. Layne lifted off me and peeked over one of them to fire back.

I immediately thought about Gary and grabbed at his arm. He shoved me down and glared at me. "What is wrong with you? I had a shot on them."

"Them?" I asked. It occurred to me at that moment that Gary hadn't planned any attacks for today. He thought the timing would be too convenient.

"Yes, two of them. Big, burly, and well-armed. We need to go now." Layne pointed to the stairs.

We crawled over to the concrete steps and used the solid wall railing for cover as we slunk down to ground level. Layne crouched down at the end of the stairway and searched the grounds. I heard the sound of wheels peeling out of the parking lot. Layne stood and fired on the escaping vehicle, but judging by the cusses that followed, I presumed he missed.

"Looks like they weren't prepared for a fighting target. They won't make that mistake again. Come on, let's go while we have the chance."

He grabbed for my hand, but I pulled it from his reach. I wasn't about to be dragged around during an emergency. He ignored the slight and jogged across the parking lot. "Why are there two now? There was only one before."

"I don't know. These guys are like cockroaches. First there's one, then there's fifty." Layne jumped into his blue Camaro and started the purring engine.

I looked over his sparkling Camaro, imagining the number of things that had to go wrong in his life to warrant getting such an ostentatious car. Meanwhile, I jumped into the puke green SUV Elise had talked me into buying, and slammed the door.

"Deja!" Layne rolled down his window and yelled at me. "What are you doing? Get in!"

I rolled down my own window. "Try to keep up."

"Deja!" he yelled again. I ignored his efforts to regain control of the situation and backed out of my parking space. I slammed on the gas, squealed my wheels, and headed out to escape my first *real* murder attempt.

60

The phone chirped in my ear as the other line rang. I heard the phone pick up, but for a moment no one answered. After a series of volume changes in the background chatter at the police station, the noise quieted down completely. "Hello?" Gary's voice sounded almost muffled. "Welch?"

"We have a problem, Gary."

"I thought you were on your way out of town."

"We are, but there was another murder attempt."

There was a long silence on the other end. "What are you talking about?"

"I'm talking about two guys, armed with guns, pointing them in my direction, and firing at me."

"But I—"

"Yeah, that's where I was about ten minutes ago. So catch up. Has someone else taken the job or what?"

"It can't be. I claimed it. Unless someone else hired them. Shit!"

"That was me about five minutes ago." I sighed and glanced in my rearview mirror. The blue Camaro was keeping up with me fine. I was surprised that he hadn't tried to pass me to take the lead. Not that it really mattered where we went now, so long as it involved the middle of nowhere. "Looks like Cantry is going to earn his money after all."

"I'm going to figure this out and call you back."

"No." I rolled my eyes at his belated due diligence. "We have to play this game for real now, Gary. Layne and I are splitsville. No calls. No electronic contact."

There was another long silence. "How am I supposed to get you out of this if I can't contact you?"

I chuckled. "When have you ever gotten me out of trouble, Gary? It's my problem, I'll deal with it."

"This was all my idea."

"It doesn't matter anymore. I just need to get somewhere safe so Elise can be protected. I'll worry about the rest when I wake up."

"I'll find you."

"Sure, Gary." I shook my head, thinking how ridiculous he sounded to me now that we had slept together. Suddenly he was my hero, and would save me against all odds.

"Deja." I heard the serious tone in his voice and I already knew what he was about to say. "I—"

I clicked off the cellular device in my ear and threw it in my purse. The last thing I needed right now was Gary's puppy love clouding my thoughts.

$$61$$

"Dear fucking bitch," I scribbled onto a piece of paper while a tattoo artist scribbled his needle onto my back. I was surprised the artist had agreed to work on me since I was several sheets to the wind and nearly capsized. However, this wasn't exactly the type of establishment that concerned themselves with the welfare of their clients. Especially since I paid him double for my tramp stamp.

Layne had had a few beers, but was managing to stay responsible in the face of my extremely irresponsible evening. He laughed and shook his head. "Are you sure you want to do this?"

All thoughts of our earlier brush with death had been cast away in lieu of my discontinued rage for Elise's betrayal. As dire as the situation was, I was going to make damn sure that Elise felt like shit when she woke up. I had even rationalized in my drunken stupor that she would be easier for Layne to deal with if she was ill. "She'll be pissed if I don't write a letter."

"You're not even writing a letter, just writing a series of expletives. Besides, I don't mean that. I mean a tattoo. Why don't we just go back to the hotel and let you sleep this off?"

"I told you before that this is happening. Unless you are considering the latter option to stop me?" I narrowed my eyes on him, which, considering they were already pretty hooded, probably just made me look tired. He got the hint though and shook his head.

"Fine, but do you really want it to say that?"

"Of course I want it to say that. She's always needed a little assistance in that area anyway. As far as I'm concerned, if she wants to have a stick up her ass, she might as well get off on it."

Layne started to laugh; he coughed, trying to cover up as much of it as he could, but he definitely found my no-nonsense humor amusing. "How about this? How about I write the letter so that it's remotely legible, and you just tell me what to write." He grabbed the paper and pen from me. He moved back to the tattoo artist working on me and whispered something in his ear. When the man shrugged, he handed him an extra hundred.

"Don't you listen to him, I know what I want."

"Alright, back to this letter now." Layne sat back down in his stool in front of me and scooted a little closer. I noticed the stretch in his pants, highlighting his hidden assets. I hadn't really taken the time to look at him, at least not in that way. He was definitely attractive. A little older than I would prefer. With his gray speckled hair and little glasses, he had a very professor-ish vibe going on. He scratched out my words on the paper and looked at me expectantly. "Let me help you start. Dear Elise."

"I have another job for you," I drawled and wiggled my fingers for him to come closer. He leaned in a little, but only to humor me. "I want you to fuck her."

Layne chuckled and leaned back. "Oh, no, no, no, I am not getting involved in that."

"She really needs it though." I thought back to the last time I could recall Elise having a boyfriend. It was always complicated when she wanted to keep them. Somehow I got stuck playing along which was always difficult because the boys she wanted to hang out with actually liked that she was smart. Not being a brainiac myself, I couldn't quite keep up the ruse long enough to fool them. And even when we tried not to fool them... Well, that never worked out either. "She would like you. You're clever."

"Why don't we just stick with business? Dear Elise."

I stared at him, my eyes already starting to loll roll back into my head. I was either going to pass out soon, or vomit. I wasn't sure which yet. "She's not like me."

"I know. I've had a chance to observe her behaviors over the last week."

I harrumphed and laid my head down. "Whatever, just keep an eye on her. She's a quick little shit."

"I'm sure I can keep up with her," he mumbled with disinterest. I chuckled at his ignorance. "Now where were we? Dear Elise..."

62

When I finally woke again forty-eight-plus hours later, I found myself tucked into the crook of Layne's arm, drooling on his chest. I ignored the background headache and focused on my craving for nicotine. I found my purse and retrieved a pack of cigarettes from Layne's duffel bag. It was the only safe place for them, since Elise always threw them away. Which I never understood, since she was also concerned about saving money.

I found my purse and searched it for the notorious note. It wouldn't be like her to forget it, especially given the situation that she had just been put through. She would need someone to vent to. Someone to blame.

When I didn't find it our usual spots, I moved over to a shopping bag that contained new clothing. Layne had obviously been nice enough to buy her some clothes—me too, I suppose—but naturally they weren't my style.

I poked around in the bag, becoming increasingly more concerned about the note's whereabouts. I hated her letters, but they were as necessary to me as morning coffee. I couldn't function unless I had read something from her. It was a sick, twisted bit of irony, but one that I had long since accepted.

I found the note rolled up in a pair of underwear and

took it outside to read while I smoked my first cigarette. It was the usual banter about privacy and the typical finger shake of disapproval at everything that I do. She had wisely already started to blame me for this attack on our lives. She was always smart, which was why I initially doubted that this plan would work, but with the addition of Layne it had no doubt become a little more real to her. It had become a little more real to me too.

Layne wandered out onto the stoop. I nodded to him before finishing the letter. I was surprised to see a rather adamant apology at the end of her communication. I was relieved to see that she didn't want to harm me, but that still wasn't the reason I was so angry. So much of my life I had spent doing what she wanted to do, living where she wanted to live. Even now, she underestimated the sacrifices I made to allow her identity to be her own. And yet, she was the one trying to secure an escape from our perpetually shared body. She was the one ready to jump ship at the first nonlethal opportunity. I was bending over backwards to keep her happy, and she still wanted more.

I bit back the bitterness that demanded I break something and handed the letter over to Layne. He leaned against the door jamb and read it quietly. As I finished my cigarette, I started to think about things as they were. I wasn't sure that there was any way to make Elise truly happy without making myself miserable. We were a married couple that couldn't divorce—we couldn't even argue properly. Two peas in a fucking cramped-ass pod.

"How did it go?" I asked when he had finished

reading the letter. "Did she flip out?"

"A little. She ran from me the first morning."

"No shit." I crushed out my cigarette. I had tried to warn Layne that Elise was a little tricky to keep track of. She wasn't one of those half-witted damsels in distress that screamed for help. When she recognized trouble, she just bolted like a wild animal. When the question was fight or flight, she always chose flight.

"Yeah, I had to call in a few dozen favors to have the local PD pick her up. After that I thought she was on board, but she ran again."

"How the fuck did you lose her twice?" I looked at Layne, astonished that he was such a slow learner. I expected a cop to be a little bit more prepared for keeping someone contained.

"Shut up, she's fast. Anyway, I think we're done with all that." He waved the letter at me. "She understands that I'm here to help."

"She'd better. I'm not paying you to play cat to her mouse. She's already got a few too many cats after her and they aren't playing." *Anymore.*

He nodded in agreement, but his mouth frowned and he looked off into the distance. I recognized a guilty conscience when I saw it.

"What?" I asked, but he didn't answer. "Don't pussyfoot around me, Layne. Just say what you gotta say."

"We had another attempt."

"What do you mean another attempt?" My mind frantically tried to think of how that could be. I resisted the urge to check my body for bullet wounds. I was clearly alive; so was Elise. "How the hell did they find you?"

"I don't know. We were only there for one night. We went shopping in one store, but I bribed the register gal. We should have been fine."

"I assume from the lack of gunshots in my body that you successfully protected her?"

"Actually, she protected herself. I made a mistake."

Mistake. The word hit me like a bomb. There was no room for error now. I had already tangled myself in a web of lies. Lies that had created their own mistakes. One more screw-up, and it might be fatal—for all of us. I stood and planted myself in front of him. I propped my hands on my hips and stared at him, waiting for an explanation about his mistake.

"I wanted to avoid cameras so I went out to fetch breakfast alone. They came by after I left. She got out through a bathroom window and hid, but they took some shots at the bed, which was where I stupidly suggested she hide if something happened. Anyway, she was pretty upset about the whole thing."

"No shit she was upset! What were you thinking? Put her in a fucking hat, go through a drive-through, and move on to the next motel. What is this, day one for cops?"

"I underestimated them or I missed something. It won't happen again." He bit back his anger in the face of my condescension, but I knew I had hit a nerve. He took his job very seriously, and he must have felt pretty guilty for endangering Elise.

"You're damn right it won't happen again. You're

here to watch my back, which just so happens to be Elise's front, so get it right. I'd like to live through this."

"You will," he ground out.

I stared at the determination in his eyes. He was the only thing standing between Elise and a gut full of bullets. He was supposed to just be a pawn in this game, but things had escalated, and he had been upgraded to a knight.

"You hungry?" he asked, no doubt trying diffuse my anger with the seduction of food.

"Yeah."

63

A half hour later, we were receiving platters of pancakes and eggs at a diner a few miles away. I stared down at the food in front of me. I couldn't even begin to concentrate. I needed to talk to Gary. I needed to find out what had gone wrong. How much danger were we really in, and for how long? I needed to know if there was any way to call off a hit once it was put in place. I had a feeling the answer was no.

I wondered how entrenched the mob was in the system, or how closely they monitored every detail of our lives. Gary and I had only wanted to use Elise to get to Moreau. Gary thought that the hit would validate her status as a valuable hacker, but perhaps it went further than that. Now, instead of seeing Elise as an asset to take interest in, they were seeing her as a threat.

"Where are we again?" I asked.

"Lower half of New Mexico. Why?"

"What do you suppose the chances are that we can make it over the border without being spotted?" I couldn't risk Elise any more than I already had. There is only one place that she would be safe from the constant surveillance that was assisting to track her down.

"Zero. Why would you consider leaving the country? Even if we could get out, we'd never get back in again. The feds will take blood and prints before they'll let us back in. You don't *want* to get back in?"

"No, of course I want back in. Where else but in the USA do I have the freedom to get a parking ticket thirty seconds after parking illegally, but yet have five murder attempts go unnoticed by anyone because the people trying to kill us own the fucking police?"

Layne frowned. "Some of us are trying to change that."

I nodded. "Yeah, I know." I did know; I happened to be one of the few that was trying to make that change. I wanted to tell him as much, but it was either too late or too soon to get into that. Until I had more information, I was at a standstill, not wanting to move in case it turned out to be the wrong move. "It just sucks that the police are only useful if unimportant people are trying to kill you."

"You should really eat. She didn't eat much yesterday."

"No appetite? Can't imagine why," I mumbled.

"Are you going to keep throwing that in my face? Cause I really don't need you adding to my guilt."

I ignored the defensive outburst. I hadn't really meant the statement as an attack on him anyway, just as an observation of how nearly dying tends to sap the appetite. "Tell me what happened last night. I woke up on your chest with cottonmouth and a headache, but judging by the amount of clothes we were both wearing, I doubt you took care of your secondary duties."

"I never accepted getting Elise laid as a secondary duty."

"You're right, it should be your primary duty. So what happened?"

He rolled his eyes, not wanting to answer. "We had a few drinks to take the edge off the day. She had a few more than me. We talked. We went back to the cabin. More talking, some arguing, we made up, and she fell asleep on me."

I rolled my eyes this time. "Fuck me, you're gay."

"What?"

"She hasn't gotten laid in a year, she almost died, and she was drunk. At what point was she going to get any riper for the plucking?"

"I wasn't going to take advantage her. Besides, this is already complicated. I don't want to add to it."

You have no idea. "There's nothing complicated about it, Layne. Just stick your dick in and push until she groans really loud." He immediately withdrew, uncomfortable with the latitude of my honesty.

"Deja, I'm not your pimp."

"Technically, you would be my whore. I would be your pimp and Elise would be my client, but since this would be a freebie, you don't have to feel dirty. Unless you want to." I winked, but he didn't smile. He was apparently losing his appreciation for my humor.

"Look, I'll protect Elise like we agreed, but anything else that happens is between her and me."

I looked at Layne, noting that there was something a little intentional about his statement. As if he had already anticipated that something might happen, even though he refused to be mandated to do it. "You like her, don't you?" He glared at me, answering my question. "You do. Why?" It didn't really surprise me. There were always people that appealed to one of us more, and likewise. Ironically—or perhaps karmically—those same people usually disliked the other one of us. It was as if our entire existence was designed to be at odds with everything around us... Or at least half of it.

However, this was the first time that I saw a commonality with a man that also took interest in Elise. I was curious how our common link of law enforcement and the fun-filled night of drinking and tattooing had been beaten out by boring little Elise Welch.

"Why do *you* like her?" he asked.

I chuckled. "Who said I did?"

"She's your backboard. She's the one that keeps you in line. She annoys the crap out of you, but I see how much you respect her for trying to hold things together, even when you're tearing them apart."

I couldn't help but smirk, thinking that Elise would be pummeling him for being presumptive enough to tell us about ourselves. I had to admit I wasn't a big fan of the psychoanalysis myself. Everyone thought they understood what it was like to share a body, but really they had no idea. It was as crowded as it was lonely. "I suppose I do. I think we both know that she severely underestimates my abilities, though."

"Yes, I think she does underestimate you, but you've never given her reason not to. Your notes are lewd, dismissive, and lacking detail. You haven't been straightforward with her about a lot of things, and I think she just assumes that you are responsible for every bad thing that's ever happened to her, because you won't back her up."

My heart started to race as I listened to his words. My territorial instincts were screaming for me to knock this guy down. If it weren't for the fact that he was right, I might have.

"Look, I'm not trying to create any friction here. I just see some misinterpretations of character that I want to correct. Even though I know you would rather I leave it alone."

"You're right. Elise does misinterpret me sometimes, but you're running under the assumption that I don't want it that way. So, yes, I would rather you leave it alone." I stared him down, making sure that he understood that his evaluation of our situation was not necessary. He didn't understand that most of what I did, most of what I didn't tell her, or lied to her about, was for her own protection. I knew what it looked like to her, and even what it looked like to him, but once again I was operating with my hero's cape hidden under a villain's cloak. And he could just bite me.

"Fine." He picked up his duffel and slid out of the booth. "But just for the record, I wasn't just talking about her misinterpretations." He walked away before I could ask him what he meant by that.

64

Layne gunned the engine of his Camaro to ninety as we headed south to Juarez, Mexico. I knew he wasn't on board with the plan but I wasn't really interested in his opinion. We needed to get out of sight, away from the eyes of Big Brother and his ugly uncle. Once we were over the border, it would be harder for us to be found. Elise would be safe, and I would have an opportunity to contact Gary and find out what the hell was going on.

I rolled down the window and dug my pack of cigarettes out. At the bottom of the purse I noticed our cellular earpiece blinking red. I frowned and looked at Layne. "I think I know why they found you."

"What? How?" I pulled it out and showed it to him. He understood the consequences right away. "Son of a bitch! I had no idea she used it."

"She must have left me a message. We never leave each other verbal messages, except appointment reminders." I pushed the phone in my ear, pressed the button, and requested playback. Elise's voice came through.

"I know you hate voice messages. It is a little weird hearing yourself update yourself on… yourself."

I listened to the oddly vulnerable message. Guilt poured over me as she admitted how scared she was.

Scared enough to want me back in control. She was right that I never expected her to say that. She had never acknowledged needing me before. If anything, she designed her life around *not* needing me. It was always a source of great pride for her to do as much as she could without my help. As much as I had to respect that determination, I also resented it. The less she needed me, the more it exacerbated how different our lives were.

I listened to the pause at the end of the recording. I knew she wanted to say more. As if she wasn't sure how to end her verbal letter: sincerely yours, cordially, best regards. Another strange thing about sharing a body was that you didn't know how to articulate your feelings toward your other half. Was it love? Was it hate? Or was it just necessity? That's why audio messages were so hard. It was weirdly challenging to your idea of independence, and assaulting to your psyche.

65

My left hand trembled against the table. I hadn't meant to hit him. I couldn't remember the last time I had used my power on someone in anger. I hated using it. The ghostly vibration that shimmered through my body always felt wrong to me. A power that was never meant to be wielded by man. At least not by one man.

I clenched my teeth, restraining the obscenities I wanted to attack him with. I knew he was just condemning me based on his interpretation of my character. It was easy enough for someone to assume that my cavalier attitude meant I was unfeeling, or indifferent to insult. Layne probably honestly did believe that I would prostitute myself—or Elise—to survive.

The waitress set down the drinks and requested her money. Once she was gone, Layne downed his drink, tossed a tip on the table, and walked out with the duffel bag.

I wanted to remind him that the money was conditional on my survival, but he needed a little space and so did I. I finished my own drink and headed outside. I scanned the dirty streets for signs of probing eyes and hidden weapons. Naturally, I found more than a few, but they didn't seem overly interested in me. I spotted a set of payphones across the street and ducked through the traffic to get to them.

I dug in my purse and pulled out my wallet. I slipped a few bucks into the machine and punched in the numbers for Gary's phone. After several rings he picked up. "Gary, what the fuck!"

"I know," he said on the other end.

"There's been another attempt on her life."

"I was afraid of that."

"What's going on? Why is this happening?"

"I screwed up."

"What do you mean?"

"I'll explain when I see you."

"I can't wait that long."

"You won't have to. Meet me at the Hotel Plaza in a couple hours."

"You're here? How?"

"I'll explain when I see you." I heard the click and stared at the receiver. Rather than call him back, I started searching the pages of the disheveled phone book for the address to the Hotel Plaza.

66

It didn't take long to get to the hotel. Waiting for Gary, however, took forever. By the time he arrived I was so pissed off I nearly decked him when he tried to hug me. I shoved him back using a little more force than necessary. "What the hell is wrong with you?" I griped. "Are you going to tell me what's going on or not?"

"Let's talk in private."

He went to the front desk and immediately booked a room. I followed him back toward the elevators and gritted my teeth as we waited for it to arrive. He glanced over at me, surveying my condition and my mood with increasing concern.

The elevator opened and I jumped inside, more than ready to have some alone time so I could scream at my partner. Unfortunately he had different plans. When the doors shut, he pounced on me, pressing me against the wall, kissing me.

Once again I shoved him off and he hit the wall on the other side with a heavy smack. He panted and stared at me with disappointment, but he didn't try to come back for more. "I'm sorry. I'm just really glad you're okay."

"No thanks to you. I thought you could get this under control."

"So did I. I didn't think it would be so technical. Who knew that requesting a hit would be so litigious?" Gary rubbed his eyes and for the first time I noticed how bloodshot they were. I wondered if he had driven straight through from Boulder. I tried to calculate when he would have had to leave to arrive now, but it didn't make any sense that he would drive straight down to Mexico.

"What am I supposed to do? I can't keep protecting Elise like this." The elevator stopped and we got off, sidestepping an elderly couple as we did. Despite their innocuous nature, both Gary and I gave them a quick once-over before continuing our conversation down the hall. "I don't think Layne is going to hang on much longer. He is getting frustrated that I don't have the answers to his questions. I'm getting frustrated that I don't have enough lies to cover up the mess that I've gotten us into."

"*We* got us into this mess. This was our decision together."

"Good, then *you* can tell Elise why we can't ever go home again." We got to our designated room Gary opened the door with his key card. We slipped inside and gave the room once-over before getting down to business.

Once again, Gary had different ideas about what our business should be. He wrapped his arms around my waist, hugging me from behind. He pressed his face alongside mine and took in a stuttered breath. "I'm so sorry," he whispered. "I didn't mean to put you in danger." I scoffed and tried to pull this hands off me.

"Just let me hold you for a second."

"We need to figure this out."

"Yes, we do, but I am not going to be able to concentrate unless you let me have my way." He kissed my temple. "I don't think you realize how worried I was." I huffed, thinking about the many reasons I hadn't slept with my partner over the years. Namely, the clinginess that would inevitably follow. "Let me show you how much I missed you," he whispered in my ear, and shoved his hand down the front of my pants.

"Damn it, Gary." I shook my head at his antics. We were in the middle of a life-and-mostly-death situation, and he literally couldn't stay out of my pants. "I did not come here to..." I started to lose focus on my words as his hand started to make some leeway for his argument. "This is serious."

"It is serious and I have a lot to tell you."

"You do? Like what?" I perked up and twisted to look at him. He smiled at me.

"There she is. There's that cop instinct."

"Tell me what you know."

His smile turned to a smirk. "How about you get down on all fours for me first?"

"How about I punch your face in?"

His smirk drooped into a sullen frown and he slid his hand out of my pants. I was a little disappointed to see that he hadn't fought harder to win his battle, but I also knew that he wasn't a fan of rough sex—especially when he was likely to be on the receiving end of the mistreatment.

He moved over to the bed and sat down. He

resituated to relieve the pressure binding his pants. "I have a little good news, if you can even call it that," he said, instantly back into cop mode. "Obviously I didn't understand what I was getting into when I put out a hit on you. Apparently, the first bidder only has so long to get his bounty. Since I never actually killed you, someone else jumped in."

"They'll just keep coming until I'm dead?"

"Essentially. We also seem to have drawn some additional attention with this stunt. As we suspected, putting out a hit on you has prompted some other key players to ante in. Whoever they are or however they are connected with the government, they seem to think that it's in their best interests to have you taken out as well. So right now we've got two competing bids. The first one, obviously, is mine and the second I believe is either from Elliott or Moreau. My money is on Moreau."

"I thought you said you had good news."

"I said I have a little good news. There's been a little talk about a third party being interested in your bid. It seems Devitti has been asking about you. He wants you brought in alive."

"Alive? You're saying we got a bite?"

"Yeah, that's what I'm saying. I'm not sure how you want to play this, though. You still have people gunning for you. Unless Devitti can get some men to you first, you are still in a lot of danger."

"What's the best-case scenario here?"

"The best-case scenario is that his men find you, take you into custody, and take you back to him."

"Then what?"

"Depends who is who at that time, but one way or another he is gonna want Elise to prove her hacker skills. If she can, then she will be our inside man."

"And I will be the mole. Holy shit!" I chuckled, thinking how far we've come, how much effort we had gone through to try to get inside this network of mobsters and back alley politicians. To think, all we had to do was use Elise as bait and shove her into the line of fire. Why didn't we do this sooner? "This could work."

"Yeah, it could, but it could also go horribly wrong. We need to think about this. We need to think about what the best choice is for everyone involved."

"What do you mean? This was practically your idea. In fact, it *was* your idea. It got screwed to hell, but we just skipped all the bullshit. We are on the cusp of taking down a major player. Why are you backpedaling now?" I stared at him as he shook his head. He looked everywhere but at me. "Crap, Gary, don't do this to me."

"Do what? Be reasonable?"

"Oh please! Are you saying all this because we slept together? Are you seriously trying to protect me? To save me, like some white fucking knight?"

"Yeah, I am." He stared at me with wide eyes. "Like that is such a horrible thing."

"We have been working towards this for years. Hell, how many men and women have died on this very same pursuit? We finally have an in. I could be feeding you information from the inside. They won't even suspect me, because I will be what everyone always assumes I am. The worthless half-wit twin soul that drinks too much and fucks too much. It's perfect!"

"You're right. It's everything that we've been working for, but you know what? I don't give a shit. I realized the other day how much I care about—"

"Oh geez, Gary!"

"Bite me, Deja! When I saw that second bid come through I got in the car and drove. All I could think about was getting to you. All I could think about was saving you. If that makes me an asshole in your eyes, then so be it. Damn if I'm going to be the asshole who doesn't show up." He stood up and moved to me. His eyes flickered over mine as he contemplated his words. "I don't want you to die. Do you understand me? You want to keep doing this, I understand, but I just want you to know before you make that choice that I would be just as happy helping you run away."

I narrowed my eyes on him. Without even knowing it, he had made my decision for me. "I don't run away, Gary. That's not what I do."

"I know," he said, looking defeated. "There's only one thing that you run away from." He brushed past me and opened the door. He mumbled something about getting a soda before shutting the door behind him.

67

I sat on the bed and contemplated my life. Not Elise's life, or the life that I currently was living, but what I really wanted. The truth was, more than anything I just wanted to make a difference. I wanted something that I did to make an impact on the world. I had a chance to be the good guy. I had a chance to bring down the bad guys. And I wanted to do it.

It took Gary nearly 15 minutes to get his soda. When he returned his hands were empty. He looked irritated, but when he saw me on the bed he frowned. "I'm sorry."

"For what?" I asked.

"For suggesting that you should give up. I know that's not you. I shouldn't ask you to walk away from this just because I let myself get wrapped up in my emotions." He paused as if he wanted to give me time to offer my own apology, but so far I didn't think I had said anything to warrant it. "I have something for you."

"What's that?"

He moved to his bag on the chair by the television and unzipped the side pocket. "It's a humper."

"If you pull a condom out of that bag, I will hurt you."

Gary chuckled and shook his head. "No, it's not a condom." He pulled out a long cylinder wrapped in pink.

"You want to give me a tampon?" I perked an eyebrow at him.

"It looks like a tampon. Nobody will be suspicious if you wanna slip off to the bathroom for your monthly business. I guarantee nobody's gonna ask twice about why you have that in your hand if you get caught."

"But what is it?" I took the package from him and slipped off the wrapper. Inside was the traditional cardboard tubing, but inside of that was a petite little memory stick.

"It's basically Elise in pocket form. If the opportunity should arise to access one of Devitti's computers, just open that baby up and stick it into an open USB slot. Not only will it download the information off that computer, but it will tap into any computer on the network. And it will broadcast its own Wi-Fi signal, allowing us to download the data without ever alerting Devitti of our presence on his system. It's going to make your job a lot easier and a lot quicker. Not to mention, if something goes wrong, we'll still be able to nail Devitti to the wall."

"You know none of this will be admissible in court."

"Doesn't need to be. All we need to do is cut off his people. De-weed the system, so the rest of us can do our jobs the right way."

"That's genius."

Gary shrugged. "I didn't invent it. I just bought it off the black market."

I put the device back in its cardboard case and then

in the wrapper. I slipped it into my purse, along with all my other crap. It would camouflage nicely with the mascara and lipstick. "I guess it's all figured out. Except the part where I have to try to stay alive until Devitti can catch me. That will be a surprise for everyone involved."

Gary bobbed his head and crossed his arms. "Yeah, I guess so."

"There is one thing that I haven't figured out yet." I pulled Layne's gun from the purse and turned it on Gary. "How the fuck did you know I was in Juarez?"

68

"Are you seriously pointing a gun at me?" Gary dropped his arms and circled out of the corner he had put himself in.

"Are you seriously blind? What does it look like I'm doing?" I circled the gun with him, keeping a solid aim on his heart.

"Your partner. Your lover."

"I'm not your lover."

"The fuck you're not!" Gary yelled back at me. "What is wrong with you?"

"Tell me how you knew I was here!"

"I already told you!"

"No, you didn't."

"Yes, I did. Right before you hung up on me. I told you that I put a tracker in your purse."

"Tracker? Why did you put a tracker in my purse?"

"Just in case."

"Just in case of what? You wanted to stalk me?"

Gary's eyes pinched shut, as if he loathed to answer the question. "I put it there as a precaution when you started going after Arthur Devitti. In case you got into trouble."

My mind slowly wrapped around that thought. I smiled at him, but the civility didn't comfort him. "Why is it still there? Why didn't you tell me about it, Gary?"

I asked sweetly.

"Come on, Deja. Don't make me say it."

"I think you are gonna have to."

"I kept it there so that I could find you. In case one of those reject one-night stands turned out to be a freak. Or in case—"

"Tell me you haven't been spying on me, Gary. Tell me you haven't been monitoring my activities on my nights off."

"I know it sounds bad."

"Sounds creepy as fuck, Gary."

He nodded. "I know. I was always going to tell you, but I just didn't. I liked being able to watch over you.

"Oh, Gary!" I dropped the gun and groaned. I stared at the floor, trying to decide how angry I was. Gary was a lovesick puppy with a cop mentality. It wasn't just good enough for him to stand outside my window with a boombox, he had to arrest the band and bring them to my house.

"I thought you heard me on the phone. I thought that was why you hung up."

"No, I hung up because I thought you were going to say I love you."

Gary's eyes narrowed into slits. "First of all, I'm not an I love you type of guy."

"What do you mean you aren't an I love you guy? You just admitted to stalking me."

"I wasn't stalking, just monitoring you for your own safety.

"You just called me your lover."

"Because I didn't think you would like the sound of

'boyfriend'."

"You are not my boyfriend."

"Yeah, I am," he argued.

"No, you are not," I said more sternly.

His vacant stare morphed into something more anguished. "Yes, I am." He moved toward me and I raised the gun again. He pushed up against it, pushing into my space despite the threat of the bullet to his chest. "Yes, I am," he whispered and wrapped me up in another kiss.

I moved the gun away so I didn't accidentally shoot him in heat of the moment. He pulled away and glanced at the bed. "Do you see that bed over there?" I rolled my eyes at his lame provocation. "You and I are going over there, to settle this once and for all. If you don't like that, then you'd better shoot me."

I grimaced and actually considered using the gun on him. It might have been easier. I liked Gary, more than I could admit. Not because of the sex—although that had definitely worked in his favor—but because he was my friend. I trusted him enough to reveal my condition to him. I trusted him with my life. I didn't even mind that he had been stalking me. In a demented way, it actually made me feel safe. Because despite the personal violation, it was all for me. He was my stalker. My very own creepy stalker.

But now Gary was asking for more. The touchy feely boyfriend/girlfriend stuff. As long as it had been since Elise had done that route, it had been even longer for me.

I wanted to tell him no. I wanted to explain how it

wouldn't work, and how history was a precursor to the future, but I didn't.

Gary pulled the gun out of my hand and dropped it back in my purse. He started to push me toward the bed, but I couldn't make my feet move. They were the only ones listening to the argument in my mind.

He didn't bother trying to convince me to move. He just picked me up and tossed me on the bed. He offered me a sly smirk. "Are you my girlfriend yet?"

I snorted and shook my head.

He crawled up on the bed and straddled me, pinning me with his hips. I smirked at the oddly nonsensical positioning. We hadn't even taken our clothes off. "Are you or are you not my girlfriend?"

I chuckled at him. "What are you even playing at? I thought you were going make love to me until I was so intoxicated with orgasm that I would say yes," I mocked.

Gary's brow knitted with the apparent naivety of my statement. "No, I'll make love to you if and when you agree to be my girlfriend."

"And how are you going to make that happen?"

"With these." He wiggled his fingers and I shook my head.

"You'd better not be doing what I—" I squealed as Gary's dexterous little digits dove at my belly and pinched my thigh under my butt. I squirmed, laughing at the absolute absurdity of his tactics. I tried to shove him off, but I could barely breathe, let alone concentrate on my strength. When all else failed, I screamed, "Okay, I'm your girlfriend!"

Gary wasted no time transitioning from tickle monster to an animal between the sheets. He ripped off his clothes and mine and dove onto me, his lips devouring every surface he could reach before inserting himself.

He pulled me up, letting me ride on him so he could watch my climax. He laid me back down and did it all again, joining me in the finale.

Nearly an hour later, I withdrew from his embrace started to collect my purse. "Wait," Gary said groggily from the bed.

"Seriously, how are you not spent?"

He chuckled and rolled over to look at me. "Not that, but thanks for the vote of confidence. I just wanted to tell you that I still have your back."

"Thanks." I put my clothes on and headed for the door. I stopped and went back to the bed. I leaned in and gave him a goodbye kiss.

"Hmm, a goodbye kiss. You might be better at this girlfriend bit than you think."

"Shut up, Gary." I smacked his shoulder.

He chuckled and lay back in the bed. "You know, I might have another round in me. If you have the time."

"I should be getting back." I glanced at my watch. I was certain Layne would be waking up from his siesta soon. "I have another stop to make anyway."

"Another stop?" Gary sat up, almost immediately concerned. "Need me to come with?"

"No." I shook my head. "It isn't dangerous. Just personal."

"Okay. Well, be careful anyway." Gary leaned back down and I headed out. If I timed my stop right, I would still make it back in time for the festival.

69

Moreau stared me down like a pig on a platter. I hadn't met the man once in my life, but somehow not only did he know my face, but he also knew my career as an undercover cop. Once again, there were no secrets in a world filled with computers, cameras and nosy pricks.

Devitti looked baffled for a moment, but his eyes eventually set on me, sinking into a dark threat. I couldn't afford a look to Layne, but I knew he was probably looking at me with shocked realization. He was only beginning to know the truth about me, along with Devitti and the rest of his entourage.

"That—" Devitti started to yell.

I punched my fist into his throat, most likely permanently damaging his vocal cords. He grappled at his neck, sputtering and choking. The room erupted into stunned alertness as Devitti flailed his arms, signaling for his men to attack me.

Moreau jumped at me, trying to use his enormous body to subdue me. He may well have been as strong as two men, but so was I—and then some. I punched his chest, pinpointing the bulk of my power on his ribcage. The bones cracked loudly.

He dropped to the floor groaning in pain. His bodyguards leapt forward to grab me. Fortunately, everyone's firearms were left at the door, so we were just down to fists and feet. At least until somebody went to retrieve them.

I knocked one man out cold with one punch. The other one tackled me, dropping me to the floor with his muscular weight. Before I could kick him off, Layne punched him in the side of the face, detouring his stranglehold on my neck. I shoved him to the side and took Layne's hand to help myself up.

"What the hell is going on?" he barked at me as he scanned the room for the next attackers.

I noticed Devitti being dragged out of the room by his loyal guard dogs. The more hoity-toity members of the party also scrambled towards the door. The women screeched and the men bellowed objections about the disruption as if they were already plotting to sue Devitti for the emotional stress.

"We're getting out of here," I answered.

Three more men arrived. Layne growled and punched one. With my knuckles already sore from broken ribcages, I shoved the palms of my hands into the two oncoming chests, relying mostly on my power. They were propelled back several yards, landing on the wood floor with heavy thumps.

"Now you want to get out of here?" Layne asked. "I thought you wanted to stay."

"We're going to have to talk about this later." I grabbed his arm and tugged him towards the door just as the lights went out.

"What happened?" Layne asked.

"I'm not sure, but I'm hoping it's the cavalry." I pulled him along as my eyes started to adjust to the darkened ballroom. There were a few candles on the table, lit in preparation for dinner, but the room was windowless, making our only option for escape the double doors we had entered through.

We shuffled forward, sneaking despite the fact that there were still screams coming from down the hall. Just as we reached the doorway a tall dark figure stepped into my path. I threw out my fist once again, this time toward the soft belly to keep my knuckles happy.

The power that I possessed should've vaulted the man into the wall behind him. Instead a reciprocating vibration deflected me like a shield.

I looked up at the dyad, narrowing my eyes on his stubborn features. Somehow I already knew the answer to the question I wasn't asking. He was far more experienced, and therefore stronger. I wasn't going anywhere unless he allowed it.

Layne made the effort to go in for a punch as well, but he was tossed back like a ragdoll. Watching a similar power as mine from the exterior was humbling. I had never met another like myself, and probably never would again. We were rare, and even rarer was one so open about it.

He raised his hands as if he was going to hug me. He clamped down on my arms and picked me up. He threw me across the room. I landed on the table, knocking down one of the candles. I moaned about the ache in my back and rolled off the table.

I hobbled a few steps before I could get myself upright and face my attacker. "Hello, Douche," I snarled.

"It's Thatcher now," he corrected with a little twitch in his lip. "Are you really a cop?" he asked with depth in his voice I hadn't noticed earlier.

"Yeah, I'm really a cop," I said from the safety of my table barrier.

"You were bullshitting us the whole time?" He came further into the room when it was clear I wasn't going to come to him.

"No, Elise was real. She has no idea what I do. I used her skills to get close to Moreau. Which, given that he knows exactly who I am, I'm starting to realize why it never worked. Actually, I'm really glad that things worked out this way. Devitti always was the biggest dick."

"Cover's blown, though. Must be disappointing that you aren't going to get him after all."

The sound of gunfire drew our attention. Thatcher looked back at me for an explanation. I didn't have one, but I had my suspicions, which made me smile.

"It's not a complete waste. All I really needed to do was get inside this house." I chuckled. "You guys brought her straight here, all the while assuming she was a prize, when in reality she was a Trojan horse." I winked at him.

Thatcher frowned, apparently not appreciating the humor of the situation. He lunged forward, shoving the entire mahogany table at me. I jumped up, barely missing being squashed against the fireplace. I landed on the table and kicked him in the face. Since he wasn't ready for me, the full impact whipped his head back.

I leapt on him while he was still distracted. I lassoed my hands around his neck and attempted to cut off his air. He grabbed hold of my hair and flipped me off. I skidded along the floor minus his fistful of my hair.

I roared in anger and jumped up to continue the fight, but froze. I stared at the barrel facing me. Thatcher was no longer interested in testing his strength on me. It was time to put an end to me. There wasn't much I could do. I considered pleading for my life. I even considered running away.

There was a first for everything.

I heard Layne scream behind me. The bullet echoed through the room, just as I was propelled forward. My chest erupted in pain. My lungs burned. The pressure on my back released as fast as it had arrived. I landed on the floor face first.

I looked up at the flashlights spiraling around the room. Men were screaming all around me, demanding Thatcher get down on his knees. The dyad looked down at me, venom still in his eyes, and his gun still aimed at my face. I shook my head, warning or perhaps begging him not to do it.

Something must've registered, because his eyes started to descend along with his gun. He carefully dropped it to the ground and got down on his knees. He carefully folded his hands behind his head. He frowned at me again. "Tell her I'm sorry I couldn't be more."

I frowned at the statement, but before I could question his meaning, the SWAT team surrounded him. They pointed shotguns in his face, barking more orders at him. They restrained his hands and legs before carrying him out of the room like a pig on a spit.

"Welch!" a familiar voice called me. I looked over and saw Gary in full SWAT gear. He moved over to me and flipped up his face shield. He carefully pulled me upright and gave me a quick kiss. He looked at my chest. "Shit, you've been hit. Looks like he got the worst of it, though." He nodded behind me.

"What?" I frowned and turned around despite the pain that electrified my every movement.

Layne was sprawled on the floor behind me, a wound similar to mine in his shoulder. It was a little too low, and there was way too much blood. He was barely conscious. The three men surrounding him were demanding that he "stay with us." They started calling in on the radios for the paramedics and my heart seized. I looked to Gary. "You can't let him die. She loves him."

Gary looked from me to the man nearly dead on the floor in front of us. I could see his eyes skirting the edges of his body where blood was pooling onto the floor. He looked back at me and nodded. "They'll get him fixed up."

"Don't lie to me." I coughed and tasted iron. Gary's eyes drifted to my mouth.

"I'm getting you out of here." He lifted me up, but I pushed him away with my power. He fell back, dropping me back to the floor.

"Layne!" I crawled toward his body.

"Goddammit, Welch!" Gary moved back to me. "You've been shot. You need medical attention."

"I have to tell him." I didn't know how to categorize my emotions; the guilty grief of a lifetime of disappointments delivered by my own hands. I couldn't gift wrap Elise's dead lover too. It was too much. It was unforgivable. I at least had to tell him.

Gary grabbed me again, but instead of taking me away from Layne, he pushed through the bevy of men to get me close to him. I turned my head and coughed blood onto Gary's neck. I grimaced and he shook his head. "Get it done, Welch."

I turned to Layne. He was barely there, but his lolling eyes locked onto mine and I hoped his fading ears could hear me. I knew he had only saved me to save Elise, but it didn't matter. He was as much my hero as hers. I owed him a lot more than a bag full of money. "Layne." I grabbed his hand.

"You're alive." He squeezed my hand.

"Yeah, you saved her. You saved Elise."

"I saved you. Elise was just a bonus."

I turned away to cough again. I could feel my lungs getting heavy with each breath. "I lied to you."

"Yeah, you're a cop."

"No, about Elise. About what she feels for you." His

brow dipped. "She loves you."

"I love her too, Deja," he rasped.

The paramedics arrived in fine form, scooping Layne up onto a gurney and inserting an IV in record time. They pushed him away, placing a breathing mask on his face and shouting medical jargon that sounded less than promising.

Soon enough I had my own cluster of paramedics. Gary placed me on my own gurney, and I felt myself fall away, as if I had fallen completely through the mattress. "I can't feel my body," I said, but I wasn't sure anyone heard it.

I watched the bed roll away, listening to them shouting the same medical litany. Before I knew it, I was gone, and yet I was still standing there. I looked around the ballroom, which was barely more than a few lit candles.

In the shadows, I could see a figure—my reflection in a standing mirror. She looked back at me and shook her head. "*Now* what did you do?"

71

I stared back at my reflection. I could tell it was Elise. Something about the eyes. Layne had commented that my eyes were beautiful, but Elise's were alluring in a different way. She always looked sweet and innocent. A window into the soul? Perhaps. Or perhaps we just put so much expectation on what we saw that we in turn created it.

"What is this place?" Elise stepped out from behind the mirror, which turned out to be only glass.

I looked around the etch-a-sketch room that had recently been shaken. The few lit candles were the only thing lighting our conversation, but even they looked elongated, like someone had smeared the image. "I think we are on the psychic plane," I said.

"What is that?"

"I think it's where we go when we aren't in control of the body."

Elise looked me over, inspecting my image for the first time without the handicap of a false reflection. "Why are we here together?" She frowned. "Are we dead? You got us killed, didn't you?"

I clenched my jaw and shook my head. "We've been shot."

"Shot? Oh my God, Deja!"

"Enough!" I yelled at her and she winced at the

volume that shook through the room like an earthquake. I took a breath and moved closer to her. "I know I've screwed up, but not for the reasons that you think. I am somebody, Elise."

"What?"

I took a breath to control the pain in my voice. "I am a person. I am not Elise Welch. I am my own person."

"I know that." She dismissed the statement.

"Do you?" I asked her. "Do you really?"

"Why are you telling me this?"

"Because I can't do this anymore. There is no way out and I'm either about to die or I'm about to go back to a life that I can't live anymore."

Elise frowned and moved forward. She raised her hand to touch me, but stopped short. She was no doubt wondering if we could touch or should touch. "Are you saying you want to separate?"

"No, forget about that shaman shit. We don't need to separate, Elise. We just need to identify ourselves. We need to just start over."

"Okay," she whispered. "Do you want to move again?"

I chuckled and shook my head. "Do you really want to know what I want?"

She looked me over and swallowed hard. "Yes, Deja. I really do."

"I want to be *seen*!"

"What do you mean?"

"I want to be seen for who I am! I want to trade in that ridiculous puke green SUV and get something black. I don't care what it is—car, truck, hybrid—but I want it to be black, or at the very least something that doesn't look like it came out of an orifice." To my surprise, Elise snorted at my joke. "I want to cut my hair." I could see her eyes light with concern so I raised my finger. "Not too short. Just short enough so it doesn't take me an hour to blow-dry it."

"Okay, what else?" Elise took my requests in stride. I was actually surprised she was even listening, let alone agreeing. I suppose at this point it was still a dream to her.

"I want..." I paused as a wave of dizziness nearly toppled me. Elise started to reach for me, but I waved her off. "I'm fine." I cleared my throat, tasting iron on my tongue again. I smiled at Elise's concern for me. "I want something else."

"What?"

"I want you to try to make things work with Layne."

She shook her head. "Deja, we both know that doesn't work."

"It will this time. He loves you. And oddly, he doesn't detest me."

"But how—?"

"It doesn't matter. You and he will figure your end out. He and I will figure out our end. I will make accommodations in my life for him."

"Why? Why now?"

"Because—" I coughed, spitting blood onto my hand. I tried to hide it, but Elise saw it and her face wilted.

"What's happening?"

"Um, I think I'm dying." She shook her head. "It's okay. I think it will just be me. When you wake up, you'll be just you."

She shook her head, tears balancing on her lower eyelid, just waiting to fall. "I don't want that. I never wanted you gone. Not forever."

"It's okay, Elise."

"No, it's not!" she yelled, rocking the room with her own volume. "I'm not ready to live this life on my own."

"You've been ready to live on your own since second grade." I took in a breath that hurt to my core. The room started to warble. My concentration, psychic or otherwise, was diminishing. "You'll do fine, Elise. When you wake up, Gary will explain everything. And when he does, just remember that I'm sorry. I'm sorry for everything." I tumbled forward, expecting to hit the ground, but Elise caught me and eased me to the floor.

I stared up at her endearing eyes. Her power in her hands prickled against my skin where she held me. She narrowed her eyes on me and raised her hand up, as if she was asking me for a high five. I slowly raised my hand to her and our palms slid into place, mirroring each other.

An electric riptide coursed through my arm and into my body, reducing my pain to a whisper. Instead of tingling stings, the connection felt like an instant adrenaline high.

I looked to Elise and the smile curving across her face. "What is that? What's happening?"

She looked down on me and shook her head. "I don't know, but I do know that you aren't going anywhere just yet."

The last thing I remembered on that psychic plane was a flare of white light and an intense heat that made hell seem like a winter home.

72

As was par for the course lately, I woke to yet a new bed. A hospital bed, by the sound of the annoying bleeps beside me. In addition to the new surroundings, I had a new pain. I grimaced at the ache in my chest, which had likely forced my still-aching finger to the backseat of my mind. I squinted at the sun streaming through the window. Despite my usual two-day break from consciousness, I still felt exhausted.

I tried to shift up in the bed, but a bolt of pain made me yelp and flop back down to my pillow.

"Take it easy, Elise," a man's voice conditioned from the foot of the bed.

I opened my eyes wide and took in the stranger seated in a chair in front of the window. I could barely make out his features amid the bright sunlight. Tall, strong, dirty-blond hair, and a shoulder holster containing a gun.

I quickly remembered my dealings with Devitti and his men. I wasn't sure what trouble Deja had gotten me into, but if it involved guns and hospitals, then we were in more danger than I realized.

Disregarding the pain that it caused, I disconnected the IV in my forearm, flipped off the bed, and ran out the slightly ajar room door. I saw the nurse's hub and turned the other way. I wasn't sure who was being paid by whom, but I wasn't about to find out.

With my ass exposed to the elements and my feet as bare as my ass, I ran down the hall and to a set of stairs. I couldn't jump the rails in my condition so I just focused on my steps so I didn't trip on them.

I heard a door open behind me and a man yelling my name, but that made no difference to me. Knowing my name didn't preclude him from being a murdering asshole. I suddenly wondered who had shot Deja. I wasn't sure why, but I had a feeling I was going to be disappointed when I found out who it was.

Since I wasn't as speedy as I usually was in my getaways, I jumped in on the next level and took an immediate detour into a room. The man in the bed was elderly and on life support. I grimaced at my own desperation, but still opened the door to his little locker. I pulled out his pants and slipped them on. He was taller than me, but not by much.

I struggled to get the shirt on. It was button-up and plaid, obviously a man's, but that didn't matter. The boots were next, but they didn't fit at all. I settled for the nonslip hospital slippers and let the pant legs cover them. After that, it was just a matter of covering my hair with a hat. Thankfully this gentleman was just old enough to be fashionable. I tucked my hair into the short-brimmed hat, and slipped on his jacket to hide my feminine curves.

I peeked out the door, but didn't see the man that was in my room. I slipped through the door, once again avoiding the nursing staff. I shuffled down the hall slumped like a hunchback and slow as molasses. I pressed the door to the elevator and rode down with a man in a wheelchair.

As he was leaving the elevator, I slipped in behind him and asked in my best rasping voice if I could lean on his chair until we got to the front door. He happily obliged, no doubt happy to serve a little sympathy for a change.

When I reached the door, I grunted a thank you and hobbled outside. I breathed in the arid, stagnant air and coughed. The pain in my lung told me more than any chart could. I would have to take this a little slower or risk opening my injury again.

I looked around the parking lot. I hadn't had a chance to grab my purse, but I didn't see my vehicle anyway. I did, however, see a bus stop and if I wasn't mistaken… I felt around in my back pocket and pulled out a wallet. I opened it and saw ample money. I cringed at the idea of robbing the old man blind as well as naked, but it was an emergency.

I walked to the bus stop and sat down to wait. I started to identify the markers of a gambling town. I finally saw the words I dreaded: Las Vegas. I was still in Vegas. Still being stalked by mob men, targeted for death, threatened into hacking, and damn it if the day wasn't hotter than hell on Tuesday.

I heard the bus creaking down the street and I pulled out a few crisp dollar bills in preparation. I felt someone sit down on the bench beside me, but I didn't look. I just kept my head down, disguising my identity.

"Oh, you're good," a man said. "She told me you were good, but I didn't think you would be *this* good."

I turned to look at the face of my would-be murderer. The features coalesced in my mind and the memory of Gary... something, sprang to my mind. The man who had put the hit out on me. The man who started it all.

The bus pulled to a stop in front of us, exhaling a waft of diesel. I glanced at it and the people filing off of it. "Don't," Gary said and patted the bulge in his coat.

I frowned as the bus doors closed and it drove away. The people around us scattered, going about the business of their day. I swallowed hard, trying not to start crying. Deja would be so disappointed if she found out my last moments on earth were spent quivering like a ninny.

"Would you believe me if I told you I won't hurt you?" Gary asked. I shook my head, staring off into the street. "Good, then we can skip that part." He stood up and offered his hand. After a moment he waggled his fingers, demanding that I stand.

I took his hand, allowing him to assist my rise. I wavered with feigned dizziness and fell against him. I tucked my free hand toward his holster and grabbed the gun. As I drew it free he grabbed my wrist and twisted the gun free. He chuckled as he returned the firearm and pulled my hands down to my sides. "Oh, Elise, you are so much more than I expected. She doesn't give you enough credit. I mean, brains and beauty, sure, but you're a little bit of a trickster too. That's good. I like that, but you really have to stop trying to get control of this situation."

I looked around the area for a way out. A good cop.

A bad boy willing to be a white knight. An old woman with a purse I could beat this man senseless with.

"You're still looking, aren't you? Stubborn in a different way. Okay, I can handle this. I've been handling Deja's shit for years, I think I can deal with you." Gary crossed his arms. "I am going to take you back to that hospital and put you back in bed. No ifs, ands or buts about it. You hear me?"

Rather than be the proper conscientious objector, I spat in his face. He gagged and wiped his face off. "Alright, now you just pissed me off. If you didn't have a gunshot wound, I would flip your ass over my shoulder and carry you back to the bed, but since you do I'm just going to ask very politely in a firm voice." Gary poked his finger at me. "Please go back to your hospital room, so you can heal and not die."

I stared at him, trying to figure out what he expected his angry voice to accomplish.

"Alright, look, I lied. I don't handle Deja. She doesn't listen to me either, but I do have to listen to her, and she'll kick my ass but good if anything happens to you."

"If anything happens to me? *You* are the reason I'm here!"

"I didn't shoot you."

"You put out the hit on me, you ass-hat!"

His mouth dropped open. "Oh, you mean... no— well yes, technically I did do that, but it wasn't actually meant to get you killed."

"I have a hole in my lung!" I screamed and immediately started coughing.

"Oh, no, no, no." Gary held up his hands in surrender. "You can't get all upset or it's going to damage the good doctor's work." He held up his hands as if in prayer. "Pretty please with sugar on top? Can we go back inside so I can explain everything? Or rather, so Deja can?"

"You have her letter?" I perked up, ready to grab onto the life preserver.

"Of sorts, but it will explain everything. Including why you shouldn't hurt me. At least not yet. We can discuss my very bad idea after you're feeling better." He put out his arm for me to lean on. "Come on, we need to get you up to speed on the last two years."

73

I watched Gary while the nurse put my IV back into place along with my blood oxygen clip. He watched me back, glancing away only when the nurse pulled my gown down to reattach my heart monitor pads and listen to my lung. When she was done, she gave me a stern lecture about the dangers of exertion after major surgery. I nodded timidly at the woman's barraging.

Gary chuckled once she was gone. "If I had known she was so stern, I would have sent *her* out to get you." He pulled his chair up close to the bed and sat down. "How are you feeling? You want any water?"

I nodded and he dutifully poured me a cup from the pitcher on my tray table. I drank in the whole glass, wondering when the last time was that I had drunk. "What day is it?" I asked.

"Ah, Monday, I think."

"Monday? I left on Monday."

"Yeah, Deja was in Tuesday." He counted the days on his fingers. "Wednesday, Thursday, Friday you were in a coma. She woke up mid-morning Saturday. And now you're waking up for the first time after the gunshot on Monday."

"So I just got skipped since she was healing up?"

"Not exactly. Technically you took over after she passed out from her wounds. I forgot to tell them that

Deja was allergic to penicillin, but when you didn't have a reaction I realized it was you." He shook his head. "Deja says that you saved her life."

"I did?" I frowned. "How?"

"I don't know. She didn't get too specific. She just said that you were looking out for her, like you always do. Like you always have. She was kind of cryptic about the whole thing so I didn't ask."

"I don't remember anything after Monday night. I barely remember—where's Layne?" I sat up and winced in pain.

"Easy, damn it." Gary pressed me back. "I'll get to all that, but I think it's best we get you up to speed on Deja and me."

"You're her probation officer."

"I was, but after that I talked her into joining the force. I'm her partner now. She's been working in my department for the last two years as an undercover cop. She's helped me take down a lot of low-level drug operations as well as some money-laundering networks. We've been trying to work our way up to the big mob bosses."

I stared at him and shook my head. "That's ridiculous. She couldn't hold a job, let alone be a cop. She drinks and gets into bar fights."

"You sure those were bar fights? Maybe she just got pinned down by a bunch of thugs intent on beating information out of her. Maybe she had a few drinks afterward so she didn't have to explain it to you."

I shook my head again, futilely trying to deny the statement, but suddenly… waking up in random places made sense. How many times had I woken up in an empty hotel room and assumed that she had hooked up, when in reality she was working undercover nearby?

Our rent would mysteriously get paid and I would assume the underhanded dealings of gambling when she was actually just gainfully employed.

When I woke up in the hospital— "My appendix?"

"Gunshot to the lower abdomen."

I gasped. "What the French!"

Gary smiled, but as he assessed the annoyance on my face he bit back his amusement. "Look, there's obviously room to be angry, and no one, least of all Deja, is denying that, but she does want a fair chance to explain herself, and to apologize."

"This ought to be a good read."

"Actually, she left you a video instead."

"Video?" I frowned. Audio messages were bad enough. I couldn't even imagine watching my other self update me as if we were sitting in the room with each other. As creepy as that was, I couldn't do anything until I heard from Deja. I needed her to give me something so I could move forward.

74

Gary handed me his phone and clicked the play button on the video paused on the oversized screen. Deja's face popped up on it. She was sitting on the hospital bed I was currently reclining in. It was surreal seeing her. Me, and yet not me. I knew the differences were subtle to others, but it seemed so obvious to me. It was perhaps just the eyes. The window into the soul always demanded its own set of shutters.

I gulped as I watched her converse with Gary behind the camera phone. Once they were both satisfied with their positioning, she looked up at me. Across the span of technology that we had always refused to use, she stared at me. I locked eyes with her, and for a moment we both stared as if we could see each other through time and space. A shiver ran through me, down to my toes and back up again. The worst case of déjà vu ever.

"Hi." She spoke. "Christ, that sounds stupid." She shook her head. "Can we start this over?" she asked, shifting her eyes away from me.

"No, just talk," Gary insisted off-camera. "If you try to perform it too much she's not even going to believe that you're telling her the truth. She's gonna think I have a gun to your head back here."

"You practically do," she remarked.

"Don't say that. Just start by introducing me. She's gonna wake up with a complete stranger next to her. Maybe she would like to know a little bit about me."

Deja looked back at the camera. "Elise, this is Gary; Gary, this is Elise." A head popped up on the screen as Gary moved the camera to get a view of his flaring nostrils and waving hand.

"Now tell her who I am," Gary instructed as he got the camera back into position.

"This is my partner."

"And?" Gary prodded.

"And what?" Deja's face crinkled.

"And I'm your..." Gary paused to let her fill in the blank. "Boyfriend."

Deja winced as if the word had actually struck her. "You are not my boyfriend."

"Yes, I am."

"No, you aren't," she argued.

Gary cleared his throat behind the camera. "Yes, I am," he said firmly.

I could see Deja's mouth trying to formulate a dozen cuss words simultaneously. Gary would be lucky if her jaw didn't unhinge and fire spew out. However, something unexpected happened. The venom in her gaze died down and with exasperated submission she looked back at the camera. "Gary is my partner and my... boy toy." Gary chuckled off-camera. "Satisfied?" she asked.

"Not entirely, but it's a start." I could hear the delight in Gary's voice, and I looked over at him listening in from his chair. I could see the subdued smile on his face as he stared down at the floor. "Okay, now time for the hard stuff. Tell her what you've been doing the last two years. The highlights, anyway."

I listened and watched as Deja retold the story of how she had taken a position on the local police force. She relayed details of her police work that had resulted in hospitalizations that Gary had helped disguise as domestic disputes and drunken brawls. I was amazed at the great lengths that she went to to hide the truth.

As I listened to the lies upon lies, my anger rose and I could barely stay seated. I wanted to jump into the screen and throttle her for her arrogance and her disrespect for our bond. As it went on though, I realized that she hadn't hidden it to defy me, or keep me at a distance. She had done it to protect me. The last week had nearly broken me. I couldn't imagine spending the last two years worrying about waking up with gunshot wounds, or being placed in a hostage situation.

She revealed her plots to infiltrated Devitti's criminal organization through his son, as well as the reasons why it didn't work. I smiled at that, happy to know that the slap I had received from him was at least at the expense of his achy crotch.

When she started to explain how she and Gary had plotted to manipulate me, and eventually use me as a pawn in their game, my anger broiled again, raising my blood pressure to new heights. The disregard she had for my safety made my chest ache. The lies that she had created just so she could do her job seemed so violating to my trust. I wanted to scream and cry, but there was no point. It was done with; this was her apology.

I knew that she was struggling to admit these truths to me, but it did prove that she wasn't without consideration for my feelings. Somewhere in the mix of things we had gotten caught up in our own lives and our own paths. The contradiction was making us both miserable, but perhaps now, with everything out on the table, we could start fresh again.

"I screwed up. I wanted to do something good. I wanted to do something important."

"You *did* do something important," Gary said off-camera. "We're about to put Devitti out of business. His empire is crumbling and half the country is going down with him."

"Do you think she cares about that? She's lying in a hospital bed that I put her in. She's not thinking about all the potential lives we've saved. She's just trying to figure out where that last witch doctor is so she can get rid of me once and for all."

"Witch doctor? What are you talking about?"

"Never mind." There was a long pause after her admission before she spoke again. "I almost got us killed. If it weren't for Layne, we would both be dead. And if he lives—"

"Don't say it like that," Gary reprimanded her. "He's doing better. A lot better." I looked to Gary and he was already nodding vigorously, reaffirming what he said in the video.

Deja nodded. "The bullet..." She pressed her hand to her chest, over her heart. "The bullet was headed straight at our heart." She paused to swallow. "Layne tried to push me out of the way, but it still hit the lung.

He got the worst of it. The bullet nicked an artery in his shoulder. He was bleeding—"

"That's enough," Gary interjected. "You're going to scare her. Just let me update her on Layne."

She took a breath. "He saved us both, Elise." She looked down at her hands, playing with her fingers. When she looked back up, she looked confused. "I wasn't doing too well either. I was sure you would wake up alone. So sure."

I frowned at the screen, my eyes already wetting at the thought of being alone. Alone for real. As much as I thought I wanted to separate myself from her, the thought of losing her entirely made me feel sick.

"I don't know how you did it." She looked back at the screen, her own eyes glistening. "Or maybe I do." She shook her head, smiling a little. "You've always looked out for me, Elise. I just had no idea how much." She smiled a little wider. "You are so much stronger than I ever thought you were. So much stronger than even you know." She stared through the screen at me, a small knowing smile on her face, as if she was immensely proud of something I had done, but I couldn't begin to know what it was. According to Gary I was in a coma after the gunshot. How useful was that?

The video stopped and I checked the feed to see if it had just gotten stuck. I wasn't ready to be done. I watched the last minute again, trying to decipher her subtextual monologue.

I stared at the blank screen for a long time. I didn't even know where to start.

"How you doing over there?" Gary finally asked.

I looked to him and filtered through every emotion running through my mind. "Are we okay? Are we still being hunted?"

"Not officially. The whole system is in an uproar. No one will have time to worry about you. Everyone is just scrambling to save their own asses. However, you and Deja will need to go off the grid for a while, until we can determine if you are still at risk."

"Can't I just hack into the system and erase the data related to the hit?"

"I've already taken care of that, but... You have to understand, you are no longer in danger per se. It's Deja now that has become the target."

"Why?"

He smiled, but quickly hid it. "I wasn't exaggerating, Elise. This stunt—as ridiculously ill-planned as it was, as arrogant and dangerous as it was —it took down a criminal empire. Thousands of men and women on Devitti's payroll are being lined up to be prosecuted as we speak. He is effectively dead in the water."

I smiled. "Does that mean the department is going to pay my hospital bills?"

Gary chuckled and nodded. "I'll be sure to send them the bill." He wet his lips and his eyes skirted my body, as if he needed to double check that he had the right twin. "Of course, since Deja is the name and face associated with this demise, there are a lot of people angry with her."

I took in a deep breath and grimaced. Gary shifted as if he might be able to stop my pain. "Should I get the nurse?"

"No, just tell me what happens now."

"What—you mean now or later?"

"Either, both. Give me a direction, Gary. I don't know what the next step is and I don't like that."

"Okay, umm, first you are going to continue to be bored off your ass and slightly drugged up until the doctor releases you. Then I will take you to a safe house." Gary leaned forward and licked his lips; the words he was trying to formulate didn't quite come out, but he was working hard.

"Spit it out, Gary."

"I'm going to be moving in with Deja. To protect her, and... because I want to."

I frowned at first, but then pushed a smile onto my face. "And she agreed to that?"

"Conditionally. You have to agree to it."

My frown returned and I nodded. "Of course."

"It's not like you think, Elise." Gary scooted forward. "I've thought about this a long time. Longer than I would like to admit." He grimaced. "The safe house is a townhouse with two units. I was thinking that you and Deja could each have one. You would just be a step away from home after you change." He cleared his throat. "The only thing is, you might occasionally wake up to my ugly mug lying beside you. Which admittedly is a little awkward." I watched him fold and unfold his hands. He was very anxious to get my answer.

"You love her, don't you?"

He frowned and nodded. "I've loved her for a long time. I never thought she would let me in. I always knew I would have to push her to get anywhere with her, but I also know that she can push back pretty hard when she wants to." He perked his brow.

"Just keep doing what you're doing. As complicated as Deja is, she's still a woman. She just wants to be recognized. To be seen for... who she is." Another palpable shiver of déjà vu went through my body.

"What is it?" Gary asked.

"Nothing." I shook my head. "Can I see Layne now?"

Gary nodded.

75

I leaned on my IV pole while I watched the nurse as she cut away Layne's old bandages to make room for the new. As she removed the pad soaked with blood, I got a good view of the bullet he had taken to save my life. Our lives. I glanced at Gary. He was politely standing at the door, giving me some space even though Layne was still too drugged to do more than smile at me and ask if my poodle got into the truck. Or something like that.

"Who did this?" I asked. "Was it Devitti?"

"No," Gary answered. "One of his men. Another twin mind."

"Dyad," I corrected and clenched my jaw. I knew he was capable of standing aside for a bullet, but I hadn't anticipated that he would pull the trigger himself. There was something ultimately insulting about that. Apparently I didn't know him as well as I thought I had. Or at all.

The nurse finished putting on the new dressing and turned back to me. "You should be in bed, miss."

I nodded. "I just want to stay a little longer." She smiled grimly and reluctantly left.

"I'll be right outside," Gary said as he pulled the door shut to give us privacy.

I sat down beside Layne and touched his hand. I

watched his beautiful slumbering face as I listened to the beeps and chirps of the machines monitoring him

I wasn't sure what had changed over the course of the last five days, but I felt different. Despite my brush with death, I wasn't afraid anymore. I didn't feel like I was alone. I felt whole, and it had nothing to do with Layne or Gary.

So many little puzzle pieces were coming together. Maybe they didn't form the entire picture, but it was more than I had ever had. For the first time in a long time, I could see a future. It didn't matter what it was, just that there was a plan. A purpose. Something that Deja and I could do together.

I had forgotten how important that was.

How important it was for two to be as one.

I couldn't help thinking about how much effort Deja had gone through to keep her identity secret. To protect me, of course, but also to protect herself. To keep me from taking it away from her.

Britt had compared Deja and me to a flipping coin. Either heads or tails. One side the face, and one side... not. But how often had that coin landed on heads, hiding the tails from view?

I stood and leaned over Layne. I kissed his lips gingerly. He stirred slightly and murmured, "I love you." I stared at him, trying to discern if he even knew it was me.

"I love you too, Layne," I whispered back even though he was long gone, back into his dreams of poodles and pick-up trucks.

As I stood back up, I noticed a pair of scissors on

Layne's tray table. The nurse had accidentally left them behind after she cut Layne's bandages off. I picked them up and examined them. The memory percolating in my mind was just out of reach, but I could feel it nonetheless.

I moved to the bathroom and switched on the light. I looked into the mirror. It wasn't the same as seeing Deja on the video. It was just me.

Maybe it shouldn't have been, though.

I combed my fingers through my hair, pulling the length down straight. I lifted the shears up, debating how high to go. I settled on a spot and snapped them shut. Several inches fell to the floor. They looked good there, so moved on to the rest.

New hair for a new beginning.

76

I needed to get back to Layne before he had withdrawals from his car, but I couldn't help stopping at the address that Elise had listed on her research about twin minds. I wasn't interested in killing her, and I certainly wasn't suicidal, but I was curious. Curious about what this guru would have to say about my kind. Despite the fact that I was a twin soul, I didn't really know anything about it.

The smell of cheap incense assaulted my nose as I looked around the so-called store. The usual metaphysical paraphernalia lined the shelves. An endless number of fat Buddhas, long dragons and crystal balls. The section on aromatherapy looked like an invitation to get nasal athlete's foot. To top it off, the woman behind the counter seemed to think that I was a shoplifter.

When I couldn't stand the stares any longer and the last of my enthusiasm disintegrated with my hope for mankind, I headed to the door. "Wait!" the woman yelled at me.

I turned back and glared at her. "I didn't steal anything."

"You here for doctor," she declared, sounding more like an angry Chinese woman instead of her own Hispanic descent.

I laughed. "Oh, a world of no, but thank you. I think I'll just get my medical care north of the border."

"You need to speak to the witch doctor!" she declared more forcefully.

I sighed and moved back to the counter. "How do you know that?"

She waved her hands around me. "Your aura is too full. You are two in one. You need advice, yes?"

"I don't know what I need."

"You are confused. You have doubts about your future. How to live a double life? How to find happiness? You are not happy."

I took a breath and nodded. She was pitching five for five. "So where is this witch doctor."

"I am the witch doctor."

"Oh."

"What, you wanted an old man with a long beard who talks in riddles? Okay, we'll try that." She turned in a circle and when she returned her face had changed to not only an old man's, but the exact old man I was picturing as she said it.

"Geez!" I stumbled away from the counter, ready to throw salt or holy water at the woman—or man. "What the hell?"

"Or maybe you prefer the irony of a deity reincarnated as a child." The old man turned and when his face returned, he was a young boy, Chinese, just as I had pictured.

"How are you doing this?"

"How do you think?" the boy asked.

"I don't know."

"You do know. You just don't want to admit it. You exist between two planes, and yet you refuse to accept the power it offers, because you prefer to ignore it. To you it isn't real. You use the power when you need it, but fight the provocation to use it at every turn. You are ashamed of who you are."

I shook my head, trying to deny it.

The boy clapped his hands and the store disappeared around me. "How are you doing this?"

"The mind is a powerful tool. Two minds are even more powerful. They transcend the realm of thought, and venture sure-footed into the psychic realm."

"Can we just go back to the woman? And skip the riddles."

The boy turned around and the woman reappeared, as did the shop I had originally been standing in. She smirked at me. "What's the matter? Don't like my parlor tricks?"

"How did you do that?"

"Easy. I tapped into your mind, and made you see it. That's the benefit of being able to access the psychic plane."

"Psychic what?"

She smiled at my ignorance. "Let's get you a drink."

I sat on the back porch of the woman's shop, which apparently was also her home. I sipped on the iced lemonade she had given me, which, to my relief, was spiked with a little vodka. I looked over at the shop owner. With her feet propped up on a milk crate and her drink in hand, she looked like she was on a beach instead of the rotting-out porch. Her sun-kissed face was also sun-aged. She couldn't have been more than forty, but the creases in her eyes said otherwise. Her long enviable black hair lay against her back in a perfect braid.

"So what do you want to know?" she asked, turning her gentle smile on me.

"I'm not sure."

"Oh, bullshit." She waved her hand at me. "You all want the same thing. You want to know what you are, who you should be, how to get along with your other self, how to unite yourselves, or how to detach yourselves, how to find love, how to raise a family." She took a sip of her lemonade through her curly straw and looked back at me. "Does that about sum it up?"

"Actually, I thought I would start with who you are, since that was never fully established."

"My name is Modesta. I am a humble shop owner and witch doctor to all that seek my help."

"Okay. *What* are you? Are you a twin mind like me?"

"I am something altogether different. I won't bore you with the details, but let's just say if two's company, then three's a crowd."

My face went slack as I tried to imagine three minds in one body. It was hard enough with two.

Modesta laughed. "Oh, honey, I already know what you're thinking, but it's not as bad as you think. Being the vessel for multiple souls, isn't a curse. It's a blessing. You just have to stop thinking about yourself in terms of two different people. You are the same person, just with a different perspective. You know what my grandfather used to say?" She leaned in to tell me. "You can't kill a chicken for dinner and still eat eggs for breakfast."

"And what does that mean?"

"It means if you want eggs don't kill the chicken."

"I meant how it applies to me."

"It applies to everyone. More, more, more, that's all anyone ever wants, but the truth is, life isn't supposed to be more of everything. It's supposed to be a series of choices. Each choice propels you into a different direction. First one, then the other. Before you know it, you are on a whole new path."

"That's all well and good, but I have two people making decisions, not just one."

"This way, that way, this way, that way. I know how twin minds make decisions. They fight each other at every turn. You want my advice? Stop fighting."

"Wow, that is some sage advice, witch doctor." I raised my glass to her.

"Oh, you think it should be more telling. More complicated. How about this: Stop lying to each other."

"Easier said than done."

"Oh, I know you have secrets. So does she, I assume. But you both have to give them up. This isn't a marriage. You actually have to trust one another. You can keep your private thoughts private, but your choices and your goals? Those have to be out in the open."

I took in a slow breath. I couldn't believe I had even considered coming to see this woman. I might as well have booked an hour with a shrink.

"What did you really come here for? What do you really want to know? "

I clenched my jaw, debating if I even wanted to ask, but why else did I come, if not to ask? "Is it possible to separate myself from Elise—without killing either one of us?"

"That depends on why you are two to begin with."

"What do you mean?"

"I mean that the universe is not as random as you might think. Everything is connected, circle of life, blah, blah, blah. Do you know if your mother gave birth to twins?"

"You mean two babies?"

"Yes."

"I guess I don't know. I mean obviously I don't have a sibling. Why?"

"There are three ways that twin minds can be created. The first type is when twins are conceived, but the bodies merge into one another before they are fully formed. Two souls are distributed, but only one body to arrive in." Modesta clasped her hands together. "The next is when one twin dies in utero. The living twin will allow the dying soul to join with it. To share the body, in order to save it."

"You mean that it's possible for a baby to choose to become a twin mind?"

"Not the baby per se, but the soul. If the body dies late in the pregnancy, sometimes an attachment is created. They just don't want to let go of each other."

"So, what option does that leave for detachment?"

"If the twin merged after conception there is no

definitive owner of the body. One or likely both souls will be ejected if a ceremony is performed. If a soul was invited in, then that soul can be rejected at any time by the rightful owner of the body."

"How do you know which is which?"

"You often don't know until the procedure is done."

"And can it be done without killing the other?"

Modesta smiled. "Yes, but you aren't going to like it. It isn't as simple as one ceremony."

"Of course it wouldn't be."

"And it's not like you get to just jump into a new body and pick up where you left off."

"Where would the ejected soul go?"

"In order to survive, the soul must go into an embryo."

"So we would have to find a pregnant woman to—"

"No, the soul cannot leave the body it was born to without leaving this plane of existence. The only way for a separation is to merge the soul with the gamete before the cell division starts and the soul arrives. The window is short, only about a day."

"But then one of us would become the daughter of another of us."

"Or a son."

"What?"

"The semen determines the sex."

"Wait a minute, this isn't about separation. This is just reincarnation."

Modesta shrugged. "Separation for one. Reincarnation for the other. I told you you wouldn't like it."

I slumped back on my chair, wondering if Elise had discovered that option and had the same reaction. I didn't want to start my life over as a baby, with no memory of my life now. What was the point? Everything I had accomplished would be erased, at least in my mind.

No, this wasn't what I wanted. I knew it wasn't what Elise would want either. As much as I wanted a miracle, I realized that Modesta's grandfather was right. You can't have everything. I was just going to have to make some choices, and so was Elise. If we stayed alive long enough to make them.

I glanced at my watch and realized that Layne was probably stalking the streets of Jaurez for his car. I drank down the last of my lemonade and extracted myself for the dipping plastic of the lawn chair. "I think I'll pass on reliving kindergarten, but thanks anyway." I offered her my hand and she gave it a gentle squeeze. I opened the back door to get back to the shop entrance, but stopped as I remembered something. "Oh, wait, you said there were three ways to become a twin soul. The merged twins, the invited twin, and what was the third?"

Modesta turned back and frowned at me. "It's very rare. Nothing that applies to you and Elise, I am sure of that."

"Now you got me curious."

"The third way that a twin mind can be created is if a soul invades a body."

"Invades a body?"

"You must understand. Shared souls don't fit into

the body the way they should. That's why you are always changing. The souls are constantly trying to squish in, but never achieving it. One gets situated and the other bumps it back out. It's a vicious cycle, but a predictable one for the most part. When a soul forces itself into a body, it isn't so much a cycle of trying to fit two souls in one slot, but rather a battle to get and keep control of the body."

"You're saying a soul can hijack a body?"

"Possess a body."

"Possess... as in...?"

"Demons."

I grimaced and then chuckled. "You're joking, right?"

Modesta smiled and chuckled with me. "Not at all," she said, holding the endearing smile on her face. My face went flat, refusing to feign any more amusement at the situation. "As I said, don't worry about it. It's nothing that you or Elise will need to concern yourselves with. At least not anytime soon." I glanced around, searching for who knows what. A creepy feeling of unwelcome had trickled into my veins and I was more compelled to run away than ever before.

THE WARDEN

FELICIA JEDLICKA

SUCCESSORS

WANTED: *A hard-working individual with a high tolerance for cold temperatures, boredom, and extreme danger. Must love dragons.*

Danato has been the designated warden for a secret prison deep in the arctic circle for as long as he cares to remember. Although he is only one in a long line of wardens, there is no one to follow him. And because this isn't a regular prison, he doesn't have the luxury of advertising in the local newspaper. He must find his own successor.

Unfortunately that means bringing someone new into his strange world. A world of vampires, werewolves, and all manner of fairy tales and nightmares. Mostly nightmares. And if that wasn't bad enough, there is a catch. There is always a catch.

The job offer is permanent. Once he decides on a candidate there is no turning back, for them or him.

About the Author

As a Nebraska native, and a small-town girl at that, I have very little to occupy my time beyond imagining a world outside of my own reality. By the grace of God and the seat of my pants, I have kept my waning attention span on the task of becoming an author.

So here I am, an indie author, peddling my words in cyberspace and enduring my comeuppances with an unwavering determination. I may not be a professional, and I certainly am not perfect, but if you've made it this far, you have to admit, this smartass yokel does spin quite a yarn.

From the self-inflicted sweatshop conditions of my unairconditioned childhood home, to the arthritis reaping positions of a sedentary lifestyle, I bring to you: my sarcasm, my oddity, and my heart. Take it with a grain of salt or a teaspoon of sugar, but take it for what it is: a story born of the mind, translated to paper, and gifted to you.

I thank you for your readership and even more for your support. Please recommend this book to your friends and family via any social media that you use. Word of mouth is still the best advertising and is greatly appreciated.

Most importantly, keep reading. I'll keep writing.

Connect with the Author:
www.facebook.com/feljedauthor

www.ingramcontent.com/pod-product-compliance
Lightning Source LLC
Chambersburg PA
CBHW031613180726
48284CB00005B/1526